VUDU DAHL

TASH HAWTHORNE

WAHIDA CLARK
P R E S E N T S
INNOVATIVE PUBLISHING

Wahida Clark Presents Innovative Publishing
60 Evergreen Place
Suite 904A
East Orange, New Jersey 07018
1(866) 910-6920
www.wclarkpublishing.com

Library of Congress Cataloging-In-Publication Data:
Vudu Dahl
978-1-954161-51-1 Paperback
978-1-954161-50-4 Hardback
978-1-954161-70-2 eBook
978-1-954161-52-8 Audiobook
LCCN: 2021916357

1. Stories about Mothers and Daughters 2. Southern Family Stories 3. Dysfunctional Family Stories 4. Stories about Emotional Healing 5. Books Set in Louisiana 6. Intergenerational Family Dramas 7. Books Set in American South 8. African American Women's Fictions 9. Emotional Reads
Cover design by Tina Shivers
Layout by Caroline Zonis
Printed in United States

"Love is divine only and difficult always. If you think it is easy you are a fool. If you think it is natural you are blind. It is a learned application without reason or motive except that it is God.

You do not deserve love regardless of the suffering you have endured. You do not deserve love because somebody did you wrong. You do not deserve love just because you want it. You can only earn—by practice and careful contemplations—the right to express it and you have to learn how to accept it."

– Toni Morrison, *Paradise*

For Grandma Martha and Mark Christopher

PART I

JUNE

1

"What is taking so long with Mrs. Jackson? The family's going to be here in fifteen minutes for the inspection," Dominique asked, storming into the prep room.

"She's too big for the casket." John readjusted the belts on the lift, setting them aside.

"What? You sure?"

"Yeah," John nodded, his eyebrows raised.

"Damn. I told the family about the Athena Rose, but they insisted on this one," Dominique sighed, placing her hands on her hips.

"Her arm is going to end up resting on the edge if I can't get her situated right."

"No, that can't happen. That'll be disturbing." Dominique looked over Mrs. Jackson and the casket. She was, indeed, a heavyset woman, but not too big for her to look like she'd been squeezed into the bed. "The couch for this line is adjustable."

"You sure?" he asked, wiping the sweat dripping from his brow.

"I better be. I've been in this business for fifteen years," she giggled. "Where's the hand crank?"

John snatched one from a prep table.

Dominique placed it into the socket in the casket and began to lower Mrs. Jackson down. "How's that?" She set Mrs. Jackson's hands, then finger curled her white, shoulder-length hair a bit. "Better?" Dominique smiled warmly.

"Much," John said, relieved. "She looks comfortable."

"That's what we want," she smiled sadly as she placed her hands atop Mrs. Jackson's. "Put her in Chapel One."

"Got it, Boss."

Dominique loved being a funeral director. Even though the industry was selfish and demanding, like a small child, it was her calling. Initially, she had plans of becoming a nurse-midwife like her mother, but life's curveballs knocked her off course. Permanently. All in all, Dominique was immensely proud of the business she and her best friend, Rose, built. Favier-Payne Funeral Home was one of few memorial parlors owned and operated by women of color in the state.

The beeping of the intercom broke Dominique's reverie.

"Ms. Favier?" the young female voice asked.

"Yes, Kelly?"

"Gia's on line two."

"Thank you." Dominique sighed heavily. She'd been wondering where her daughter was. She walked over to the wall, picked up the phone from its cradle, and pressed the blinking red light to line two. "Gia, where are you? You were supposed to be here an hour ago."

"Mommy."

Dominique's antennas immediately shot up.

~

DOMINIQUE MARCHED out of the West Orange Police Precinct tight-faced and rigid-bodied. Gia and Amari trailed behind with their heads hung. She hadn't muttered one word to them upon learning the news of their arrests. They were charged with one count of Indecent Exposure. As if that wasn't bad enough, Amari had also been charged with Aggravated Assault on an officer. They wanted to keep him and would have had Dominique not known the police director. She'd handled his father and brother's funerals. Not too long after, they began to date. But because of their hectic schedules, they couldn't go further than a friendship. However, he didn't hesitate to take care of the kids' misadventures that day. And she was grateful.

In truth, Amari's mother had been at the forefront of her mind. Dominique had gone to the extreme of asking the favor *for* his mother because she knew the woman was a single mother, a *good* mother who was doing the best she could. She, like Dominique, woke up every day fighting; fighting against time and nature, badges and batons, corners and guns, society, miseducation, and herself. Dominique called her after squaring things away with the police director. As expected, she was disappointed and embarrassed, but thanked Dominique and apologized for her son's behavior. Dominique reciprocated the apology, assuring her that their ties would remain unsevered.

Dominique unlocked her SUV with the touch of her hand and slid behind the wheel. She gripped it tightly as she waited for the teens to follow suit. Once she heard the clicking of seat belts, she pushed the START button, put the truck in drive, and made her way to the reservation.

Dominique studied Amari's six-foot-two frame as he placed the picnic blanket, basket, and trash into the back of her truck. He was a good-looking young man, baby-faced. His lips were full, nose strong, and he had bedroom eyes with perfectly arched eyebrows. His smile was gap-toothed and broad. Even with the bit of acne, she thought he was a cutie. Out of all the boys who came through her house in the last two years, she liked Amari the most. Loved him, matter-of-fact. He was dependable and strong. He was good with her sons and daughter. He had a pure heart. It hadn't been hardened by all he'd seen and endured at the hands of his abusive uncles. And she believed it never would. And what Dominique admired the most about him was his honesty. He never wavered when he stood in his truth, regardless of whether she agreed with him. Today, however, she didn't know what to think of the boy.

"You could have gotten yourself killed today," she glared up at him. "What were you thinking?"

"I don't know. I wasn't . . . thinking," he said just above a whisper.

Dominique sucked in a bit of air as she closed the trunk. "You and Gia need to take a little break."

"Ms. Favier, please. No. Just let me explain," he replied with furrowed brows.

"There's nothing to explain, Amari," she smirked. "I trusted you with her."

"I know. I know you did." He shifted his weight. "Please, let me explain."

Dominique crossed her arms at her chest and pursed her lips.

"It wasn't our intention to come up here and have sex. The plan was to have a picnic, and that's it. Gia was hungry, and I thought it would be a nice idea to do something special for her."

Dominique blinked, unmoved by his confession.

"I take full responsibility for my part in what happened today, but I don't regret what we did. I love her, and she loves me."

Dominique raised a brow. "There are other ways to show your love."

"You're right. You're right," he nodded.

"I gave you permission to date my daughter, not spread her wide in a park," Dominique snapped.

Amari gulped. "I'm sorry, Ms. Favier. I never meant to disrespect her or you."

"I'm going to drop you off at home. Whatever you need to say to Gia, you say it before you get out of my truck. Is that understood?"

"Yes, ma'am." He wiped his wet eyes.

"You will not have access to her after this. I'm taking her phone, tablet, and laptop. And don't think about coming by the house because she won't be there."

Gia's body quavered as she cried quietly, listening to her mother abruptly end her relationship. Even though she and Amari had only been dating for six months, she'd fallen for him and fallen for him hard. He wasn't like any other boy she'd met or dated, even befriended. To be quite honest, she thought he was way out of her league. With everything she'd been through in the past with other boys, drugs, and her mother, she just knew Amari wouldn't want anything to do with her. She'd done too much, too soon, and she was sure he would see her sins. Eventually. Every last one of them. Then, he would look at her like her mother did, with dejection and disappointment. But he never did. He saw her goodness and was amazed by her beautiful mind. She was a deep thinker and possessed an old soul. He loved everything she hated about herself. And that was more than what she could ever ask for in a lover and friend.

Gia shook her head as she struggled to wipe her eyes and runny nose.

Things couldn't end like this. They just couldn't.

DOMINIQUE STEPPED into the arms of her home with Gia in tow. She threw her purse and keys on the kitchen island before making her way to the refrigerator, where she retrieved a bottle of water, opened it, and took a much-needed swig. Gia had since stopped crying but began to fold into herself. Dominique couldn't stand the sight of her. She wanted to lay hands on her child, but she knew that wasn't an option. Not anymore. The two had been through so much within the last two years. She was sure they'd both learned from their mistakes, making strides in the right direction. But the day's events obviously proved her wrong.

Life was funny. Unforeseen patterns in behavior showed themselves in the next generation, almost always at the most inopportune times. Dominique was Gia once upon a time. And her mother had been her. She couldn't help but reflect upon the night of her seventeenth birthday. She'd gone out to celebrate with her high school sweetheart and stayed out past her curfew—*hours* past. She crept into the house, careful not to shut the front door too loud. But when she turned around to escape to her room, there was her mother, sitting on the steps. Waiting. Her mama—Corrine. A woman who was strict yet always fair. Caring and compassionate yet matter-of-fact and tolerated nothing outside of the truth. Dominique could hear her voice just as clear as day.

"Before you put yo' lips together and take one of yo' God-given breaths to lie to me, I want you to figure. Is it worth it? Is it worth da slap I'm gonna give you across dat face of yours? Is it worth pickin' yo' teeth up off dis flo'? Is it worth throwin' away yo' self-respect? Now, you can throw away yo' self-respect . . . but as long as I can stand straight, you not gonna disrespect me and my house."

Dominique remembered her mother daring her to speak after that. To explain herself, but she didn't. She couldn't. The woman was no fool. She already knew what she'd been out doing. Her innocence was gone. And so was her mother's trust.

"As of today, dat boy is dead to you. And I swear, on yo' grand-mama's Bible, if I find out you actin' sly and sneakin' 'round corners wit' him behind my back, you gonna have to find another place to live."

8

At the time, Dominique only understood deception's pain from a daughter's perspective, as the deceiver. Today, she was standing on the other side, as the deceived. She placed her hands on the edge of the island and stared at her daughter long and hard. She didn't know what to do with her. Dominique often wondered if things would have been different, *easier* for her, had she not left home. Not that she had much of a choice then, but she'd thought about it, nonetheless. The North was nothing like the South. Down South, the people were kinder, the pace was slower, and the living was much easier. Northern living was difficult and unapologetic. Everything was fast-moving. People walked around with grimaces and scoffed at you if you greeted them with a smile. It took several years to adjust. And for the most part, she had. But Gia, Gia had fallen in step with Jersey's madness the moment her feet touched its hard soil, moving with the rough tides of city life like a pro.

Dominique didn't know if she wanted to scream or take to her bed until the pain passed. One thing was for sure. She was happy her sons were spending their summer break in the Dominican Republic with their father. She didn't want them to be witnesses to any more of her and Gia's bloody wars. Even though the boys were fourteen and twelve, the ongoing battles affected them deeply. They never moved steadily between the two. Always torn.

"Give me your phone."

Gia retrieved it from her back pocket and handed it to her mother.

"What do you have to say for yourself?"

"Nothing," Gia whispered.

"Mmm. I'm sure you had a lot to say when you had that boy bust you open up on that mountain," Dominique sneered.

She knew her child well enough to know Gia initiated the public rendezvous. Amari, unfortunately, hadn't enough willpower to refuse her advances. Gia was young and ripe, very

9

much attuned with her sexuality. She embraced it fully. But when one looked at the girl, you wouldn't think butter melted in her mouth. She'd come on strong to that boy, fervent and savagelike in her approach, and Dominique knew it. Amari didn't have a chance.

Finally, Gia looked up at her. The tongue-lashing had begun.

Dominique's nostrils flared as she met Gia's gaze. "What? Did I strike a nerve?"

Gia remained silent.

"Well, that's too damn bad. Because any nerves that I had are all gone, thanks to you," Dominique professed. "I haven't had a moment's rest since you transferred to that goddamn school. But it ends today, you hear me, Gia? Your shit ends today!"

"Mommy, I made one mistake. One!" Gia mustered up to say.

"Which part? Not coming to work so you could sneak off and have sex in public or getting arrested?"

"I can't talk to you. Not if you're going to be like this." Gia shook her head.

"Like *what*?" Dominique fumed. "Like what?!"

"Mean! And-and-and unreasonable! You're acting like you weren't having sex at seventeen!"

"And what happened? Huh? What happened? I got pregnant with you!" Dominique hollered, throwing the water bottle at her head. She missed. "Is that what you're trying to do?! Is *that* what you want?!"

"I'm not you," Gia trembled.

Before she knew it, her mother had run up on her and backslapped her.

"You damn right ya not me. You could *never* be me. 'Cause da hell I've been tru would have killed you." Dominique's New Orleans accent dripped from her lips like crawfish juice. It was heavier now, exposed and permanent with her rage. She didn't want to hit the girl, but her mouth was reckless. It was one of the many traits Gia inherited from her. Make no mistake about it; she adored her daughter and loved her more than she could ever express in words. But Dominique had to regain control over the situation. She watched Gia struggle through hiccupped sobs to wipe her wet eyes. Her cheek was flushed from the slap. As sensitive and pale as her skin was, Dominique knew it would bruise.

She put her hands on her hips and shook her head. "I am so afraid of losin' you. You have no idea."

Gia looked up slowly and met her mother's eyes. Tears were brimming there. She hated seeing her mother cry. It was rare when Dominique did. But those few occasions always hit Gia hard. Her mother was the strongest woman she'd ever known. Her beauty and wisdom, in Gia's eyes, were unmatched. Dominique was her "safe place". And if the foundation of her safe place was unstable, she, her brothers, and the household were as well.

It was never Gia's intention to disappoint her mother, but it was a daily struggle to meet the woman's expectations. If someone asked her mother if she expected too much from her children or her standards were too high, she would undoubtedly say no. Gia, of course, would say otherwise.

The chiming of Dominique's cell phone broke their trance. She pulled it from her pocket and read the name on the screen. It was her oldest sister.

"Hey, Toni."

"Hey, suge. You busy?" the raspy-voiced woman whispered.

"A little. Why? Wassup?" Dominique walked over to the sink and wet a paper towel. She wiped Gia's face, then made her way to the fridge. She opened the freezer, retrieved a Ziploc bag of ice, and pressed it against Gia's cheek.

Toni sighed heavily on the other end. "Daddy had a heart attack this mornin'. He's at University Medical in ICU."

"What?" Dominique placed her hand on her forehead. She'd spoken to him just the previous night and he sounded fine.

Then Dominique took a moment and thought about it. This wasn't the first time her father suffered a heart attack, nor was it the second or third. He was a big man who had poor eating habits. He stood at six foot seven and weighed well over 300 pounds. Hence, the name "Duke", as his closest friends and family called him.

"He's stable for now and talkin'. And . . . askin' for you."

Dominique looked over at Gia. She was concerned, so she changed her facial expression and signaled for her to go upstairs. Once she disappeared, Dominique sat down on one of the stools at the island.

"And Mama?" She braced herself. Her relationship with her mother hadn't been the same after she'd become pregnant with Gia. Their conversations were few and far between. Mother and daughter often found themselves in a tug-of-war with their thoughts and opinions, emotions always on high. Dominique expected the worst.

"She's the one who told me to call you."

Dominique blinked back tears. "I haven't spoken to her since Christmas."

The holiday visit had been swathed with fire, her mother's words igniting the flame. Her father found himself caught in the middle, struggling to keep peace between the two.

Toni sucked in air.

"How bad is he?" Dominique asked, annoyed.

"His heart's givin' out, *cher*. It's weak. The doctors say we need to prepare ourselves."

DOMINIQUE SAT on the edge of her Jacuzzi, watching the steady water rise. Dawn was approaching. She'd spoken to Toni for over two hours and caught a migraine. The more information she learned about her father, the more her head throbbed. He wanted her back home. He needed to put his affairs in order before he closed his eyes for the final time. And regardless of whether Dominique liked it, she was a major part of those affairs.

Fourteen years. It had been fourteen years of sunrises and sunsets, full mooned and eclipsed nights since she'd been home. Home, her beloved NOLA. She missed the early-morning sights of hummingbirds and the sweet smell of magnolias, night-blooming jasmine, and lavender settling under her nose as she hopped on the St. Charles Streetcar to get from one part of town to the other.

She was a daughter of New Orleans. And that meant growing up in a place people took for granted and wanted to let sink. It also meant coming back to a place that no one thought would survive. Having NOLA blood meant beating the odds, being filled with the magic of a city that refused to stop fighting. Dominique was strong and resilient, just like her city. There was no other way to grow. And she truly believed it was because of her Nawlins roots that she'd survived the hard living of the North.

NOLA showed you what it meant to be resilient and what it meant to have people who would not go down without a fight. Being New Orleans-born meant being born with a heart below sea level. Dominique wanted to pass all of that on to her babies.

Barefoot and draped in white, she slowly looked around the room and took in the sight before her. It was aglow with candles and incense. Smoke from the bundle of sage burned on the windowsill wafting in and out from the open window. She'd told Toni what happened with Gia, and her sister instructed her to go back to what they were taught, what always worked

—*spirit medicine*. But, unfortunately, Dominique had to confess that she hadn't practiced any of their mother's familial traditions in years. She'd abandoned them the day their mother abandoned her. Toni understood but insisted nonetheless that she dig deep and put Gia's well-being first and foremost—before she lost her forever.

So, here Dominique was, pouring the liquefied herbs she'd steeped and strained into the warm bathwater. She closed her eyes and began to pray, calling upon the *Lwas* and ancestors to bless the water. Gia appeared in the doorway, her eyes heavy with exhaustion. She looked around, uncertain about what was in store for her with this spiritual bath.

"Come," Dominique said softly.

Gia took a deep breath, then blew it out before walking toward her mother.

"Take off ya robe."

Nervous, Gia did as she was told. She hated for her mother to see her in the nude. It wasn't because she looked at her in a way that made her self-conscious. It was just normal teenage insecurity. Gia felt her mother had everything she lacked. Her skin was a creamy vanilla, while her mother's was a sun-kissed caramel. Her thick, coarse hair stopped at her shoulders and was too hard to manage.

On the other hand, Dominique's hair was a finer grade, wavy, and hung down her back, brushing her tailbone. Her mother had sensual, captivating eyes, high cheekbones, a thin nose pierced with a tiny diamond stud, and full lips that were blessed with a beauty mark to kill for. Her eyebrows were set high and meticulously arched, one studded with a ring. Gia's cheekbones were undefined. Her freckled nose was thin at the bridge, then widened at the tip and nostrils. Even though her lips were full as well, the upper lip was heavier than the bottom and protruded some. Her mother was statuesque with sculpted arms and legs and strong, moderately wide hips. Gia's body was much softer and younger, her hips round. She had dimples in both cheeks, while Dominique had only one. The only qualities they shared were their broad smiles and quick tongues. Unfortunately, that wasn't enough for the seventeen-year-old. Her mother was everything she wanted to be, and more. But Gia just kept falling short.

Dominique extended her hand for Gia to take. She did and held it tight until she was seated.

"Close ya eyes."

Gia did as she was told as her mother retrieved a bowl from the sink.

Dominique submerged it into the water and poured it over the girl's head. She watched it run down her body, then poured the water over her again, repeating it several more times.

Gia wiped her eyes and took another deep breath. She was well aware of her mother's southern roots but dared not ask her if what she was doing was normal. Nor was she going to ask how much longer the ritual was going to take. So, she remained quiet.

Dominique took a washcloth from her pocket, dipped it into the bath, and then washed Gia in a downward motion. "I'll be back in twenty minutes. Use this time wisely." She rose to her feet and placed the washcloth on a rack before leaving Gia to her thoughts.

Gia lay back and found her eyes pulled to the ceiling. There was nothing there, but she wanted to focus on something other than what she'd just experienced. She was scared to death. She didn't understand why her mother was dressed in all white, head wrapped, and tranquil in the eyes. It was too early in the morning for all of this, but Gia remained still, nonetheless. She missed Amari and wondered what he was doing. The sun was rising, and she hoped he was watching it rise too.

Dominique stepped back into the bathroom with an African licorice stick in hand. She chewed on it for a moment, then held it in the corner of her mouth as she rested against the threshold.

"Time's up. Step out and stand here so that you can dry properly."

Confused, Gia sat up and cringed. "I can't dry myself with a towel?"

"No," Dominique shook her head. She watched her daughter step out of the tub and stand before her.

Gia refused to look her in the eye. She was ashamed of herself. Ashamed of not telling her mother how she felt about Amari from the beginning. Ashamed of not telling her how serious they had become sooner. Ashamed of being more comfortable under his gaze and touch than hers. She began to tremble from the cool breeze blowing in. Her mother looked from the sun's peeking light to her, a shrinking violet.

Dominique walked toward her slowly and lifted her chin. "I don't expect you to understand what I've done this mornin', Gia. Not yet, at least. But I do expect you to *remember*. *Always remember* that I'll do whatever's in my *power* to keep you and ya brothers covered. You got me?"

"Yes, ma'am." Gia shuddered.

Her mother hadn't batted an eye.

2

Gia plopped down in her mother's high-back swivel chair and rolled it toward the bay window's seat in her office. Several folders and gift bags were lined up there. She looked back at the items stacked on her mother's desk that needed to be placed in each bag. Every family received the memorial book from their loved one's service, unique gifts made by Rose and her mother, extra funeral programs, prayer and thank you cards. Gia appreciated the time her mother and "aunt" took to create things from nothing for people they didn't know. They always went above and beyond for the families who stepped through their doors.

Gia read the name on the first folder, then rolled back to the desk to retrieve and pack the items for the decedent's bag. She was tired. They'd been at the parlor since six that morning. Her mother had two bodies released from the medical examiner's office that needed to be put back together. And that process was going to take over five hours. Dominique had instructed her to clean the entire funeral home before opening. Gia dusted every office, polished every chair, washed every window, vacuumed both chapels and the selection room, disinfected the visitor and staff bathrooms, then lit scented candles in each room. The only room she didn't touch was the prep room. She never stepped foot in there. Gia hated the way it smelled, an unnaturally sweet scent of death mixed with chemicals. And she hated the sight of the deceased even more.

The families would drop their loved one's clothes off, and Gia would be forced to go downstairs and deliver them to her mother. In the beginning, Dominique would leave the prep room door open to make it easier for her to dash in and out. But when she received a disaster case, that wasn't an option. So, Gia would just keep the clothes upstairs hanging in her mother's office. And, of course, that method didn't last long because a new family would come in to make arrangements, and she would have to remove the clothes and take them downstairs anyway. So, Dominique had wall hangers installed outside the prep room door, where Gia could hang the person's garments.

She'd been able to take a little nap in the car on the drive over, but she was still a bit stirred from the ritual that morning. She didn't feel any different. Her nerves were still shot, and her longing for Amari worsened as the hours passed. They spent every day together. But today—today, he was still gone. Every breath she took without him was just as painful as the last. She might as well have been dead.

Gia blinked back tears as she continued to stuff the bags.

"Morniiing!"

She looked up and forced a small smile at the young, doe-eyed woman standing before her. "Morning."

"Everything okay?" Kelly asked, genuinely concerned.

She, in her early twenties, popped her gum at the back of her mouth. Kelly studied the sadness behind Gia's eyes as she took a silver Favier-Payne broach out of her pocketbook and pinned it to her black suit jacket.

"Yeah, I'm okay," Gia lied. She'd done her best with concealing the bruise on her cheek with foundation. "Just tired."

"I hear you. But school's out for you now, right?" Kelly began to spin her ponytail into a bun.

"Yeah."

"Well, then you can catch up on some sleep this summer." Kelly placed one last pin in her bun.

"True."

"You worked hard this year. That's all your mom's been talking about. She's so proud of you. We all are."

Gia's shoulders slumped a little. Deflated. It didn't matter how well she'd done. Yesterday's fiasco officially trumped it.

"She downstairs?" Kelly continued.

"Mm-hmm," Gia nodded.

"Any calls?"

"Only from people who wanted to know the time of Mrs. Jackson's service."

"All right. Good. I'm gonna go use the restroom. See you in a little bit!"

"'Kay," Gia smiled small again.

"How long do you think you're going to be gone?" Rose asked as she searched for the femoral arteries of the man lying at their hands.

Dominique sighed. "Two weeks. I can't do more than two weeks." Just the thought of returning home under the dire circumstances made her stomach churn.

"And if they want you to stay longer?" Rose eyed her knowingly.

Dominique closed her eyes and shook her head. "They won't. And I can't. My life is up here."

"But—"

"This wasn't my doin'. This was my mama's," Dominique retorted. "She forced this hand on me."

Rose set the spring forceps down and inhaled. She waited for her best friend, her *sister*, to look over and find her eyes. Rose's yellow skin glowed under the fluorescent lights. She licked her heart-shaped, glossed lips as she took in Dominique's frustration. *Home* was a sore spot for her, just like Gia's behavior. She seemed to unravel almost immediately at the thought of her family . . . the thought of her mother.

"Dom."

Dominique, with pursed lips, sniffled back tears.

"Look at me," Rose demanded gently.

"I'm sorry. I didn't mean to bite ya head off." She found Rose's tightly slanted eyes, her beauty instantaneously pulling her in.

"Look what you did with that hand she dealt you, sis. Look around. *You* built this. *We* built this," Rose smiled in awe of their accomplishments. "If it wasn't for you, I would have drowned years ago. Lost myself in Dwayne's foolishness, stayed walking in his shadow. My babies are proud of me because you showed me how to fight. You never let me settle. You're always pushing me to go for what's meant for me and showing me how to do it along the way."

Dominique wiped a tear from her bottom lid.

"You've been angry for a long time, boo. Maybe you'll get the chance to let it all go when you get home. You *should* let it go when you get there." She grabbed her hand. "And as far as Gia goes . . . She made a mistake. I'm sure she won't do anything like that again. You have to have some faith in her. You put her on birth control, which she takes religiously, right? So, now, all we can do is hope that when she lies down again, her little boyfriend is on point on his end."

"You right," Dominique shrugged. She loved Rose with all

of herself. Her tone and delivery were as gentle as a lullaby. Sinfully soothing.

"I know," Rose teased, picking up the forceps once again.

Confused and disgusted, Gia and Kelly watched a few of Mrs. Jackson's grandchildren take pictures of her with their cell phones. Neither one could understand the purpose or benefits of such an invasive act.

"Should I go in there and tell them to put their phones away?" Gia asked with furrowed brows.

"No. It's their prerogative to do what they want with her," Kelly sighed. "As long as no one is trying to climb into the casket or fighting, we're where we're supposed to be."

"Okay." Gia turned back to the desktop computer and continued updating the dates of upcoming homegoing services on the funeral home's website.

The bell atop the front entrance door jingled. A short, muscular man in a baseball cap and matching uniform strutted in. The letters "USCG" were sewn onto the center of his cap and above the upper left pocket of his shirt. He took a quick glance around the bustling waiting area before running his chestnut-brown hand along his manicured goatee. He didn't see who he was looking for, so he walked up to the concierge window in hopes of some assistance.

Gia caught sight of him in the corner of her eye. She knew exactly who he was. He was the man who had been walking in and out of her mother's life for the last six years, never committing to her, always leaving her with the hope of a happily ever after. Yeah, she knew who he was. His unexpected and unwanted presence shifted her mood. She kept her eyes forward.

Kelly looked up from her desk and greeted the man with a wide smile.

"Good morning."

"Morning," he smiled back.

Kelly was thrown by his handsomeness. "How may I help you?"

"Is Ms. Favier here, by any chance? I'm a friend of hers," he cooed.

"Why, yes, she is. She's in the chapel at the moment with a family. But if you're not in a rush, you may have a seat and wait while I pull her for you."

"Thank you."

Kelly rose from her chair and made her way out of the office. "Of course. Your name?"

"Louis." He removed his hat.

"Just Louis?"

"Yeah. She knows who I am," he chuckled.

"All right," Kelly grinned and nodded.

Louis crossed to a set of chairs resting along a wall decorated with framed news articles about the funeral home. His eyebrows raised, impressed by the write-ups. He slow-turned on his heels and glanced at the young lady at the computer.

Gia could feel his eyes on her. Attitude at full throttle, she met his gaze and smirked.

"Hey, Gia. I thought that was you."

She grunted. "So you can think now?"

"That's funny. You're funny," he grinned. "But on a serious tip, what's your problem with me? I've never done anything to you or to your mother. What's the problem?"

"You're the problem," she spat.

"Me?" Louis pointed to himself.

"Yeah, *you*. You come in here like you own shit, like you own my mother, and you don't."

Louis ran his hand over his mouth, peddling back. "Wow."

Dominique turned the corner, her eyes locking on the twosome. She wasn't certain what was wrong, but she could sense some tension. "Is everything awrite?"

"Couldn't be better," Louis lied as he smiled through his annoyance and opened his strong arms for her to walk into.

"Yeah, everything is fine. *Lovely*," Gia followed sarcastically as she walked out of the office. The look of disbelief on her face spoke for itself.

Dominique studied her briefly, her lips pressed before turning her attention back to Louis. "What are you doin' here?"

"I just left my mom's house. Thought I'd stop by and see how you were doin'."

Dominique basked in his scent. Egyptian Musk. She was so comfortable in his embrace, she almost forgot where she was. Heat began to rise between her legs. She shifted her weight, attempting to simmer it. "I'm, uh, I'm awrite. Busy, as you can see."

"Yeah. Looks good in here. And you . . . You're always lookin' good," Louis teased, licking his lips.

"Eww, this nigga," Gia mumbled under her breath as she walked back into the office, an extra set of prayer cards in hand.

Dominique stiffened under Gia's condemnation.

Kelly grinned as she went back and forth between filing paperwork and watching the exchange. Gia remained silent. The nerve of her mother to have come down so hard on her when she was entertaining the likes of this man, at her place of business, no less! She knew what was to come afterward. They both did.

"Thank you. Ya not lookin' too bad yaself."

Louis licked his lips again. He loved the drawl of her tongue. It reminded him of the way she made love to him, slow and steady. She always took her time with him, attentive to his needs. His body was obedient under her touch, his mind blown.

"Appreciate it." He became lost in her eyes. Spellbound. "But listen, I'm not gonna keep you. I know you're on a service."

"Yeah."

"Can I call you later?"

"If you'd like," Dominique nodded.

"Cool. Talk to you later then." Louis pulled her in for another hug and kissed her on the cheek before waving goodbye to the girls.

"Damn, Ms. Favier! Who was that?" Kelly squealed.

Dominique tilted her head, her face fixed in a grimace. "Watch ya mouth."

"I'm sorry. I didn't mean to curse. But . . . wow. You've got zaddies! I mean, *men* coming at you left and right, like *every day*. That's not normal. You know that, right? Right? They are coming to your *business* looking for you!" Kelly laughed.

Gia shuddered. Everything her coworker was saying was true. For as long as Gia could remember, men fiended for her mother. Dominique was always cool, very much a lady about the attention. But in Gia's eyes, she thought her mother should have been firmer with them. She didn't like the way they looked at her, undressing her with their eyes, luring her in with their unspoken sexual desires. Nor did she like the way they spoke to her. Their tongues were slick, lust-filled, and uncensored.

"It's that New Orleans voodoo, isn't it? You castin' love spells out here?"

Dominique couldn't help but laugh. "Girl, get back to work."

"Yup, you on some Eve's Bayou-ish," Kelly giggled as she bounced back and forth in her chair. "You made him a *special gris-gris* bag, huh?"

Dominique dismissed her with the wave of her hand as she walked back into the chapel.

"I wanna be like your mother when I grow up." Kelly swiveled around to face Gia, who was not moved by either woman's antics. "Damn, GiGi. You've got a face that could kill, girl. I'm just playin'."

"It's no fun and games when it comes to him and my mother."

DOMINIQUE SAT on the side of her bed, pressing her feet deeper into the shag rug. She looked over her shoulder. Louis was lying on his side, his body rising and falling in a rhythm. This was a no-no for her. She never let him or any of the others fall asleep there. In fact, she didn't entertain them at all when her children were home. But tonight—tonight, she'd fallen under lonesomeness's spell and received much-needed conversation.

Louis. A rebound in the beginning. He replaced the kids' father in the bedroom after they parted ways, filling the void of his absence, filling her ears with sweet nothings, and the cove between her legs with the extension of himself, pouring nothing but lies into her over and over again. She learned years ago that she would never *really* have him. And that was okay with her because she didn't want him. His purpose was to satisfy her, feed her insatiable sexual appetite. And he did. She allowed him to make her forget her reality of singlehood, her *loneliness* when her kids were away. Even if the moments spent with him only lasted a couple of hours, they were enough for her.

She placed her hand gently on his shoulder and shook him lightly. He stirred a bit before waking. Smiled at the sight of her. She told him he had to go. She and Gia had to leave for the airport in a couple of hours, and she needed to finish packing. Louis rose without a fuss. Dominique grabbed the empty wine bottle and glasses, then led him out of her room. She floated across the catwalk and down the stairs. Gia was standing in the dark dining room with a glass of water in hand, watching her.

Dominique averted her eyes quickly. She opened the front door for him. He kissed her on the corner of her mouth, then walked away. Dominique closed the door behind him and locked it. She stayed there for a while, her forehead and hand pressed against the cool mahogany wood. She was going to have to face this girl and explain. It didn't matter if she was the adult; her child had caught her with her slip showing.

"Do you let them all spend the night or just him?"

Dominique's neck twisted slowly in Gia's direction. Her eyes cut. Gia's tone was low and dark—judgmental.

Dominique wasn't aware, but Gia remembered Louis as a little girl. She remembered peeking out from her room and watching her mother lead him into her bedroom. She remembered hearing their muffled voices move between conversation and laughter. Then the sounds of unadulterated passion. Her mother's moans. His profanity. The tears that followed. And then silence. He would disappear for months at a time, and she would get to know someone else.

There had only been four in his absence. Gavin was married with a wife and baby girl. A union man who was respected at his job and in the community. He'd lusted over her for years, and she finally gave into him one time. They shared a kiss—a passionate one. But the guilt ate at her for months, so she cut all communication with him afterward.

Kenny was an entrepreneur and marine vet who took pride in his many jobs. He cared for his family and friends, but he hated kids and loved the attention of other women. He didn't like to take responsibility or apologize for entertaining them. And Dominique refused to settle for anything less than what she deserved. Their courtship ended as quickly as it began, but he still texted her from time to time.

Angelo was a high school history teacher who had an insatiable appetite for sex as well as an on-again, off-again girlfriend. He was fun to be around and doted on her. But he begged for her time and attention when they were apart. His neediness interrupted her peace and the little freedom she had.

Ramone was a warehouse worker by trade, poet by God's calling. He lusted over her just like the others, often smothering her with his insecurities and residue from his past failed relationships. He hadn't moved on from them and refused to see how they affected any potential future he had with not only Dominique but also any other woman who caught his eye.

When Louis returned, he forced the others to retreat; they fell to the wayside. And Dominique always welcomed him back. Back into her home, back into her ocean.

"I beg ya pardon?"

"Does he always spend the night?"

"That's none of ya business."

Gia folded her arms across her chest, raising an eyebrow. "Mommy, *you are my business.* What happens here, while I'm home . . . while the boys are home, *is* my business. He's using you."

"We're usin' each other. He just doesn't know it." She made her way into the kitchen and placed the glasses in the sink. Then threw the bottle into the trash. "I'm entitled to have a life outside of you and ya brothers, Gia. Outside of work. I'm human. I got needs just like everybody else. And I've chosen *that* man to meet 'em. Now, I'm sorry that he came over while you were home. That was my mistake. It won't happen again." Dominique turned to walk away.

"I don't like him. He's trash."

Dominique stopped at the bottom of the steps, her back taking in Gia's confession.

"To be honest, I don't like any of them. But *him* . . . I really don't like."

"Well, luckily for you, he's not a permanent fixture here or in my life."

"He shouldn't be a temporary one either."

"Excuse me?" Dominique asked, turning in her direction.

"Why is he still coming around?"

"You don't question me. *You* are a child." Dominique's brows furrowed.

"Who is trying to understand my mother. I deserve an answer."

Dominique dropped her head and sighed, searching for words she could not reach. Thoughts of one-sided exchanges with her mother came to mind. She could *never* go back and forth with her like Gia. It hadn't been an option for her and her sisters. Expressing an opinion or emotion in response to her mother's rules was considered back talk. She ran a tight ship in her home. With five girls, she had to or else she would have played the fool.

"What you do affects me. It affects my brothers, whether or not you realize it," Gia confessed. "Why do you keep allowing him to come and go as he pleases?"

"I don't—"

"You do! He was here right after you and Papi broke up!" Gia met her, daring her to lie to her again.

Dominique remained rooted. "Ya daddy . . ." her voice trailed off.

Gia waited for her to finish her sentence. Waited for her face to soften. But neither happened. She was instead unraveling. Her father, Esai, had been the love of her mother's life and she his. But familial obligations had set the foundation for the relationship to fail, cursed it . . . *forbade* it. And then time and distance killed it altogether. The two were still very much friends, their love and respect for each other unbroken.

"Did you tell him what I did?"

"No."

"Thank you," Gia said into her chest.

Dominique knew Esai would have booked the first flight up from the Dominican Republic and scolded them both, then found Amari and castrated him. Telling him had not been a thought.

"Mm-hmm," she muttered as she began to ascend the steps.

"I'm ashamed of loving Amari. For the way I *chose* to show my love for him," Gia grumbled. "I don't wanna feel this way anymore."

"Then have more respect for yaself, Gia."

"Respect? Who are *you* to say that to *me* when *you* don't have any? At least, not when it comes to *him*. You keep bringing this man into our home, a man that you're not even in a relationship with—disrespecting me and my brothers over and over again."

"He's not a fuckin' stranger, Gia! If ya mad at me because you feel like I replaced ya daddy with him, then just say that! But don't stand up here and make me out to be some whore because I'm not!"

"You're disrespecting *Papi!*"

"Ya daddy disrespected me when he walked out that door!" Dominique placed her hands on her hips. "Now, I know you love 'im. I know you do. But he ain't perfect, baby. Nowhere near it. And you hold 'im in such high regard, all the while lookin' down on me."

"No—" Gia shook her head.

"Yes, you do. And I'm tired of it." Dominique retied the belt on her robe, then made her way toward the steps again.

"Where was he when you lost the baby? That was his baby too," Gia growled.

The baby. Dominique lost her early on. A cold March morning. She was at work, sitting with a family, when she began to experience sharp cramps. They were rolling in like waves, constant and intensifying as each minute passed. She excused herself and went to the bathroom. When she checked her underwear, she saw clots of blood. So many. Too many. The pain was unendurable. She emerged, asking Rose to take over, then called her OB/GYN for an emergency appointment. It was in that Montclair office where her doctor confirmed she was miscarrying.

Dominique didn't cry. It was a year later, and she still hadn't. And the only reason why Gia knew anything about the baby was because she overheard her telling Rose about it. She didn't have time to mourn. Didn't make time to do so. Her emotions and thoughts about it were buried way down deep, covered in stone.

A loud silence crept between mother and daughter. Dominique's jaw clenched and unclenched. She didn't have the nerve to hit her again. She was weary. Fighting had become their norm. Her head swam. The heat that began to rise in her chest was suffocating. And it made the pain there too heavy and unbearable. "When did you get to be so mean? So hurtful?" Dominique asked just above a whisper.

Gia cast her eyes to the floor. "I-I just don't like the way he carries himself. He's cocky. How he believes you can't do better than him or don't deserve better than him. How he didn't think enough of you or your feelings after you lost her," she sniffled.

A tear rolled down Dominique's cheek. She wanted to tell Gia she hadn't told Louis about the baby. That if she had, she knew their years of dealing with each other would officially come to an end. She and Louis would have to face the loss together, then settle in the inevitability of parting ways. She wanted to tell Gia she hadn't let him or any other man touch her since that dreadful day. She'd been celibate and liked it. She wanted to tell her she had no intention of leaving him alone because she enjoyed his company. He was her escape. Of course, she missed the way he turned her inside out when her body surrendered to his.

But like so many other women, she knew the dangers of losing herself behind a man's loving (or lusting), which was why she was so hard on Gia, so against her engaging in sex at this age. Even though Dominique had only given herself to three men, each took a piece of her with them and never put the piece back. They couldn't be put back. Each of them had a different piece, so none knew what piece belonged where.

And Gia—Gia was already missing four pieces too many. She, unlike her mother, had yet to face the feeling of worthlessness that came, often with giving a man all of oneself or a part of oneself, and it not being *enough*. His appetite growing bigger, and you, as a woman, growing tired because you can't keep up, or your need for other displays of affection from him become unimportant, then nonexistent. Dominique had so much more to offer Louis and the others, but she didn't want to. They weren't Esai. And her pain spilled over into Gia's relationship with Amari. Dominique needed to protect her from the same heartache. She'd tried last year, but Gia didn't listen. The year before that, she'd failed as well.

HOPE—that was what kept people in relationships longer than they should. Holding on to the hope of BETTER. Hope that their beloved will *change* for the better, *do* better, *walk* and *talk* better, *BE* better. And maybe that was what Dominique was holding on to with her memories of Esai. The hope that he'd come around and love her like he should. Love her RIGHT.

She was full. Her emotions coursed through her like a tornado. Gia's words stung. The *truth* stung. But she wasn't going to admit that tonight. She wasn't ready.

"It won't happen again," she sniffled before climbing the stairs.

3

Dominique wrung her hands as the plane touched down. She wasn't prepared to see her sisters and nephews. She didn't feel strong enough to see her father hooked up to machines, weak in mind and body. And she couldn't bear the thought of her mother's impending grief. It was all too much.

"I can't do this," she groaned, looking out onto the runway.

Gia looked over at her and saw the lines of worry deepening between her brows. "Everything's going to be all right, Mommy. You'll see." She placed her warm hand on top of her mother's. Her mother always fidgeted when she was nervous. Gia couldn't blame her. The last time they'd been in the Crescent City was the day they moved away from there for good. Fourteen years ago. Since then, her grandparents, three of her four aunts, and cousins always flew up to see them, to which they never reciprocated. And Gia didn't know why. She didn't know why her mother left at twenty-one and never returned. She didn't know why she hadn't spoken to her one aunt since then either. She'd asked her mother and aunts over the years, but they changed the subject every single time. So she stopped asking.

Dominique relaxed some. All Gia had to do was touch her to calm her down. It didn't matter if it was just a simple hug, kiss, or scalp massage. Gia's gift of touch always brought Dominique to a place of solace. Their relationship was funny like that. Just as quickly as Gia could anger her, she could soothe her just the same. Dominique brought Gia's pale hand to her cheek and kissed it. Everything was going to be all right with her baby girl there. It had to. Because if it wasn't, she would never return after this.

Mother and daughter stepped into the parking deck of the Louis Armstrong International Airport and found three women who favored Dominique standing against a Ford F-150 truck.

"Here dey come!" Jackie clapped.

"Awrite, hawl!" Big GiGi shouted with excitement.

Dominique and Gia couldn't help but smile as they closed the space between them.

"Where y'at, girl?" Toni asked as she enveloped her baby sister in her arms.

"Awrite," Dominique replied in submission.

"You be dat," Toni hummed, rubbing her back.

The three sisters looked their youngest over. They thought she looked regal in her emerald-green, strapless maxi dress. She'd styled her ginger hair in a messy topknot and adorned herself with silver.

"Ya home now. Back where you belong," Toni nodded matter-of-factly.

Antonia, or Toni for short, a curator for the New Orleans Museum of Art and manager of their mother's apothecary and botanical shop, was the eldest and tallest of them all. Her posture and presence were strong, commanding. Her amber complexion had a natural glow against her hazel eyes and ginger dreadlocks. She smelled like lavender birch. And she spoke with the eloquence of an aristocrat. She favored a cotton Ankara print tunic and pant set with sandals.

Jacqueline (Jackie) and Genevieve (Big GiGi), the twins, were the color of copper and ginger. Jacqueline, a master chef and restaurant owner, was the second-born and unapologetically militant. Her voice was gravelly, accentuating her tough exterior perfectly. She was a proud lesbian who favored menswear and cologne. She wore a tank top with oversized khaki cargo shorts that stopped at the knees and a pixie cut.

Genevieve, for whom Gia was named, was an OB/GYN with her own practice. She was born two minutes after her twin and was warriorlike. Her voice was much kinder on the ears. She was a two-time breast cancer survivor who'd placed nutrition and health at the forefront of her life. She loved to dance and loved her family even more. She stood comfortably in a fitted baby doll T-shirt with yoga pants that stopped below the knee. Her bob cut was covered with a bandana.

Three shades of brown. Three shades of beauty. Three shades of magik. It was almost overwhelming to be in the presence of such royalty. This was the stock from which Gia sprang. And she was never so proud.

"And look at this girl, here," Big GiGi beamed, taking a step back in awe.

"Ain't she beautiful?" Jackie cosigned.

"Lookin' just like Mama," Toni smiled sweetly.

"Fo' true," the twins agreed.

Their accents were as heavy and melodic as her mother's. The "th" at the beginning of words was replaced with a hard "d." Gia felt a wave of peace wash over her as she settled into the arms of each aunt. They were safe places, just like her mother. Unquestionably.

"She's gonna be beside herself when she sees you," Toni began.

"Aw yeah," Jackie pinched Gia's chin.

Dominique bit the inside of her cheek. Any mention of their mother made her uncomfortable. Time had not healed anything for her. She'd just learned how to live with the open wounds.

Gia noticed her mother's discomfort and placed her hand on her back. "I can't wait to see her!"

"Well, let's get up outta here then," Toni replied.

DOMINIQUE HATED HOSPITALS. The smell of sickness and disinfectant . . . The crowdedness that came with certain seasons forcing patients out into the hallways on stretchers. The cacophony of coughing and beeping heart monitors, random announcements of coding patients, paging doctors over the PA system, and shifting of doctors and nurses throughout the days that turned into nights all made her sick to her stomach. But here she was. Walking beside her eldest sister down a wide hallway with newly waxed floors to see a man who allowed his wife to disown her for loving her unborn child more than his wife's stipulations.

She could see a woman standing at the nurse's station dressed to the nines in a poncho-style cotton animal print kaftan and white leggings, bejeweled arms, and her hair slicked back into a bun at the nape of her neck. The woman was giving the nurses grief about something. And Dominique knew she was next.

"I'm gonna run to the bathroom."

Toni looked over at her, thrown by her sudden need to depart.

"You awrite?"

"Yeah. I'm just a little—a little hot. I need to go wet my face and chest."

"Don't let Simone run you outta here. You know she got more bark than bite."

Dominique began to fan herself. "I know. It's just . . ."

The air-conditioning was on blast, but Dominique was overheating. Her face began to flush, and her hearing was starting to go. The voices around her were muffled now. She could feel her breathing change; it was rapid and jagged. A panic attack. Never in her life had she had one of these.

"This ... This was a bad idea," she shook her head.

Toni pulled a chair from the wall and sat her down. Dominique closed her eyes, throwing her head back, and struggling to slow her breath.

"You got this, suge. More than you know."

A nurse, who had been watching from a distance, approached with a cup of water and wet paper towel in hand. "This should help some," she smiled at Toni as she placed the damp rag on Dominique's forehead.

"Thank you," Toni nodded as she took the cup of water from her. "Take a couple of sips of this."

Dominique opened her eyes briefly, then closed them again. She took the paper cup and put it to her lips.

"Well, the prodigal daughter has returned," a sultry voice jeered.

It was close. Too close to her for comfort. Dominique slowly opened her eyes and sighed. The gray-eyed devil was standing over her with arms folded and lips pursed.

"Took Daddy to be on his deathbed for you to come home. Mmm. Still selfish, I see. Still playing the victim."

"Stop it, Simone. Nobody got time for ya shit right now," Toni warned.

"No, it's awrite, Toni." Dominique removed the paper towel from her

forehead and crumpled it in her hand. "It's good to see you too, Simone. Ya still bitter and miserable."

Simone grinned devilishly, her milk chocolate skin shimmering. "My honey calls that 'fire' and 'spirit.'"

"Ya honey?"

"*Yes, my honey.*"

Dominique smirked. "Well, he obviously doesn't know you."

"Oh, I would say Antoine knows me *very* well."

"Antoine?!" Dominique looked back and forth between them. "*Antoine Brevard?*"

Toni placed her hand on Dominique's back, sliding it to her shoulder. She squeezed gently.

"Do Mama and Daddy know?"

"Of course not. They don't even know he's back in town. Hell, they don't know he's even alive," she laughed.

"He's back for good?"

"Mm-hmm. But enough about me and mine. You still seeing that Negro, Louis, right? Is that his name? No, no, it's Quintin. No, that's not it. Chase? You know what? It doesn't even matter. You never could keep your legs closed. And I hear that daughter of yours can't either."

Dominique began to rise from the chair. Toni gently pushed her back down.

"You watch ya tongue about my child before I split it," Dominique hissed.

"Are you threatening me?" Simone smirked.

"I'm *warnin'* you," she snarled low. "*Gia* is her name. And she ain't no different from any other girl her age. So, as a mother, as *her* mother, I'm handlin' it accordingly. Now, I know you don't understand what that means because ya not a mother. But that ain't my fault. That's *yours.*"

Simone peddled back some. She looked back and forth between her sisters, her glossed lips parting and brows knitting together. Toni ran her hand across her forehead and swiveled on her heels. Dominique remained. She was sitting forward with her arms resting on her lap, daring her sister to say another smug word.

The two were like night and day. They never liked each

other, not even as little girls. Simone was mean and surly. She had always been that way. But it seemed Dominique endured the worst of her cruelty. Especially after she became pregnant with Gia. Simone held on to their parents' shame and disappointment as tightly as Dominique.

"How's Daddy?" Toni asked, breaking the tension.

Simone closed her mouth and met Toni's eyes. "Same as yesterday. Mama's in there showing the nurse how to give him a proper sponge bath."

"No, she's not." Toni began to chuckle.

"Yes, she is, honey. You know she wasn't going to let anyone touch her man. Especially, not a young tender like the one in there with her right now."

"Lawd."

Simone shifted her pocketbook's strap on her shoulder. "I'm going to run now. Gotta go get ready for the Urban League's Annual Gala tonight."

She and Toni exchanged a cheek kiss.

"Awrite."

Simone looked down at Dominique and smirked before marching down the hall.

Dominique and Toni locked eyes.

"See, I told you. You had it."

GIA REMOVED the remaining articles of clothing from her bag and placed them in the tall dresser adjacent to the queen-sized sleigh bed. The guest room in her aunt Toni's bungalow-style home was cozy and quaint. She stayed behind as instructed while her mother and aunt ventured off to the hospital.

Gia closed the dresser drawer and made her way into the living room. It was decorated with African masks and statues, unlit candles, and wooden bowls of potpourri, familial photographs of those she knew and loved, and others she didn't know but respected. The cream-colored sectional had modcloth pillows and a kente cloth throw blanket tossed over it. A baby grand piano sat in the corner decorated with many of her aunt's and cousin's awards. Magazines and books were spread across the wooden coffee table set before the couch. The space truly reflected her aunt's personality.

Gia plopped down on the sofa and picked up a magazine. It was too hot to go outside, so she decided to relax until the women returned. She lay on her side and began to flip through the first couple of pages. The ringing of the house phone resounded. She jumped up and trotted into the kitchen, where it rested in its cradle on one of the counters. She picked it up and pressed the "ANSWER" button.

"Hello?"

"Hey, GiGi. You awrite?" Toni asked on the other end.

Gia smiled. "Yes, ma'am."

"Good. I just wanted to check in wit'cha. Mommy and I are about to go in and see Mama and Daddy."

"Okay. Is she okay?" Gia asked, unsuccessfully hiding her mounting anxiety.

"She's hangin' in there." Toni exhaled.

Gia knew by her aunt's response that her mother was struggling. "Can I talk to her?"

"She's in the bathroom, but as soon as we leave here, I'll have her call you."

"Kay," Gia said, sounding and feeling like a little girl again.

Her mother needed her right now. Something as small as hearing her voice would make all the difference, but her aunt didn't understand that. And she was certain she didn't care to.

"Ya mama's got to do this on her own, GiGi," Toni said gently as if reading her mind.

"Yes, ma'am," Gia replied softly.

"Give us an hour."

TASH HAWTHORNE

"Okay."

The line went dead. Gia pushed the "END" button and placed the phone back in its cradle. She wished Amari were there. He always helped her navigate through the waters that were her and her mother's disputes. She stared at the phone, wrestling with thoughts of calling him. If she decided to, what was the worst that could happen? She was thousands of miles away. He had no way to reach her.

And she would be honest and tell her aunt what she'd done in hopes that she didn't relay it to her mother. Life was about taking risks, right?

"Hello?"

Gia melted at the sound of his voice. "Amari."

"Baby?"

"Yes, it's me," she smiled.

"Where are you calling me from?"

"Louisiana," she sniffled back tears.

"Louisiana? What type of shit . . .? I didn't know she was gonna take you to Louisiana. Are y'all staying down there for good?"

There was fear in Amari's voice. Something she'd unfortunately grown accustomed to under her mother's reign.

"No, we're down here because my Papaw is sick, and he wants to talk to my mom before he goes."

"Oh, I'm so sorry. I'll keep him in my prayers."

She could see him making the sign of the cross. Her mother always said a man who prays is a powerful man. God appreciates and always takes notice of his faithfulness.

"Thank you."

"Of course. I hope he passes peacefully."

"Me too. I miss you," Gia whined.

"I miss you too, babe."

She smiled small. Sad. "Me and my mom had a fight. And to be honest, it was pretty bad."

"Did you talk it out with her?"

"No," Gia shook her head.

"Why not?"

"Because I don't want to talk about it, and neither does she. We're just sweeping it under the rug, like usual," Gia sniffled again. "I'm so tired of this."

"Give her some time, baby. She's your mom. She's not perfect, you know? She makes mistakes like all of us do. And she loves you. Whatever it is, I know you guys will work it out."

Gia sucked her teeth. "I guess. How's it going up there?"

"Pretty good. Wishing you were here, though."

"Same." Gia wiped her eyes.

"Should we be talking right now?"

"No, but you're my best friend. Who else am I going to talk to?" Gia huffed.

"You're right. I'm feeling guilty about it, though."

"Me too. You think I should tell her I called you?"

"Yeah, but just wait a little while. She's already messed up behind your grandpa being in the hospital. Let her get herself together first."

"Yeah, you're right. I don't want to cause any more problems." She placed her hand on her forehead and began to rub it.

"Are you going to call me again?"

"I don't know. I'm gonna try. Just don't call this number. It's my aunt's house phone."

"Okay. You know I'm always here for you, babe. I love you."

"I know. I love you too. Just bear with me."

HER BACK WAS FACING the door when they entered the room. She was dressed in a white, cotton, buttoned-down blouse with the sleeves rolled to her elbows, denim blue jeans secured by a leather belt with a silver and jasper-encrusted wrestling buckle, and white sneakers. Her black hair was styled in a loose French braid that stopped just below her shoulders. Her nails and lips were painted red. She didn't hear the girls come in. She was too focused on buttoning the remaining buttons on their father's pajama top.

"Hey, Mama," Toni smiled.

Corrine's back remained turned. "Hey, baby. You just missed Simone."

"Oh no, I saw her."

"Oh, good. I told her to go on to the gala. Stand in fo' Daddy and me."

"You told her right. Didn't she, Domi?"

"Yes, she did," she nodded.

Corrine spun around, her mouth slightly agape. She hadn't expected her youngest child to make it in time. In fact, she'd expected her to make excuses not to come at all. But she had to remind herself that the love her daughters had for their father was unconditional. And even the youngest one, whom she warred with the most, would move heaven and earth to be with him . . . even if that did mean sharing space with her.

Dominique cracked a small smile.

"You came," Corrine whispered, her voice quivering.

"Yes, ma'am."

"Get over here, girl," Corrine smiled, her arms outstretched.

Dominique walked into her mother's strong arms without hesitation. The embrace was firm. She took in her scent of lavender and honeysuckle. Drowned in it as their hearts found a steady rhythm, beating as one. Her mother rubbed her back, squeezed her tighter, almost instinctively, to close the time and space that had come between them. It had been so long since Dominique last felt her touch that she almost forgot what it felt like.

Corrine pulled back gently and took her in, caressing her

face with her thumbs. She wasn't one to brag about her daughters' beauty, but she surely couldn't help but beam with pride at the sight of them. "You've lost yo' softness."

Dominique grabbed her mother's deep cocoa-brown hands and held them. Then, she closed her eyes and prepared herself for what was to come after her response.

"No fault of my own."

Corrine raised a brow as she removed her hands from her grasp. "Oh, no?"

"No, ma'am." Dominique watched her mother transform, *retreat* to the apathetic woman she'd come to know and fear at seventeen.

"Well, I beg to differ."

"Awrite, you two. That's enough," Toni whispered.

Corrine moved toward Duke's bed and proceeded to tuck him in. "He's been holdin' on fo' you."

Dominique looked over at her father, then shifted her weight from one foot to the other.

"Duke, open yo' eyes, baby. Look who's here to see you."

He lay under a small mound of white sheets and blankets, an oxygen line taped to his freckled cheeks. Countless wires were attached to his massive chest and arm. The beeping from the heart monitor was slow and steady. Dominique lingered at the foot of the bed as she watched Toni plant a kiss on his freckled forehead, then rub his white hair.

Dreux slowly opened his eyes and focused on the figure draped in green. He smiled small and genuine, then his eyebrows creased. Then, fighting against heartache, he smiled once again.

"Domi? Is that my Domi?" his voice gravelly.

"In the flesh," Toni grinned.

"Hey, Daddy," Dominique finally spoke.

"Doesn't she look good?" Toni continued.

"Mm-hmm. Leave us," he kindly demanded.

"Awrite. Come on, Mama."

Dreux and Dominique watched Toni and Corrine leave, closing the door behind them. Dominique carried her eyes into the hallway. It was quiet. The occasional page over the intercom system resounded. But where there should have been activity, there was stillness.

Dreux signaled for her to move closer. She did. He patted the vacant spot beside him on the bed. She sat. They stared at each other for a long while. Like her, he'd been a ginger once upon a time. She missed his red curls. So much had changed in the last six months. And it hadn't been kind to him like it hadn't been to Simone.

"Are the children . . . outside?"

"No. Gia's back at Toni's. Dominic and Michael are in DR."

"Mmm. I wanted . . . to see them . . . too." He closed his eyes momentarily. "I've missed you."

Dominique choked back tears. Her father, her hero whom she worshipped, was now a shell of the man she once knew. It was almost too much to bear.

"I've missed you too, Daddy."

He smiled sadly, his eyes tired.

Dominique sniffled. "You got to fight. We not ready."

"Ya more ready . . . than . . . you know. Ya strong, Domi. All of you . . . girls are. But you . . . you've always been . . . the stronges'. I'm so proud . . . of . . . you."

"Thank you, Daddy," she wiped fallen tears from her cheeks.

He gripped her hand tighter. "I want . . . you to . . . do . . . somethin' for me."

"Sir?"

"I want you to . . . make peace. I need you . . . to." He struggled to swallow.

Dominique tilted her head. She winced as she struggled to

wrap her mind around his request. "I can't do it, Daddy. I just . . . I can't."

"Ya . . . mama don't know . . . how to let things . . . go either."

"There's been exceptions. There's always exceptions," Dominique countered.

Dreux stared at his youngest for a moment. She'd blossomed overnight, it seemed. "Forgiveness. I taught you . . . that."

"Yes, you did. But you also taught me that it doesn't happen overnight. It took you awhile to forgive me for conceivin' Gia the way I did."

Dreux closed his eyes and shook his head. "That's not . . . fair."

"Why isn't it?" Dominique shifted her weight. "It's the truth."

"Pride. Shame kept me . . . from doin' so sooner," Dreux blinked.

Dominique rose from the bed and placed her hands on her hips. She began to pace. "I'm not ashamed of my child. I'm only ashamed of how she got here."

Tears began to roll down Dreux's cheeks.

"I'm a good mother, Daddy. A *good* mother. I am. But as a woman—my daughter thinks I'm a whore."

Dreux closed his eyes.

"Look at me, Daddy."

He did.

"She thinks every man I date, I lay with. And that's just not true. I entertain 'em. I entertain 'em by feedin' their egos with empty praise and insincere interest. I entertain 'em to forget that I wasn't enough for her daddy to stay. That she and her brothers weren't enough for him to come home for good. You tryin'a force the past back on me . . . and the past is the reason why I'm this way at all."

"Daughter . . ."

"I am *ashamed* of myself. Of what I've *become*. Of what *he* made me."

"Don't . . . please."

"I am a *disgrace* to myself and to my children. To Mama. *And it is eating me alive*." She rubbed her chest.

"Dom—"

"I lost my power."

"No—"

Dominique could feel the heat spreading through her body. Her chest tightened. "I love you, Daddy. I do. But I can't honor ya wish. I won't."

"Have mercy . . . have mercy on . . . him."

"Mercy is not for me to give," her voice sounded dark and empty.

Toni entered with a sandwich, chips, and bottle of water in hand. "Mama ran to the bathroom. And I got you somethin' to eat." She studied them for a moment, ingesting the awkward silence.

"Thank you." Dominique grinned as her eyes pulled away from Dreux. "I'm gonna go get him some fresh water." She retrieved the pitcher on the windowsill and kissed Dreux on the forehead. As she moved toward the door, he called out to her.

"Domi."

She turned around to face him. "Yes, Daddy?"

"There's somethin' . . . fo' ya . . . at the bank. Speak to Delacroix . . . about it."

Dumbfounded again by another request, Dominique simply nodded before exiting the room. Emergency lights blinked, and machines beeped in a distant room. She walked through a flock of nurses and a doctor running past her to aid a coded patient. In her rage, blanketed in it, she never broke her stride.

MAISON LE SAINT-FAVIER was located Uptown on Nashville Avenue. Built in 1866, the classic center hall-style home sat in the middle of the block. It had a grand foyer, high ceilings, chandeliers, double parlors, dining and breakfast rooms, a gourmet kitchen, master suite, and five other bedrooms with en suites. Dreux had spared no expense in providing an affluent home and lifestyle for his wife and daughters. They had the best of everything, from clothing to education.

Born into a wealthy Creole family, Dreux understood the value of money, how to earn it, invest it, watch it grow, and (most importantly) keep it. He attended Dillard University, where he studied biology (pre-med) and met his beloved wife, Corrine. Corrine, or Cori, as she was lovingly called. She was also Louisiana-born, but that of the Bayou Teche. She had dreams of becoming a nurse, using her mother and grandmother's traditions of spiritual and holistic medicine to heal their people. Break cycles. Mend traumas. Preserve their history. And she did. Dreux became a dentist, and she a healer. Forty-five years they'd been together. And now, Corrine was forced to live her remaining years without him.

Dominique busied herself by serving her sisters their dinner and drinks. Her mother was in her room lying down. Her father had gone into cardiac arrest in the midnight hour, slipping away like a thief in the night. She was numb. Father or not, he'd wanted her in the arms of the wrong man. One who had already forced her to fend for herself in a world that hated Black women, was intimidated by them, hunted them like prey, and expected unrealistic superheroic saviorism from them. He'd let her go. Unprotected. She had no tears for her father. Not now. Not yet. And she had no words of comfort for her sisters. None of them had slept since getting the call. It was only a matter of time before they crashed.

Her brother-in-law Devere, Big GiGi's husband, decided to throw an impromptu seafood boil. He was a firm believer in the power of comfort food. Dominique peeked out the window above the sink and watched the disastrous game of UNO between Gia and her three nephews unfold. Young, strong voices rose and fell, hands slammed cards down, backsides left seats. One would have thought they were playing a game of Spades. Their joy brought a smile to Dominique's face. She was happy to see Gia having a good time. Lord knows she needed it.

"What time is the appointment tomorrow?" Jackie asked.

"Nine o'clock," Toni replied as she cracked a crab leg.

"Damn, I'm not gonna be able to make it. I have two events to cater."

"You want one of us to text you the particulars while we're there?" Big GiGi asked.

"Naw, I'm not gonna have time to check my messages."

Toni dipped a piece of crabmeat in her butter sauce. "Then, how about this? I'll ask Mama if you can take care of Daddy's suit and accessories while we handle everything else."

"Awrite. That'll work. I know just which one to put him in too."

"Damn, Jackie. You ain't wastin' no time, huh?" Big GiGi chuckled. "You ready-ready."

Jackie became serious. "I ain't mean it like that."

Toni, shaking her head and giggling, waved her hand. "We know, love. Pay her no mind." She wiped her mouth with a napkin. "Leave her alone, GiGi."

Genevieve surrendered, her hands up.

"I'm not goin'," Dominique professed.

Her sisters' smiles faded.

"Dominique," Toni began.

"What?" she snapped over her shoulder.

Toni set her plate down on the end table beside her cushioned chair. She crossed her legs at the knees, then interlocked her fingers. "You know that's not an option. Mama expects you to be there."

"I know, but—"

"You have a responsibility."

"And so did Daddy. In fact, y'all did too. But instead, you had me come all the way down here to get blindsided by him and Simone."

Jackie cleared her throat. Big GiGi took a swig of her wine.

"You right," Toni admitted. "Daddy was wrong. Simone is too. Hell, we all dead wrong. We should'a told you."

"We're sorry," the twins added.

Dominique removed the dish gloves and placed them on the edge of the sink.

"Look, I'll stay until the readin' of his will, but after that, I'm gone."

"Good riddance," Simone sang from the kitchen's entryway.

All eyes fell upon her.

"Simone!" Toni, Jackie, and Big GiGi yelled in unison.

"Simone, nothing. She's been itching to leave since she got here. If she doesn't want to stay, then let her go."

Simone, dressed in a sundress and espadrille wedges, walked to the island and placed her bedazzled clutch on it.

"It ain't that simple," Toni smirked.

"Why isn't it?" Simone said, confused.

Toni looked at the twins, then Dominique. "Because with Daddy bein' gone now, Mama's gonna retire and hand the botanica over to her."

Dominique turned around, holding Toni's gaze. "What?"

"No, she's not. If anything, she's going to continue working to keep her mind off of him being gone," Simone went on.

"Naw, Mama's gonna take this time to do what she wants. That means doin' some travelin', gettin' back to her mornin' walks . . . Everything she wasn't able to do while Daddy was here," Jackie stated matter-of-factly.

"And you all know this for certain?"

The three eldest nodded.

"Mama's gonna hand that shop over to Domi, give her and the kids this house, then move in with me so she can do whatever the hell she wants for the rest of her born days," Toni continued. "Her and Daddy made that decision years ago after he had his first heart attack."

"It sounds like they had a slight lapse in judgment. I mean . . . It just doesn't make any sense," Simone sneered.

Internally, Dominique agreed with her. She'd been gone for fourteen years. Her relationship with her mother was volatile. And she already had her own business to run.

"Why doesn't it?" Big Gigi asked before taking another sip of her wine.

"Because Toni's been managing the botanica since we were teenagers. And the house . . . wait, is she going to—?"

"We don't know. She didn't mention it."

"Look, I ain't come back to take Mama's place and dig up no bones," Dominique confessed.

"Good. 'Cause you could *never* be Mama. And we all know those bones are nothing but lies anyway," Simone scoffed.

Before anyone could comprehend what was happening, Dominique slammed her hand down on her wineglass, snatched a shard of glass, and charged at Simone.

"Bitch!"

"Oh my God!" Simone screamed as she steered backward. Her sandals slid along the wooden floor, forcing one of her ankles to give way.

"Domi!" the twins hollered, running after her.

Dominique caught Simone by the neckline of her dress. She dropped the piece of glass and slapped her twice, then wrapped her hands around her neck.

Blood flowed like a faucet. "Ain't nothin' dishonest about me, bitch!"

Toni, Jackie, and Big GiGi struggled to pull her off of Simone, who was losing consciousness.

"Dominique! Dom-i-nique!"

"Let her go!" the twins cried.

Hearing the commotion from outside, Gia, her cousins, and uncle ran in to see what hell had broken loose. Gia watched her aunts struggle with her mother. Someone was bleeding. She wasn't sure who.

"Mommy!" she screamed.

"Get a good look at my child," Dominique jeered through gritted teeth.

"She can't breathe, Dominique!" Toni shouted.

"*Look at her,*" she stressed.

Simone, her eyes flooded with tears, did as she was told.

"Now, call me a liar again."

Corrine emerged from her room, wrapping her hair in a tignon. "What the hell . . .?" She charged at the group, pushing everyone out of her way. "*Laissez-la partir, Dominique! On donna la vie, pas on prend! Laissez-la partir!*" Corrine affirmed in her ear.

Dominique released her. "Fuckin' bitch!"

"Enough!" Corrine barked as Devere helped her to her feet.

Simone turned on her side, holding her throat and gasping for air. Her lips were swollen and bleeding. Toni and Big GiGi's sons pulled Dominique to her feet. Her right hand and arm were covered in blood.

"Hold ya arm up. Hold it up," Toni ordered as she grabbed a rag from the sink and tied it around her hand.

"You babies go on back outside and finish playin' yo' game," Corrine instructed, her hands on her hips.

Gia hesitated until her grandmother met her gaze and gave her a gentle nod.

Corrine looked at each of her girls and shook her head. "I feel like I'm in a goddamn time warp."

"Mama—" Toni and the twins began.

"I don't wanna hear it! Yo' daddy's body ain't even cold yet, and y'all in here fightin' and carryin' on like you ain't got the good sense God gave you!" Corrine spat.

"Y'all get this one up and get her some warm saltwater for her throat. I'll take this one wit' me."

DOMINIQUE SAT on the edge of her parents' double sink with her injured hand under her mother's magnifying mirror. Small wooden bowls of turmeric powder, honey, and coconut oil were set beside her mother's nursing kit. Dominique watched her push her glasses up on her nose before proceeding to remove a shard of glass from the open wound with tweezers.

"Gia should not have been subjected to that back there."

"I know, Mama."

"Do you?" Corrine stopped, looking at her over the rim of her glasses. "Because what I just saw says otherwise." She put the tweezers down, then retrieved a saline flush. "You need to be ashamed of yo'self. What kind of example are you settin' fo' that chile?"

"Mama, you the one who taught us not to take no shit from nobody—family included."

"Watch yo' mouth," she patted the cut with a piece of gauze. "And you right, but I ain't mean fo' you to put yo' hands on anybody, Dominique. I meant to handle them wit' yo' words."

"Well, Simone don't understand words."

Corrine threw the bloodstained dressing in the waste paper basket at her feet. "What could she have possibly said that was so bad? Hmm?"

"Don't matter. It won't happen again," Dominique sighed as she slid off the sink.

"Uh, we not through here. Sit down."

Dominique rolled her eyes as she obliged.

Corrine began to apply the turmeric powder to the laceration. "This is the hardness I was talkin' about at the hospital. Whatever's eatin' at you, you gonna have to let it go. My grand-babies need their mama to be available to them."

Dominique stared at her mother in disbelief. *Is she serious? She* was what was eating at her. During their last visit, all she did was condemn the way Dominique ran her household. She didn't approve of Amari's daily visitation, nor did she agree with him being entertained by Gia in her room. When Dominique tried to explain to her why he spent most of his days at her house and why she allowed him in Gia's room, her mother accused her of having no control and enabling poor behaviors in Gia. A screaming match ensued, leaving Dominique embarrassed and in tears.

"I *am* available to them."

"Like you are to those men you got comin' in and out of that house of yours? Sure are a lot of souls to have tied to you."

Dominique shot her a look.

"Don't look at me like that. Yo' sister told me all about 'em."

At that moment, Dominique swore to herself that she wouldn't tell Toni another thing ever again. "They're just friends, Mama. I ain't sleepin' with any of 'em."

"Does Esai know about these *friends*?"

They locked eyes.

"He don't ask about mine. I don't ask about his."

Corrine grunted in disapproval. "What about the one Gia saw you wit'? You know, that ain't really safe to have some man in yo' house while yo' daughter's there. Niggas be sleepin' wit' the mama but dreamin' about the daughter."

"Jesus Christ, Mama!"

Corrine pressed down hard on Dominique's hand, causing it to bleed again.

"Ouch!"

"I don't give a damn how you talk up there in New Jersey.

But down here . . . in *my* house and in *my* presence, you gonna watch yo' mouth and keep the Lord's name out of it. Is that understood?"

"Yes, ma'am," Dominique winced. "Louis—"

"Louis, huh?"

"Yes. He isn't like that."

Corrine grunted again.

"It was a mistake, Mama. One that I have already apologized to Gia for."

"Well, you really in no position to be makin' any more of those, are you, baby girl?"

Dominique wanted to crawl under a rock. There was no way to please this woman. It didn't matter how well she'd done for herself under the unfortunate circumstances. Her mother would always remind her of the hurt and humiliation she caused.

"Gia is *not* a mistake," Dominique countered meekly.

"I ain't talkin' 'bout Gia."

They locked eyes once again.

"Mama—"

"The next couple of days are gonna be overwhelmin' fo' all of us. But I expect you to be on yo' best behavior."

"Of course."

"And yo' gonna take care of yo' daddy's body, right?"

"I'm leavin' for the funeral home in an hour."

"Good, good. Don't let Andrew touch 'im. Please."

"I won't."

"I ain't never been a fan of their work at Broussard's, but ya daddy insisted he go there. So . . ."

Dominique watched her eyes gloss over. "I got it, Mama. I'll take good care of 'im."

"I know you will," Corrine sniffled as she finished wrapping Dominique's hand, then removed her glasses. "All done."

Dominique slid off the sink, watching her mother gather

her instruments and place them back in her bag. "Thank you," she said, her hand raised.

"Yo' welcome. Give it a couple of days to heal."

"Okay. I'm gonna go check on Gia."

"Good idea."

Dominique stopped in the entryway, then turned back to face Corrine. "Mama?"

"Yes?" Corrine continued cleaning the counter.

"Toni mentioned somethin' about you retirin' now that Daddy's gone. Is that true?"

Corrine stopped in midwipe. "Yes."

"And?"

Corrine proceeded with her regimen, avoiding eye contact with her. "And we'll talk about it another time." She took the soiled rag and threw it in the waste paper basket. Then looked her square in the eyes. "'Til then . . . we mourn."

THE BANGING on Toni's front door jolted Dominique out of her sleep. She heard Toni's feet hit the floor, then drag into the living room. It was a little after three a.m. She couldn't imagine whose rage settled on her sister's doorstep. Dominique sat up, throwing her legs over the side of the bed. She grabbed her short cotton robe from off the bedpost and put it on.

Toni flipped on the living room lights. She yawned as she made her way to the door, looking through the peephole. She swore under her breath before unlocking the latches. A tall, fair-skinned man with a modern quiff and well-groomed goatee stood before her. Towering. He was dressed in a black T-shirt, tattered jeans, and matching Vans sneakers.

"She here?" He, unaware there was a line of red brick dust outlining the doorsill, shifted his weight from one foot to the other on the doormat.

"Antoine," Toni said flatly.

"Simone said she's here." He squinted his bloodshot eyes.

"And she's asleep. Where you should—"

"Wake her up for me," he sniffed.

Toni folded her arms across her chest. "No."

"Please? I'm askin' nicely, Toni."

"And I'm tellin' you 'no' nicely. Go home."

Antoine planted himself. "I'm not leavin' until I see her."

"She ain't got nothin' to say to you."

"Dominique!" he hollered over her head.

"Nigga!"

Dominique appeared. Her red hair tousled and cascading down her back. She was calm. Unnervingly calm. "I didn't call for you."

Toni turned around, startled. She and Antoine settled their gaze on her. His eyes widened. Taken aback. He wasn't prepared for the woman version of Dominique. She was refined. Fully grown. But she'd hardened. He could see it in her

eyes. Yet, the rigidity hadn't overshadowed her beauty. A fire began to rage in his loins.

"Yes, you did. When you went ape shit and put ya hands on ya sister."

"She deserved it," Dominique sneered.

"That may be so, but you know better."

"And she didn't. So now what? You gonna put ya hands on *me*?"

A cunning smile grew along Antoine's face. "I wanna do more than that to ya."

Dominique cringed.

"Aww, hell naw!" Toni started to close the door on him, but Antoine stopped it with his arm.

"Antoine, go home!" Dominique hollered.

"I love the way you scream my name," he chuckled.

Gia stumbled into the room, wiping her heavy eyes, her Afro wild with curls.

"What's going on?"

Panic began to creep into Dominique's chest. She didn't want Gia to see it, so she stayed focused on Antoine.

Toni sensed her sister's anxiety. And, as if on cue, made her way to her niece.

"GiGi, baby, let's get on back to bed."

"Who is he?" Gia looked from her aunt to her mother, then to the man studying her.

"Nobody," Dominique retorted over her shoulder.

Toni subtly shook her head. "This is an old friend of the family, Mr. Brevard."

"Oh."

Antoine placed his hand over his heart and bowed. "Miss Gia. My apologies for wakin' you, darlin'."

"GiGi," Dominique began, "everything's awrite, I promise. Go back to bed."

"Do as ya mama says," Toni followed.

"The fuck . . .?" Gia mumbled underneath her breath. She backed away into the darkness, deep enough to hide in it. And she remained there. Still and quiet. Listening. Watching. He was handsome, she thought. And familiar. She wasn't sure if it was his voice or his face. But she was certain she knew him from somewhere. Couldn't place him, but their paths crossed at some point in time.

"She's beautiful, Dom."

"I know."

"You really a mama," he smiled. "That's really . . . really somethin'," he nodded as he pressed his lips inward.

"Are we done here?" Dominique asked, ready to retreat to her room to fall apart.

"We ain't never really been done, baby. You know that." Antoine reached for her, but she slapped his hand away.

"Don't."

"You still trouble, girl. Always have been, always will be. But that's what I loved most about you. You were a thrill. *My* thrill. My li'l magnolia," he grinned. "Remember when I used to call you that?"

"That was a long time ago," Dominique sighed.

"Yeah. Yeah, it was." Antoine gave her a once-over. His eyes then resting on her bare legs.

Dominique shifted under his gaze.

"I never stopped lovin' you, ya know? Simone . . . Simone ain't you."

"And ya not Esai."

Antoine grunted, placed a stick of chewing gum in his mouth, and turned on his heels. "Behave, now. Or else."

Dominique slammed the door behind him. She was shaking. Toni moved toward her and took her face into her hands.

"It's okay. He's gone now. He's gone."

Her stomach was upset. She began to dry heave.

"Domi. Domi, calm down," Toni hushed.

Dominique broke free from her sister's grasp and ran into the hallway's half-bath. She lifted the toilet seat and lid before falling to her knees and submitting. Tears stained her cheeks. Her heavy sobs bounced off the bathroom walls. Toni and Gia gathered in the doorway. Toni stepped in and knelt beside her baby sister. She pulled her hair away from her face and rubbed her back.

"It's awrite, *cher*. It's awrite."

Toni looked up at Gia. She was still. Nervous and confused. Helpless almost. The hurt she was seeing in her mother, hearing from her was the kind of hurt people buried for a reason. The kind many didn't bounce back from. She was scared for her mom. For herself and her brothers.

Toni forced a smile through her dejected, wet face.

"She's gonna be awrite, GiGi. She is. Go get me a rag from the linen closet and wet it for me."

Gia did as she was told. She ran back, turned the faucet on, and placed the washcloth under the running water.

Dominique lifted her head out of the toilet and rested it against Toni's shoulder. "Call."

"Call who, love?" Toni rocked her gently as she wiped her nose and patted her face.

"Call 9 . . . 9-1 . . . 1," Dominique muttered before slipping into a seizure.

GIA SAT on a blanket watching her cousin and brothers jump waves. The beach ridge that was Grand Isle was sprinkled with people. They'd gone fishing earlier on the pier and caught some bass and redfish. Her aunt Toni thought it would be a good idea to get away from the familial madness for a day. Gia had never been to the edge of Louisiana. Wading in the warm Gulf waters felt like one thousand hugs. So she lay still and allowed the ebb and flow of the small tide to carry her beneath the sun's lips.

Dominic and Mikey flew in the previous night, grateful to be back in their sister's care. The boys. They had good heads on their shoulders. They excelled in school, athletics, and the arts. Dominic was a wiz in science and math. Mikey loved English and history. Dominic played the drums while Mikey strummed anything from a guitar to a ukulele. Dominic could build anything with Legos and erector sets, and Mikey could fix anything broken others may have thought had no value. The love Gia had for her brothers transcended space and time. She'd do anything for them, and they for her.

Her mother had been in the hospital for three days now. She'd suffered two more seizures since being admitted. Her grandmother was holding vigil at her bedside like she had for her grandfather. She was both vigilant and weary at this point. When she asked Gia and Toni what happened, they told her Dominique had suddenly become overwhelmed with grief and began to seize. Of course, it was an absolute lie, but that was the story they told and had to stick to. Without giving her much of anything else to go on, Toni stressed to Gia there was no way they could ever tell her grandmother the truth because the truth would turn her world and theirs upside down.

Gia almost found it ironic. Living in Jersey was nothing but stressful, yet her mother's body never reacted the way it had here in Louisiana. Louisiana was supposed to be slower and much kinder to its native sons and daughters. Yet, Gia had seen nothing but pain and sadness since being here. And she slowly understood why her mother never returned after leaving so many years ago.

"I can't get over how tall ya brothers have gotten since I last seen 'em." Toni said as she sat down beside her.

"Yeah, I know," Gia smiled again, basking in her brothers' lithe statures. "I still can't believe Dominic's taller than me."

"At fourteen, no less!" Toni shook her head.

"I know, right?"

They shared a laugh.

"I won't ask you to lie to ya grandmama again, GiGi. I just can't bear the thought of her knowin' what caused ya mama to get sick."

"Don't you mean *who*?"

"Yeah. Who." Toni looked toward the sky and sighed. "What do you know about trauma?"

"Well . . . It's something people don't talk about very much. And it's misinterpreted as stress a lot of the time, especially in our community."

"I'd say you know a lot," Toni smiled. "So, with that bein'

said, you need to know that what you saw the other night, what surfaced in ya mama, was trauma. And she gotta lot of it. We all do. Most, if not all, Black people do. That's why her body and spirit responded the way they did. But . . . She is where she needs to be to begin her healin'."

Gia processed her aunt's words. "Is he the reason why we haven't been back here in fourteen years?"

"Partially," Toni replied.

Gia looked over at her, then back at her brothers. "Did he hurt her?"

"Worse." Toni shook her head slowly. "He broke her. And that's all you need to know," she sighed. "Mmm . . . Before I forget, I thought you might like this back." Toni handed Gia's iPhone to her.

"You don't have to blackmail me, TeeTee."

"I'm not. I know ya word is good," she grinned. "I just can't have you runnin' up my phone bill."

"I was gonna tell you. I was just waiting for the right time," Gia confessed.

Toni waved her hand dismissively. "Don't worry about it. I was young and in love once. We all were."

"Mommy doesn't act like it."

"That's because she lost herself under its spell and had one helluva time findin' her way back."

Gia looked out into the distance. The sun's rays were dancing atop the water.

"I miss Uncle Charles."

"So do I, baby girl."

"Are you angry with him . . . for the way he left?"

"No. Mostly sad. I had to come to terms with the fact that I lost him long before he turned that gun on himself. Katrina is to blame. So I do blame her. He never recovered from all the devastation she left behind." Toni wiped her wet eyes. "You want a future with this boy?"

"Yes, ma'am," Gia replied, her face flushed.

"And he wants the same?" Toni asked.

"Mm-hmm," Gia nodded.

"Then you got to mind ya mama when she tells you to keep the most precious part of yaself *to* yaself, GiGi. She *knows*. Don't question it."

Gia shook her head, fighting the urge to cry. "It's not fair. I can't love my boyfriend the way I want, but she can fuck whoever?"

"Watch ya mouth."

"She's nothing but a hypocrite."

"That's enough, Gia. That's my baby sister, my heart you talkin' bad about. And if you keep it up, you gon' be walkin' this journey alone." Toni stared at her intensely. The child was angry. Hurting badly. She'd obviously seen some things, but her perception had been misconstrued. "How many partners do you think she's had?"

Gia shrugged her shoulders. "I don't know. A lot. Too many."

"You sound like ya grandmama," Toni cringed. "That's a terrible light to see ya mama in." She lifted Gia's chin, turning her face toward her. "And ya wrong."

Gia shook her head.

"You hear me? *Ya wrong*," Toni stressed.

"I don't understand her."

"What don't you understand?"

"Why she's so hard on me."

"Because ya just like her, *cher*."

"But I don't think I am, TeeTee, because Mommy holds onto things, and I don't. I like to forget and move on."

"Memory can be a dangerous thing," Toni said carefully.

"And painful," Gia added. "I know I've made a lot of mistakes, but I don't like feeling trapped by them. I hate it. I feel like I'm drowning. And I know if I'm forced to keep holding onto them and reliving them, the weight will get heavier and heavier. I can't live like this—I can't. I'm starting to fall into myself again and see the broken pieces. And they hurt more than what actually caused me to break in the first place."

"Ya mama means well, GiGi, but I don't think she realizes that you've got ya own hurt too. Some that she's caused even. She needs to understand that her way of healin' is not ya way. That her sufferin' shouldn't be yours or ya brothers. I'll speak to her about it when the time is right."

Gia picked at her sandwich.

Toni looked over at her niece and brushed a wisp of hair away from her forehead. "What else is on ya mind?"

"I don't know," she said quietly.

"Yes, you do," Toni replied, rubbing Gia's thigh.

"It's a lot of things. Everything," Gia confessed.

"Well, maybe I can help you make sense of some of those things."

Gia looked over at her aunt briefly, then picked at her sandwich again.

"What happened between Mommy and Mamaw?"

Toni sighed heavily. "Where do I begin? Well, ya mama was ya grandparents' pride and joy. I mean, we all were, but she being the last of us, the baby, they just adored her. She could do no wrong in their eyes." She sat back against the tree and sighed again. "Ya granddaddy, as you know, was a very proud man. He was one of the first Black successful dentists in NOLA. And he was one of very few business owners who were able to rebuild after Katrina and flourish. Because of his hard work and dedication to the community and us, we were afforded the best education and opportunities. One of those opportunities was marryin' men who shared the same social status. Mr. Brevard just so happened to be one of those opportunities. Papaw chose him specifically for ya mama."

"They dated," Gia said flatly.

"Correct," Toni replied. "And Mamaw disapproved from the very beginning. She didn't like him and didn't care who did. They dated for about a year. But then ya mama made the mistake of breakin' curfew one night, and ya grandmama ended the relationship."

"Oh."

"Yeah. She didn't play. So much so, she didn't allow ya mama to date anyone else after that."

Gia thought about how much her mother was like her grandmother at that moment. Quick to head someone off at the pass.

"But . . . Ya daddy came along and swept ya mama off her feet. And because she didn't want to lose him like she had Mr. Brevard, she kept their relationship hidden from ya grandparents."

Gia smirked. "I don't blame her."

"We didn't either. We were happy for her. But, unfortunately, her secret didn't stay that way for too long."

"What happened?" Gia asked hesitantly.

"*You happened*. And they didn't take it too well."

"How'd they find out?"

"Well, Mamaw gotta call from one of her colleagues who worked as a nurse at the Planned Parenthood we went to. We thought we were doin' somethin' by drivin' all the way to Baton Rouge. But you see, we had no idea ya grandmama's network reached beyond the waters of the Southshore. Anyway, she told her she'd seen me, the twins, and ya mama come in, and she'd given the youngest prenatal brochures on the way out. When we got home . . . all hell broke loose." Toni waned. Reflecting. Agonizingly.

"Ya grandaddy just . . . fell apart. We tried to console 'im, but we couldn't. Ya grandmama wouldn't let ya mama explain herself. As far as she was concerned, she had made a conscious decision to defy her and her rules, knowin' the consequences."

Toni tried to shake the memory . . . mute the sounds and smells. "And my poor li'l sister fell victim to ya grandmama's fury. She whipped her so bad. So, so bad. I can still hear the crack of ya granddaddy's belt buckle against her body." Toni wiped a creeping tear.

Gia shivered at the thought. She'd never known her grand-mother's anger, only her joy. As she processed everything, she began to feel sorry for her mother. Understanding *now* more so than ever that she still carried the memory of that night with her—the pain from it. The scars. Visible and invisible.

"Then . . . What happened?"

"Well, then ya grandmama told her to pick herself up off the floor and leave."

Gia shook her head in disbelief. Memories of her early childhood years in New Orleans started to resurface.

"That's why we lived with you, Corey, and Uncle Charles."

"Mm-hmm," Toni nodded.

"She hasn't forgiven her for it still. That's why they fight so much and why we don't visit," Gia professed, a lightbulb turning on.

"You got it," Toni sulked. "But ya granddaddy . . . He forgave her."

"This is a lot," Gia said, rubbing her neck.

"I know. But you're strong enough to handle it."

"Okay. TeeTee Simone . . . How did she end up with Mr. Brevard? Isn't there some kinda sister code or something to follow?"

"Ya aunt Simone ain't never been loyal to anybody, and she's always been jealous of ya mama."

"Why?"

"Nobody knows. But jealousy and envy are a dangerous combination for Spirit to have. And believe it or not, ya mama's tried to kill Simone with kindness over the years. But she's understandably grown tired of her shit."

"But why is he with her if he still loves my mother? That's what he told her."

Toni cut her eyes. "You weren't supposed to hear that. You were supposed to be back in ya bed."

"I wanted to make sure she was really okay," Gia lied.

"You were being nosy."

"A little," Gia blushed.

"Mm-hmm." Toni shook her head.

"He looked at her the same way the other men do. That isn't love."

"No, it isn't." Toni held her breath. "None of 'em tried anything wit'chu, have they?"

"No, ma'am. She never brings them around us. Well, except this one nigga, I mean *guy* . . . Louis. He's the worst of them all." She paused. "Mommy had a miscarriage last March. It was his baby, and he disappeared right after. Then out of the blue, he popped up at the funeral home right before we flew down here."

Toni looked into the distance. "I didn't know about the baby."

"You didn't?"

"No," Toni shook her head.

Gia scratched the back of her neck. "She really has kept it to herself."

"She'll tell it in her own time."

"You're not upset? She tells you everything."

Toni shook her head. "I'm sure she had her reasons. Still does. And I respect that."

Gia grunted.

"What?"

"Your patience. You're just so laid-back and chill about everything. Like, nothing bothers you."

"A lot bothers me, GiGi. I've just learned to carry my cross with a smile."

EVERYBODY WHO WAS anybody attended Duke's homegoing. From the mayor to representatives of the National Dentist Association and NAACP, the man who had been "bigger than life" to his friends and family had gone out in style. Two trumpeters led the family and mourners out of the church, then into the care of the Zulu Social Aid and Pleasure Club, who led a dirge second line to the cemetery. Standing side by side with heavy hearts, the LeSaint-Favier family laid their patriarch to rest. Gia stood with her grandmother, aunts, brothers, and cousins staring in the distance at the stretch limo that kept her mother. She'd decided against taking part in the committal ceremony, insisting Gia and the boys stand in for her. The twins tried to sway her, but she remained immovable.

Under the high sun's gaze, Gia watched and waited for her mama to emerge. But she never did. She'd watched her throughout the service, as well. But Dominique had been stoic the entire time. Afterward, the family rejoined the public in another celebratory second line along Esplanade Avenue and into New Orleans City Park to the New Orleans Museum of Art, where they gathered over comfort food and drinks at Café NOMA.

Dominique stared at her reflection in the bathroom mirror. She adjusted the veil on her fascinator, cocking it to the side and securing it with another hairpin. She checked her face. Flawless, her lips painted in red. She'd been released from the hospital just in time for her father's service. Her sisters had taken care of her and the kids' outfits for the occasion, and for that, she was grateful. Dominique behaved today, and so had Simone. She was proud of herself. And even though she was tired and ready to retire for the night, doing so wasn't an option. Not only would leaving be an insult to her father's memory, but also to their culture. The partying had just begun. It didn't matter if most of the guests were over seventy. They were going to eat, drink, laugh, reminisce, and dance until the midnight hour.

The bathroom door creaked open. The sound of its lock securing in place followed. Antoine turned the corner with his hands in his pockets.

"What are you doin'?" Dominique cringed.

He raised his hands in submission. "I come in peace. I swear."

"I don't care. Get out."

"We need to talk," he said seriously as he walked toward her.

"This isn't the time or the place. Please leave before my mama finds out that ya here."

"She won't. She's too busy takin' care of everybody right now." Antoine made himself comfortable, leaning against the sink.

"Simone see you?"

"Maybe. But for the record, we're not serious."

Dominique grunted. "She seems to think otherwise."

He shrugged with little care or concern and continued to take her in. Every inch. Dominique sighed.

"Has anyone told you how beautiful you look today? Even in ya sadness?"

"What do you know about sadness?" She cut her eyes at him.

He chuckled. "I know enough."

"What do you want?" Dominique sighed again.

"You. It's always been you. And Gia."

Their eyes locked.

"I apologize for my behavior at Toni's. Forgive me?"

Dominique pursed her lips.

Antoine crossed his arms and shook his head. "I think it's time to tell her the truth."

"The truth ain't in you."

"And what about you? Is it in you?" He removed a speck of lint from her hip.

"I'm not gonna upset my child with this shit." She began to place her makeup back in her clutch. "I'm not."

"Well, then I am."

"Over my dead body."

"I want a relationship wit' my daughter."

"Oh, *now* she's ya daughter. You are a piece of work. You know that?"

"It's the right thing to do."

"The right thing to do." She laughed incredulously. "Wasn't nothin' right from the time that girl was conceived. Not even before it. You have lost ya mind. Have you forgotten that ya with my sister?"

"I just told you it's nothin' serious." Antoine reached for her hand. She tucked it under her arm. "I'm not the same teenage punk I was nineteen years ago." He rubbed her arm with the back of his hand. She shifted her weight to the other leg.

"I don't believe you. I'd be a damn fool."

Antoine rose from the counter and stood behind her, staring back at their reflection. He moved forward, filling the space between them. He pressed his hardened nature against her back and watched her chest rise and fall.

"Then let me show you."

GIA SAT at a corner table watching her brothers and cousins play football outside. She ate the last piece of her salmon cake, then wiped her mouth with the cloth napkin in her lap. She didn't realize how lonely it was being the only girl until that moment. Her grandmother and aunts moved through the room, greeting and entertaining guests with grace. It was almost effortless. She caught her aunt Simone staring at her from time to time, causing her to squirm in her chair. Her gray eyes were unsettling. Almost spooky against her chocolate skin. Gia didn't want any trouble. She wasn't in the mood for Simone's foolishness and surely couldn't promise to mind her manners if approached.

Gia flipped her phone over and scrolled through unanswered text messages from her friends back home. She replied one at a time, then decided to Facetime Amari. His smiling face appeared on the screen.

"Amari."

"Hey, ma-ma! You got your phone back?"

"Kinda."

"Kinda?"

Gia wanted to share in his joy but couldn't. She was miserable. "Yeah. I . . . I wanna come home."

"What you mean *you wanna come home*? You're on vacation."

"I can't do this anymore. It's hot and humid. I have mosquito bites on my ass. I'm ready to come home," she sulked.

"All right, hold on. Chill out. What's going on?"

"I'm tired. I don't like being here. My mom just came out of the hospital. She's down here having seizures and shit."

"Wait, what? Seizures? Is she all right? She good now?"

"No." Gia rubbed her forehead absentmindedly. "She's fucking crazy for bringing us down here. Like, it's supposed to be different from up North, but it's not. Shit here is worse. Like, I have never seen so much coonery in all my life, babe. My mom has never had a seizure before. *Ever.* And she's had three, baby . . . *three.*"

"Three? The fuck goin' on down there? Do you need me to come down?"

"No. She's gonna mess around and have another one if you do that," Gia simpered.

"Well, is she all right, though?"

70

"No. The doctor said she's unstable and might have more."

"Oh my God. You serious?"

"Yeees. She's *not* all right. And my aunt's not helping. She's making it worse." Gia caught eyes with Simone yet again.

"Wait. Which aunt?"

"Simone. Mommy fucked her up."

"Wait. You telling me your mother got into a fight with your auntie?"

"Yeees."

"Did she win?"

"Amari!"

"What? I'm serious. Did she win?"

"Yeah, she did," Gia laughed. "She fucked her shit up. Oh my God. Like, on some crazy shit. She held a piece of glass to her throat and everything."

"Daaamn. I can't believe I missed it."

"Yeah, it was over some old beef they never squashed."

"Wooow. So, everyone down there is just on some shit, huh?"

"Yup," Gia sighed.

"Well, listen, I understand it's a mess down there, and you can't control too much, but you gotta try to push through that shit and take care of your mom."

"I'm tired of taking care of her."

"She's sick, babe."

Gia rolled her eyes. "Mm-hmm."

"Don't 'mm-hmm' me. I don't care how much she gets on your nerves. She's still your mother. You have to stick with her during times like these, baby. She needs you."

"You're right," she sighed again. "Listen, I gotta go. My Mamaw's calling me."

"A'ight. I love you."

"I love you too, baby. Bye."

~

"No." Dominique struggled to maintain her composure.

He wrapped his arm around her waist and slid his other hand between her breasts before massaging them.

"Let me go."

Antoine leaned into her neck and kissed it tenderly. "I can't." He licked the nape of her neck, kissing the other side the same, then latching onto it. He sucked.

Dominique blinked back tears as she grabbed Antoine's hands with her own. Peeling and pulling, trying to match his strength with hers. Antoine ran their clutched hands from her breasts, past her stomach, to the forbidden place between her legs. He broke free from her tight grasp, bringing his hand to his mouth. He licked his fingers and forced them between Dominique's skin and the fabric of her panties clinging to it, encircled her hooded pearl and listened to her purr. She was losing the battle, reverting to the love-stricken seventeen-year-old girl again.

"I missed you," he panted in her ear.

"Stop," Dominique moaned.

"Bend over," he groaned.

An image of Dominique's teenage self in Antoine's embrace flashed against the darkness of her closed eyes. Then another. Waves crashing. And another. She beneath him; his weight suffocating her. And another. Water rising. And another. His hands full of her hair, head thrown back. Then another. Trees swaying in heavy, wet winds. And another. Tear-stained cheeks with swollen, bitten lips.

Dominique's eyes fluttered open. She settled briefly on her reflection, then that of a woman standing beside them. Terror washed over her, then a surge of heat.

Blood began to run from her nose.

Antoine, through hooded eyes, caught sight of the bloody

mess and stopped.

"What the hell?" He removed his hand from her panties and grabbed some tissue. "You awrite?"

Dominique snatched the Kleenex box out of his hand, throwing it onto the floor.

"What's wrong wit'chu, girl? I'm tryin' to help you!"

"I don't want ya help! I don't want nothin' from you!" Dominique peered back at him as she pulled her dress down and pinched her nose with her handkerchief. "Stay away from me. Stay away from my daughter."

"Ain't gonna happen," he sniffed, then smiled.

Dominique snatched her purse off the sink. He grabbed her by the arm, then leaned in close.

"Ya mine."

She jerked her arm free, unlocked the restroom door, then hurried out.

"Oh!" Toni squealed as Dominique collided with her.

"Oh my God! I'm sorry!" Dominique grabbed her sister's arms to steady them.

"Ya nose is bleedin'? Hold ya head back."

"It's stoppin'," Dominique pinched it harder.

"You feel another seizure comin'?"

"No. I'm—I'm fine. Really," Dominique smiled briefly. "What did I miss?"

"Nothin'. Mama—"

The bathroom door swung open. Antoine stepped out, smiled, and excused himself. Toni watched him slither away.

"—is lookin' for you."

Toni, her eyes afire, met Dominique's abashed gaze. She looked her over, tilted Dominique's head, and ran her thumb across the passion mark on her neck.

Then she pressed down on it. Dominique flinched, grimacing in pain as she met her sister's fiery glare once again.

"Where else did he touch you?"

"Nowhere."

Toni flung the bathroom door open and grabbed her sister by the elbow. "Get back in here."

Dominique sat on the edge of the sink, pinching her nose harder.

"Where's ya concealer?"

Dominique slid her clutch to her. Toni opened it, pulling out the tube of makeup.

"We don't need nobody seein' this . . . especially Mama and Gia. They already think—"

"I know what they think."

Toni watched as a veil of desolation blanket her baby sister's face. She cupped it. "And they wrong. I told Gia she was *wrong*."

Silence settled between them. Toni began applying the concealer to her neck.

"You know better."

"I tried to fight him off," Dominique's voice was small.

"Well, you got to fight harder. He's goin' to keep comin' for you, suge. And he's not goin' to stop until he gets what he wants."

Dominique knew that to be true.

"I saw Manman Marie," she confessed.

They locked eyes.

"Nobody else ever seen her but Mama. We gotta tell her."

"Mmm-mmm. Nooo. We not tellin' her nothin'—*especially you*. You've already told her enough."

"I know, I know. But I need you to believe me when I tell you that Mama draws her own conclusions from our conversations."

Dominique shook her head. "Which is why we're not tellin' her."

"Not tellin' whom what?" Corrine asked from the doorway with one hand on the door and the other on her hip.

Dominique cursed herself for not locking the door. She stared back at her mother as Toni struggled to place the makeup back in her clutch quickly.

Corrine slowly moved in their direction, settling beside Dominique. She examined the bloody handkerchief, then took her chin and turned it toward her. Studied her keen features, the perfect application of her makeup, then her neck. Corrine took her thumb and smeared the concealer. Dominique recoiled in pain.

"Who left their mark on you?"

Dominique lowered her eyes.

"I asked you a question," Corrine said, her eyes staring through her.

"Antoine," Toni professed.

"Toni," Dominique grumbled.

"What?" Corrine stared at Dominique, then Toni. "He was here?"

"Yes, ma'am. Just a li'l while ago."

Dominique shook her head and cringed.

"I was tellin' her that we needed to tell you so that you could prepare her," Toni went on. "Manman Marie appeared to her too."

Corrine's eyes stayed on Dominique. Dominique never met them.

"She's the one who made yo' nose bleed. It was a diversion."

"I didn't need her help. I don't need *anyone's* help. I can—I can take care of myself."

Corrine gently cupped her daughter's face and began to rub her cheek. "No, you can't, beloved. Because if you could . . ." she pressed down on the hickey. ". . . *this* wouldn't be on you."

Tears began to well in Dominique's eyes. "I tried to fight 'im off, Mama. I swear."

"Well, you didn't try hard enough." Corrine's voice was low and unyielding. "He gon' start preyin' on you now. And you gon' have to dig *deep*. Deeper than you ever have befo'. So that when he comes fo' you again, you will have *la force* and *savoir faire* to *remind him...WHO...YOU...ARE*."

Corrine then turned to Toni. "Make the calls."

GIA'S full bladder woke her from a sound slumber. Her arms and legs were entangled with her brothers'. Corey lay sprawled out on the attached chaise. They'd fallen asleep on the over-sized sectional after indulging in repast leftovers and watching a slew of anime movies. She retrieved her phone from the coffee table and checked the time. It read: 1:15. Then she care-fully slid her arms and legs from the web of limbs and made her way to the hallway bathroom. With an empty bladder, Gia stepped back into the hallway and looked around. The house was dark and still. Since they'd been here, her mother and aunt would stay awake for hours talking and laughing in the kitchen or her aunt's bedroom, but there was no detection of life now. Just quiet. She figured they both were asleep, exhausted from the day's events. She decided to check on her mother. Under her aunt's directives, Dominique retreated to her room as soon as they got in from the repast eight hours ago.

Gia walked to the guest room and cracked open the door. Dominique wasn't there. She opened the door fully, moved inside, and checked the bathroom. Empty. She made her way back to her aunt's room. The door was wide open, the room vacant also. Gia went back into the living room and looked out one of its windows to see if the women were on the porch. They weren't. Strange. Neither had left a note. Gia turned her phone on and checked to see if she had any missed calls or texts from either of them. There were none. She pressed "MOMMY" on her Favorite's list and waited for her to pick up. No luck.

Confused, Gia ended the call, then did the same for Toni. Her phone went straight to voicemail.

"What the fuck?" she said to herself.

She looked over at her cousin, contemplating if she should wake him. She decided against it, settling on not wanting to worry him. Panic was beginning to set in. Then she remembered. She had her mother's location set on her phone. Gia pulled it up. "St. Charles Avenue"?

She ordered an Uber before jogging back to the room and throwing her hair into a messy topknot. Quickly, she threw on a hoodie, leggings, and sneakers, then placed a sheet from the linen closet atop her brothers and tucked them in before stepping onto the porch. A dark car pulled up. She jumped in.

DOMINIQUE TRACED the wood grain on the front door to *Au-Delà Du Voile*. It was painted royal blue. One of the many shades of blue that her mother loved. The sweet smell of vanilla and lavender, frankincense and myrrh swept through the warm space. She followed her sisters into the warmth of childhood and teenage memories.

The brick-shelved walls were stocked with mason jars of colorful herbs and spices, conjure/fixed candles, oils, and Florida water. Small, round, wooden tables set around the room were decorated with wooden and woven bowls of sage, palo alto, incense, gris-gris bags, tarot cards, and conch shells. Free-standing bookstands were full of hard and soft-cover literature about hoodoo and voodoo. Huge floor plants sat in each corner. Two ceiling fans spun at a moderate pace above. Metal chairs adorned with decorative pillows, and tables were placed in the sun parlor as a designated reading space. A portrait of her mother hung over the fireplace adjacent to the cashier's counter.

Dominique approached slowly. The portrait's wooden frame was lit with threaded lights, her mother's chocolate skin aglow. Her hair was wrapped in an ocean-blue-colored tignon, her neck adorned with multicolored beads that rested upon her heavy breasts. The white cloth she wore against her dark skin carried the secrets of her mother and mothers before her. Peace emanated from her eyes. Power. Without a smile to compliment them.

Dominique outstretched her arms, placing her hands on each end of the mantle and bowed her head in humble submission. A storm was brewing inside—a war between wills: hers and that of her mother.

GIA THANKED the Uber driver before stepping out and onto the sidewalk. She read the sign on the wrought iron gate and realized she was at her grandmother's shop. Bright lights from behind the quaint building created a halo around its frame. She could hear drumming and voices singing. The language foreign to her. Gia's heart began to race. She was unsure if she wanted to complete her quest. Uncertain of what was in store for her, she placed one hand on her hip and rubbed her forehead with the other.

"Fuck it," she mumbled.

Finally, Gia lifted the latch on the gate, ascended the steps, and turned the knob on the door. It opened. She stepped inside, closing the door behind her. It was hot and dark in there. Too dark for her liking. And too hot to stay in one place for long. Lit candles danced on the mantle below her grandmother's portrait above the fireplace. Gia neared it and looked up. She thought her grandmother looked majestic. A familiar pain began to build inside. Memories of her beloved Mamaw's visits uprooted themselves. Gia blinked back tears.

Suddenly, she felt the soft blow of someone's warm breath on the back of her neck. Startled, she spun around only to see no one there. Gia turned back around and noticed the candles' flames leaning in the direction of the shop's backspace. She obeyed, moving through a narrow hallway past the guest bathroom and storage closet. The drumming grew louder with each step, bouncing off the walls. The cacophony of men's laughter and women's weeping created a primal symphony. Gia stopped. A colorfully painted screen door separated her from the mysterious world on the other side.

Her grandmother's backyard. A secret garden. Two oak trees adorned in Spanish moss and wisteria towered over the fenced-in space. Bushes of magnolia, hibiscus, Louisiana iris, and gardenias outlined the grassy enclosure. Four tiki torches burned against the night's suffocating heat. A fire pit was ablaze, centered. And an altar draped with a white cloth was adorned with colored ribbons, bottles of wine, bread, and pastries. Her mother was kneeling before it. She was dressed in all white, and her red mane flowed down her back. A circle of people, men and women, young, old, and everything in between sang and swayed to the beat of the talking drums. They all were dressed in white.

Gia saw three elders. Women who shared her grandmother's features sitting side by side in wooden chairs. Beautiful, smiling, aged faces. Proud. Her grandmother's sisters. She remembered meeting them at the repast. In fact, many of the people she was watching at that moment had been at the repast. Her aunts were also there, standing side by side with their long, white skirts raised and fanning in rhythm.

Then Gia saw *her* emerge from behind the altar. A snake coiled around her left arm. She was also shrouded in white. Her neck adorned with beads, layer upon layer of blues and greens. Her wide hips swayed and rolled seductively as her back contracted and flexed, the arch deep and perfect. Her bare feet pounded the ground beneath them, syncopated with the drums' heartbeat, never outstepping the pulse. The song. It had her entranced. Spellbound like that of a lullaby to a baby. Her eyes were closed. And she moved. Floated almost.

Provocatively.

Fluidly.

Unapologetically.

Freely.

Gia watched her grandmother dance before the fire and watched everyone else fall deeper under her spell. She looked in the direction of her great-aunts again and gasped. Her great-grandmother was standing behind them, holding a baby girl in her arms. Watching her grandmother with tears of joy, Gia squinted, then rubbed her eyes in an attempt to remove what she thought was an illusion. When she reopened them, her great-grandmother was still there. The baby too.

Another woman caught Gia's attention, her fair skin reminiscent of her own. She was standing at the altar smiling, as well. Her head and shoulders were covered with red scarves. A single black curl rested against her forehead. Gia watched her watch her grandmother closely. Then followed her as she stepped forward and began to mimic her moves. Just as quickly as she fell in step, she fell out of it, hopping into a fierce spin. And she continued to spin until she was encircling her grandmother like a human cyclone. She spun faster and faster. The throbbing of the drums intensified while her momentum built. She spotted and twirled. Her grandmother flexed and contracted. Harder. Quicker. Faster . . . until the two women collided. The drumming stopped. The attendees gasped. And Corrine stood with her back bent, head aligned with her backside and arms outstretched to the sky. Still. The snake uncoiled itself from her arm and slithered across her chest, to her right shoulder, behind her neck, then to her left shoulder.

"*Ase*!" cried an elder.

The other two nodded in satisfaction.

"*Ase*!" cried another.

The master drummer tapped his drum three times as a call to change the rhythm.

His pupils responded. A polyrhythm of sound was born. And her grandmother came alive once again. Her eyes opened, and she grimaced. Body parts moved, isolated from each other, but all responding to a beat only they could understand. She moved toward Gia's mother with her aunts following behind. She handed the snake over to one of her drummers before giving each of her aunts a candle and bowl full of water and herbs to hold. Her grandmother tilted her mother's head back, then caressed her face. She pressed her forehead against hers before kissing it. She was singing, *chanting* in a language foreign to Gia, but her mother understood its phonology perfectly. She watched tears fall from her mother's eyes as she closed them. Her grandmother dipped her hand in the bowl her aunt Toni was holding and immersed her mother's hair in it. Then the crown of her head. Then her forehead. Her hands moved in a washing motion.

Gia's phone vibrated. She retrieved it from her pocket and cursed herself again. Corey was calling.

4

The ringing of Dominique's phone pulled her from a deep slumber. She reached for it, then held her head. It was aching badly. She sucked in air, cringing in pain before pressing the ANSWER button on the screen.

"Hello?" her voice hoarse.

"Heeey, sissy! What you still doin' asleep?"

Rose was cheery as always.

"What time is it?"

"Noon."

Dominique sighed. "Yesterday was long."

"Aww, I figured so. You okay?"

Dominique rolled onto her back. Slowly. Her body ached. "Yeah. I should be back sometime next week."

"Good." Rose breathed a sigh of relief. "Things aren't the same without you. We miss you."

"I miss y'all too. You have no idea."

"I think I do."

The two shared a laugh.

"Listen, a family just walked in. I'll call you later."

"Awrite. Bye." Dominique pressed the END button. She

noticed she had two missed calls from Esai and an unopened text message from Louis. She sucked her teeth, then threw her phone back on the stand. She needed a shower. She didn't remember much from last night. It was all still a blur and tonight, part *deux* of the ritual, would be much of the same. But what she did know was that she needed to get out of her ceremonial gown before any of the kids saw her.

When she emerged from the bathroom, Dominique found Gia lying along the foot of the bed and Toni at the dresser, preparing a natural healing remedy for her headache.

"Well, good mornin'," she smiled, trying to play off her exhaustion and discomfort.

"Good mornin'!" Toni threw over her shoulder.

Gia forced a small smile. "Morning."

"I didn't expect to walk out into a party," Dominique chuckled. "Everything awrite?"

"Aw, yeah. Everything is fine, suge. How's ya head?"

"Throbbin'."

"Come. Sit down."

Dominique shuffled over to the upholstered chair adjacent to the bed and eased down into it.

Toni walked over to her with two pills and a treelike object in hand. "Here, take these, then chew a little on this bark."

"Willow?"

Toni nodded. "Mm-hmm, and the pills are butterbur."

Gia remained. She was watching her again. Her eyes penetrating. Demanding answers. Dominique caught her gaze, then quickly popped the pills into her mouth

and swallowed. "Did you and ya brothers eat?"

"Yeah. TeeTee made breakfast."

"Okay." She smiled at her sister. "Thank you."

"Oh, don't mention it." Toni looked back at Gia and signaled for the hot cup of tea. They exchanged a look before she passed it to her. "Umm . . . GiGi wants to speak to you about somethin'."

"Is that right?" Dominique tilted her head.

"Mm-hmm," Toni nodded as she began to hand her the mug.

"Ya not pregnant, are you?"

"Oh my God, no!" Gia frowned.

"You sure?"

"Why do you always think the worst of me?" Gia tensed.

"I don't," Dominique giggled, guilt-ridden.

"Yes, you do."

"Look, I'm still a work in progress, okay?" Dominique shifted uncomfortably in her seat.

"So, you admit it? You have no faith in me."

"I'm not doin' this with you right now, Gia. I'm not." Dominique placed the cup down beside the chair.

"Unbelievable." Gia shook her head, smiling.

"Awrite, you two. That's enough." Toni gently placed her sister's hand in hers.

"What GiGi has to tell you isn't bad. It isn't bad at all."

"Well, awrite then. What's up?"

Gia considered, then reconsidered telling on herself. What she'd seen last night was nothing short of a phenomenon. Time stopped. Her grandmother transcended space and time with a spirit, a spirit Gia dreamt of many a night as a little girl. She concentrated hard on the importance of knowing what she saw.

Toni nodded at her reassuringly.

"I saw Mamaw last night. At her shop. I saw all of you. A couple of spirits too."

Dominique looked over at Toni, then back at Gia. Her lips tightened in defeat.

"Why didn't you tell me? Why didn't you take me with you?" Gia continued.

"What I do remember tellin' you is to never leave this house without me or somebody else in the family," Dominique replied firmly.

"I know, but—"

"You know? Then *why* didn't you listen?"

"You're avoiding my questions."

"GiGi," Toni cooed.

"She's avoiding my questions, TeeTee—like always." Gia rose to her feet, her voice rising. "She's wrong! For once, just admit you're wrong!"

Toni finished tending to Dominique and turned her attention to Gia. "GiGi, calm down. Sit."

"Not until she admits she's wrong!"

"You had no business leavin' this house that time of night," Dominique exclaimed evenly.

"I tried calling you both, but you didn't pick up your phones. Neither one of you left a note. I thought maybe you had another seizure or something. Maybe Mr. Brevard came back and did something to you. I didn't know what to think."

"Gia Corrine," Dominique began.

"What?! I was worried about you, Mommy! I'm always worried about you now. It's like nothing has been right since we got down here. It seems like everything is worse than it ever was. You're sick and getting into fights with people. TeeTee Simone looks at me funny whenever she sees me. I don't know anyone down here outside of the family, and I can't go anywhere without a chaperone. I don't understand anything. I just . . ." Gia fell apart.

Dominique moved toward her, catching her before she crumbled to the floor. She gathered her baby girl in her arms and pressed her child's head against her chest. "Don't cry, baby. It's okay. It's o-kay."

"I wanna go home."

"I know," Dominique rocked.

"How did you find us, love?"

GiGi sniffled back tears as she tried to regain her composure. "I traced Mommy's location from her work phone. Then called an Uber."

Toni shook her head and giggled. "Somethin' special, you are." She handed Dominique a couple of tissues.

Dominique lifted Gia's chin. She wiped her cheeks and nose. Then stroked her temple with her thumb. "Listen to me. *I am o-kay.*"

"No, you're not," Gia hiccupped.

"I am. And you will see that in time. But understand . . . I would *not* have been okay had somethin' happened to you last night. You could have been raped or killed, Gia. Do you know how many little Black girls are missin' in this country right now? How many of them have been kidnapped and are bein' trafficked for sex?"

"Yes."

"Then please . . . Do what I ask of you."

"We were wrong, GiGi. We should have left somethin' behind. Somethin' to let you kids know we were awrite. We're sorry."

"*I'm* sorry," Dominique stressed. "I was goin' to tell you . . . eventually."

Gia wiped her face and nose with the back of her hand. "When?"

"When the time was right."

"When, Mommy?"

Dominique sighed, holding steadfast to her patience. "On ya eighteenth birthday. I was gonna bring you down here and let ya grandmama tell you everything that makes us who we are." She looked up at Toni. Toni signaled for her to continue. "But before I say anything else . . . I need you to tell me what it is that you saw last night."

Gia hesitated again. "I saw Mamaw pouring water over your head."

"You saw her performin' a ritual," Dominique replied calmly.

"A voodoo ritual?"

"Yes. A ceremony called a *lave tet* or head washing."

"Almost like the bath you gave me before we left."

"Yes. Almost."

"Am I supposed to feel...*different*?"

"Yes. But more work has to be done on you. And you have to be ready for it."

"Oh." Gia pressed her back against the chaise at the bed's foot. "So, like, does everybody in the family do it?"

"We don't *do*, Gia. We *are*," Dominique countered.

"That's right," Toni nodded. "Voodoo is who we are. We live it. We are the embodiment of it."

"Oh," Gia blushed.

Toni mumbled something under her breath in Kouri-Vini about Simone.

"Toni."

"It's true," she shrugged.

"I thought voodoo was evil. Like, people are brought back from the dead and—"

Dominique cringed. "Zombies?"

"Yeah. And you can hurt or kill people by sticking pins in dolls."

The sisters laughed, almost hysterically.

"Where'd you get all these lies, GiGi?" Toni wiped her wet eyes.

"TV ... social media. Most of the tour guides here."

"Society," Dominique groaned in disgust.

"Damn shame, ain't it? But don't believe the hype, okay? Voodoo is good. It is spirit medicine. It is sacred. And it is in ya blood."

"And the snake? Is that part of it too? Because I've never

seen Mamaw handle a snake before, and that one was big as shit."

Toni laughed again. "Mind that tongue."

"I'm sorry."

"The snake represents strength. And Damballah, who is one of the most important *Lwas* in our tradition." Dominique informed her.

"Okay. But like . . . Where did she even get a snake from?"

"Enough about the snake, Gia," Dominique huffed.

"Well, I wanna know where it came from. Did somebody just give it to her and say, 'Here, take my snake.' Or did you she go out and buy it? That thing was like five feet long."

"He was given to her as a gift from ya granddaddy. And he's named for Damballah, the sky father."

"Oh."

"Now . . . The ritual you saw her performin' had to be done so that my head could be cleared and my foundation strengthened. I need to protect myself from—"

"Mr. Brevard."

"Anything and anyone who means me no good," Dominique responded carefully.

"Mamaw and ya mama are more than what and who you think they are," Toni added.

Gia shook her head, still confounded.

"Mamaw's a voodoo priestess, Gia," Dominique said softly.

"The *Queen*," Toni followed seriously. "And ya mama is her successor."

Gia rubbed her forehead and stared at her mother for a long time.

"You can't repeat any of this information to anyone. Understand?" Toni stressed with her eyes.

"Yes, ma'am," Gia replied quietly.

"Tell us what ya thinkin'," Dominique urged softly.

"There was a woman there last night watching Mamaw

dance. But she wasn't . . . alive. I dreamed about her when I was little, but I didn't know who she was or why she came to me in my dreams. She was wearing a red tignon."

Toni threw a look of disbelief at Dominique. "I'll be damned." She shook her head. Then she waited for Dominique to be as surprised, but the emotion never surfaced. "Why didn't you tell this girl who she was or why she was visitin' her?"

Dominique said nothing.

"Mama know?"

"No."

"Why not?" Toni asked sincerely.

"Because I didn't want her forcin' somethin' on Gia that she didn't want or wasn't ready for, that's why. I didn't want her to have no parts of this life," Dominique replied matter-of-factly.

Toni, taken aback by her sister's truth, nodded slowly in understanding. With voodoo came great responsibility and discipline. With their mother came pressure to be great. And since Dominique considered voodoo and her mother to be one entity, the option for Gia to have anything to do with them, in that capacity, was out of the question.

Dominique didn't know, but Gia told her grandmother about "the lady in the red tignon" during one of her summer visits up North. Corrine promised to keep the secret to herself and explained that the woman was her guardian angel, keeping a close eye on her.

"What's so special about that lady?" Gia asked, still confused. She'd repressed a lot from her childhood.

"*That lady* ya speakin' of is ya great-great-great-grandmama, Marie Laveau, New Orleans' most renowned Voodoo Queen," Dominique affirmed. "A woman who was both feared and revered."

"Yes, she was. Truly a force to be reckoned with," Toni continued.

Gia heard the name before but never imagined she had

direct ties to the infamous black magic(al) woman.

Dominique's phone rang, breaking the trio's sacred exchange. "Hold on."

She shuffled over to the nightstand and peered at the name.

"Who is it?" Gia asked, slowly coming out of her state of shock.

"Ya daddy."

Gia shifted uncomfortably. She briefly locked eyes with her aunt. It was then, Toni knew Gia had made the mistake of calling him.

Dominique pressed the speaker button. "Hello?"

"*Donde has estado?* I've been trying to reach you all morning," Esai barked, his accent thick.

"I slept in. Why? What's the matter?"

Toni passed Gia her mother's empty mug, then nudged her to make a run for it.

"You tell me," he jeered.

"What?" Dominique said, confused.

Gia moved toward the door but stopped abruptly at the sound of her mother's snapping fingers. She turned to face her.

Dominique mouthed, *"Don't take another step."*

"Gia called me and told me what happened."

Dominique cut her eyes at her. Her blood was boiling. "Wait a minute. Wait. What exactly did she tell you?"

"She told me that *pedazo de mierda* came to your sister's house and threatened you."

"Esai."

"I just wanted to let you know that I am catching the next flight out."

"What? No. No, that's not necessary."

"Yes, it is. He had no right. You hear me? No right! I'm going to kill him!"

"Esai, please? I have it under control."

"Well, I'm flying in to make sure it stays that way. And I have some other business to tend to as well while I'm there."

"*Esai—*"

"I knew this shit was going to happen. I knew he was going to step out of bounds while you were there." He breathed heavily. "Take me off of speaker, please."

Dominique honored his request, placing the phone to her ear.

"Has he said anything to you about Gia?"

"Yes."

"Can you talk about it now?"

"No."

"All right, then we'll save it for when I get there. I'll call you when I touch down."

"Awrite."

"Bye." He disconnected the call.

Dominique pressed the END button and slapped the phone against her thigh. "Jesus Christ, Gia! Why would you tell ya daddy about Antoine comin' to the house?"

"Because he threatened you."

"It was an empty threat, honey. If he wanted to do somethin' to me, he would have."

"But he did. He put you in the hospital without even touching you."

"Did you tell ya daddy that too?"

"No."

"Well, you might as well have. Dammit, Gia! I'm dealin' with enough as it is down here!"

"I know that! That's why I called him! He wants to help you, so just let him!"

"I don't *want* his help!"

"Why not? You *need* it!" Gia watched her pace the floor. "Why are you acting like this?"

"Because you just woke a sleepin' dragon!"

"Papi's harmless. He probably won't even show up!"

Dominique waved her hand dismissively. "Hush, now. Hush. I need to think."

"You're overreacting, Mommy. Like, for real."

"You think *this* is overreactin'? Baby, you ain't seen nothin' yet," Dominique hissed before storming out of the room.

$\sim$

THE LESAINT-FAVIER SISTERS sat quietly side by side in their father's study.

They watched Mr. Delacroix, his lawyer, place his reading glasses on his nose and remove their father's Last Will and Testament from his leather briefcase. The silence was thick. Thicker than the blood they shared.

Dominique was deep in thought. She didn't know how she was going to keep Esai away from Antoine. He despised the man. She sat, leaning to one side, flexing and straightening her injured hand. Toni and the twins glanced over from time to time, but she was too far gone to meet any of their gazes. She couldn't wait to get through the reading so that she could get back to Toni's and talk Esai down.

"Will your mother be joining us?" Mr. Delacroix asked.

"No, she decided to spend the day with the grands," Toni smiled warmly.

"Of course. Well, before we begin, would any of you ladies like a bottle of water or . . .?" Mr. Delacroix smiled back.

"No, thank you," they said in unison.

"Awrite, then." He perused the first page, then turned it. "Jacqueline, Genevieve, Simone, and Dominique, it is imperative for you to know that because Antonia is your father's power of attorney, she already knows what his wishes are, as she was with him and your mother when this document was amended."

They nodded.

"Ready?"

"Yes, sir."

"Good." He lowered his glasses on his nose. "And so it goes:

I, Dreux Jean-Paul Favier, resident in the City of New Orleans in the State of Louisiana, being of sound mind, not acting under duress or undue influence, and fully understanding the nature and extent of all my property and of this disposition thereof, do hereby make, publish, and declare this document to be my Last Will and Testament, and hereby revoke any and all other wills and codicils heretofore made by me.

I devise and bequeath my property, both real and personal and wherever situated, to as follows:

My first beneficiary, Antonia Desiree Favier-Dumas, currently of New Orleans, as my firstborn daughter, with my art collection, which contains original prints by Jim Blanchard, Rolland Harve Golden, Jean-Michel Basquiat, Kevin A. Williams, and Kara Walker. You are to do whatever you wish with them.

My second and third beneficiaries, Jacqueline Angelique LeSaint-Favier and Genevieve Anais Favier-Pierre, currently of Mandeville and Covington, as my second-and third-born daughters, with my positions of Chairman of the Board and President at Parish National Bank, of which I organized and founded. Should you decide not to, I advise that you speak to my lawyer, Mr. Delacroix, and Antonia about prospective candidates for those seats. It is my hope that you will appoint your sons, my grandchildren, Wesley Favier and Stephan Pierre, to those positions upon their graduation from college.

My fourth beneficiary, Simone Vivienne LeSaint-Favier, currently of Baton Rouge, as my fourth-born daughter, with the condominium in Savannah, Georgia, and cottage in Oak Bluffs on Martha's Vineyard that belong to your mother and me. Maintain them both with love and care.

My fifth and final beneficiary, Dominique Corrine-Marie LeSaint-Favier, currently of Maplewood, as my fifth and last-born daughter, with Maison Favier and Au-Delà Du Voile Botanica and Apothecary Shop, two places my darling Corrine, your beloved mother, calls home, both of which I built just for her. It is my hope that your love for me far outweighs the discord between you and your mother. And in that love, with time, you will find it in your heart to make peace with her and the past.

"Now, there are other sections to be discussed, like that of expenses, taxes, debts, and the monies that he has divided between you all and your children. But we don't have to get into all of that just yet. Does anyone have any questions before we continue?"

Dominique raised her hand.

"Uh, yes, I have a question," Simone quickly interjected. "Why does *she* get to have the main house and our mama's shop?"

Mr. Delacroix pushed his glasses up. "Well—"

"We've already been through this, Simone. Mama and Daddy want her to have 'em," Jackie chimed in.

"And because she *deserves* them," Toni corrected.

Simone uncrossed her legs and continued, "She disgraced this family having a child out of wedlock at eighteen, then leaving here without looking back."

"Mama told me to leave, so I did," Dominique smirked.

"Look at her. She's not even a bit remorseful," Simone smiled in disbelief.

"Why should I be? I owe Nawlins nothin'. I owe this family nothin'."

"See, now, *that's* where you're wrong. You owe Mama and Daddy—for breaking their hearts the way you did."

"I've already paid the price for hurtin' them. A hundred times over, maybe more—I don't know. But I wasn't gonna stay here and be reminded of how much of a disappointment I was. Or kill my baby to save the family's name—like you."

"Ladies," Mr. Delacroix interpolated.

"I did what was best for me."

"Yes, you did. *Four* times," Dominique scoffed.

"Dominique."

"Yes, Toni?"

"That's enough," Toni warned.

"I'm sorry. I am. But she's called me everything but a child of God over the years."

"We know."

"So, then, why am I not allowed to remind her that *she* is the reason why *she* can't have children?"

"Because this is neither the time nor the place," the twins cooed.

"Why not here and now? All this is mine now, ain't it?" Dominique's ponytail swung back and forth like a pendulum.

"Where did you get that mark on your neck?" Simone asked, her eyes squinted.

The room grew quiet. All eyes fell upon Dominique. She never flinched. She'd put concealer on her neck before coming, but the sweat that was running off her must have removed it.

Cool, calm, and collected. Dominique leaned back in her chair and raised a brow. "You know where."

Jackie shook her head. "Damn."

Simone cleared her throat in an attempt to keep her tears at bay. She gathered her belongings and rose to her feet. "Are we finished here, Mr. Delacroix?"

"No, but—"

"I'll sign whatever you need—"

Mr. Delacroix stood slowly, removing his glasses from his nose. "Simone—"

"I have to go." She struggled to maintain her composure.

"Simone, don't leave," the twins begged.

"I'll call you all later." She stormed out, her heels leaving an echo behind.

Mr. Delacroix plopped back down in his departed friend's chair and patted his wet face with his handkerchief. "Well . . . Why don't we take a little break, ladies?"

~

GIA WALKED onto the porch with her brothers' lunches in hand. She placed the food down beside them, careful not to interrupt their intense game of chess. She'd been teaching them, like their mother had taught her, for the last six months, and they'd caught on quickly.

"Remember, Mikey . . . Your goal is to safeguard the king. Don't let Dominic threaten him."

"Okay."

Gia made her way to the porch swing and sat down, throwing her knees up. She flipped her phone horizontally, placed it against her thighs, and then pressed the PLAY button on her selected Netflix movie.

"Who's winning?" a deep voice chimed in the distance.

The kids looked up, following the voice. Dominic and Mikey smiled.

"It's *Papi!*" yelled Mikey.

"Hey, *Papi!*" Dominic followed.

Esai smiled and waved from his rental car. His pale skin whitened under the sun's light.

Gia slowly put her legs down and turned her phone off. She didn't think he would really show up.

"*Hola, chicos!*" He stepped onto the porch and gave them kisses on the tops of their heads. "*Hola, niña linda.*" He brought Gia close and squeezed her with one arm, then kissed her on the forehead.

Gia looked up at him and took in his freshly cut hair and lightly oiled beard which was sprinkled with white hairs. It smelled good. So did he. She thought he looked handsome in his powder-blue linen short set. The white tank top beneath matched perfectly with his Air Force 1s.

"Heyyy, *Papi.* You really came." Gia nervously slid out of his embrace.

"Of course, I did. Wasn't that the whole point of calling me in the first place?" he asked in confusion.

"I mean, yes. But I think we may have a little problem."

He crossed his muscled arms, tilting his head back. "*Que es eso?*"

"I may have overreacted—just a bit. And I think because I overreacted, Mommy's going to beat my ass. That or she's going to cast a spell on me or some shit. I don't know. But I'm totally regretting this now. So, yeah . . . She's gonna flip out when she sees you, and all I'm saying is I don't want no parts of that."

"You know about her being—?"

"Yes. And either way you look at it, she's gonna fuck me up."

Esai cringed. "Ay, *princessa*, you curse so much."

"Sorry, *Papi*," Gia replied quietly.

"*Escuchar*, I will take care of your mother," he smiled slyly. "No matter how you say she feels, you did the right thing by calling me. And after tonight, everyone is going to be able to sleep better. *Porque lo estoy matando.*"

The boys looked up with wide eyes, uncertain of the situation yet intrigued by the exchange.

"I just don't think it's that serious."

"So your mother getting threatened isn't that serious?" he asked, running his index finger and thumb along his mustache.

"I mean, I was half-asleep when it happened, so maybe it was a dream. I don't know."

"Gia, she confirmed it, and so did your *Tia* Toni."

"Okay. But I need you to *understand* what I'm trying to tell you, *Papi*. I'm scared of her!"

Esai looked down at the boys. They nodded their heads up and down, agreeing with their sister.

"Mommy doesn't play," Mikey said seriously.

"See! Even Mikey knows. Why can't you accept this?"

"Because I cannot imagine your mother putting her hands

on you. *Simplemente no puedo.* She has never said anything to me about fighting between the two of you, Gia. Ever."

"You know what? Forget it. I'm hungry. How about you? We have leftovers," she stated before disappearing into the house.

Esai looked down at the boys again. Dominic shrugged his shoulders.

"Women," Mikey sighed as he shook his head in disbelief.

DOMINIQUE SASHAYED onto Toni's back deck with a pitcher of iced tea and plastic cups in hand. She placed them on the table beside a bowl of ice and a pack of bottled waters before wiping her neck and chest with a wet paper towel. She'd thrown her hair into a high, loose bun and changed into a white tank top and tattered Daisy Dukes. Gia sat under the table's umbrella, eyeing her. She took in every detail of the outfit. The tank top was too tight, and the shorts were too short. Yes, it was hotter than hell out there, but even she had the decency to put on a T-shirt and basketball shorts.

"Don't hurt yaself now," Dominique teased Esai. She had a plan. She was going to butter him up, then sweet-talk him to death until he had no choice but to leave as quietly as he'd come.

Esai looked up at her, taking in her glistening arms and legs. He noticed her lips were swollen from the heat. He smiled. "Never that." He attempted to charge the hoop and dunk, but Dominic jumped up and slapped the ball out of his hand.

"Gimme dat!" Dominique, Gia, and Mikey hollered with excitement.

"That's a foul!" Esai huffed.

"I didn't touch you!" Dominic bounced the ball between his legs.

"He didn't touch you!" Mikey followed.

"I know, but it is still a foul!"

"How?!" the boys laughed.

"Estoy en desventaja! You are too tall for your age!"

"No, you're just shrinking," Dominic smirked before doing a crossover and dunking the ball.

Dominique shook her head. She missed moments like this with Esai and the kids. Pure joy. "Awrite, you two. Game over. Go on inside and shower. We're gonna leave here in fifteen minutes for Carousel Gardens."

"Okay!" The boys grabbed their shirts, towels, and water bottles before disappearing into the house. Gia followed, eyeing her parents on the way.

Dominique extended her arm, offering Esai the towel in her hand.

"You know, you are the reason why I fouled."

"Me?"

"Sí, tu."

"How? I was standin' all the way over here," she grinned.

"Yes, but those legs were in my peripheral the entire time. How much are you pressing now?"

Dominique blushed. "About 260. Maybe 280 on a good day."

"Se ve bien en ti."

GIA STUFFED her iPhone at the bottom of her mother's suitcase, careful not to blow her and Toni's cover. She climbed back into bed and settled beneath the thin sheet. A humid breeze fought against the coolness of the ceiling fan spinning above.

Slowly, the bedroom door groaned open. Esai's head emerged. He peeked through the darkness, then titled his head when he noticed Gia staring back at him.

"Hey, you," he whispered.

"Hey, *Papi.*"

He walked over to the bed and sat. "What are you still doing awake?"

She lay her head on her bent arm. "Just . . . thinking."

"Thinking about what?"

"How good of a day this was," she said softly.

Esai smiled. "It was, wasn't it? It felt like old times."

"Yeah."

Sadness crept between them. Esai caressed her arm, then took her hand in his. "Well, I'm going to let you in on a little secret," he squeezed her fingers. "Your *Tio* Fernando sold me his half of the business. He is going back to DR to take care of *abuelo,* and I am coming back here for good."

"Does Mommy know?"

"No. But once things get squared away, I'm going to tell her . . . then ask her to marry me again."

Gia sat up. A glimmer of hope glossed over. "Really, *Papi?*"

Esai kissed the back of her hand. "*De Verdad.* Your mother is the only woman I have ever loved. She gave me three beautiful children who I would lay my life down for if I had to. And they deserve to be happy," he smiled, tears brimming. "I was so busy taking care of everyone else that I lost sight of you and your brothers . . . your mother. I was selfish, *mariquita.* I should have kept her . . . you and the boys first. *Lo siento por eso.*"

Gia leaned in and hugged him. Tight.

Dominique stretched her legs along the porch swing. She was spent. She, Esai, and the kids stayed at Carousel Gardens until closing time. The kids rode every ride and played every game imaginable. She watched them wear Esai out, spend his money, and tease him for not being able to match their energy with his own. They were a happy family again. A rare moment in time.

But it fleeted quickly. So, Dominique held on to every smile, sound of laughter, full hugs, and wet kisses.

Esai stepped onto the porch with two bottles of water in hand. He gave Dominique hers as he settled on the swing, placing her legs across his lap.

"The kids are knocked out."

"I knew they would be. They not used to this kinda heat." She took a sip.

"Neither am I. It has never been this hot."

"Aww, it's not that bad."

Esai raised his brows. "Oh no? Then explain to me the steam rising from you."

"Ain't no steam comin' off of me."

"Yes, there is."

"You need to stop," she grinned.

"*Lo digo en serio.* That is why I brought you some water. It is to keep you from melting."

"If anything is comin' up off of me, this Louisiana heat ain't the cause," she teased, giving him a once-over. Then took another swig of her water.

Esai watched her pull the bottle from her lips. He caught a running droplet with his finger, then rubbed it in with his thumb.

Their eyes locked. Dominique blushed. Smiled shyly.

"I'm sorry I didn't—"

"Don't," Dominique stiffened. "Don't ruin this moment."

"I should have been here for you."

"Well, you weren't. And we both *knew* you weren't gonna be here. You've never been *here*." Dominique sighed as Esai shook his head.

"*Lo siento, mi amor.*"

"I don't want any more of those, Esai. There's no more room left for them here," Dominique said just above a whisper.

"Okay." Esai rubbed her foot, then grabbed her hand just as

he had Gia's and kissed it. He began to massage her legs. "May I ask how it was?"

Dominique looked over at him and smirked. "It was . . . It was fit for a king."

"That is beautiful. *Dios lo bendiga.*"

"Yeah. I'm sure one of the kids got footage of it on they phone."

Silence settled between them.

"Were you able to compromise with him?" He hated to ask, but he remembered how upset she was upon learning the news of his hospitalization and what would be asked of her. Esai was well aware of how her father felt about Antoine and knew he would leave those feelings with Dominique.

She looked over at him, shaking her head. "No. He pushed to the very end. And I pulled. He didn't care about my mama's worries and wishes. Said she never knew how to keep the past in its place."

"Maybe he was wrong in his approach, but being the type of man he was, I don't think he would have even brought it up after fourteen years if he didn't think Antoine possessed *bondad*. Or changed for the better."

Dominique cut her eyes at him. "This is how you really feel?"

"It's just a thought. Forgiveness . . ."

Dominique exhaled.

". . . forgiveness is mighty, Dominique."

"So is denial. My daddy's biggest flaw was seein' what he wanted to see in people. Antoine ain't no good. You and I both know that."

"He was thinking of Gia."

"Was he? If he was thinkin' of Gia, he wouldn't have brought it up at all. Blood don't always make you family."

"I know that."

"Then why are you sidin' with him?" Dominique threw her legs down and sat on the edge of the swing.

"I'm not. I'm just trying to put myself in his position . . . look at this situation from every angle."

"*You* are her father, Esai. *You. Not* him. She doesn't know anyone else *but* you."

"I know."

"Then why are we havin' this conversation?"

"Because I believe everything you told me he said to you at the repast. He meant every word."

Dominique sighed. This was a losing battle. She sat back on the swing and began to rock it. "Then what do you wanna do?"

"I already told you what I am *going to do*. He disrespected you, and he has to pay for that."

"You can't put ya hands on 'im."

"Why not?" Esai's tone screamed of fury.

"Because beatin' 'im within an inch of his life isn't gonna solve anything."

"Yes, it is. It's going to make me feel better."

Dominique stared at him for a moment. He'd turned, or fallen, into darkness, and she was struggling to reach him. "I don't ask you for much. I never have. Not even ya forgiveness . . ." she placed her hand on his thigh. ". . . but right now, I'm *beggin'* you. As the mother of ya children . . . *Please*, just *talk* to him."

Esai looked over at her, biting the inside of his cheek. "I'm not making any promises."

Dominique looked out into the street, past the neighboring houses, through the oak trees. She lost herself in the jingling bell of a streetcar moving along the track in the distance.

Ain't no good gonna come from this. That's what my mama said to me after she laid eyes on Gia. She said, "Ain't no good . . . gonna come from this."

5

Gia rinsed her fork and plate off in the sink before loading them into the dishwasher. She and her mother were leaving for Jersey tomorrow, her father and brothers for the Dominican Republic. She was so happy she could hardly contain herself. Their lives were going to go back to normal. She and Dominique were going to return to work, get back into the ebb and flow of death and the waves of grief that came with it. Then enjoy the familiar sounds and smells of their house.

Her mother had been asleep for the last three days, this being the fourth. She worried in the beginning, but Toni explained it was normal. Actually necessary, for her to rest for days, as it was the proper way to realign her spirit and mind. Regenerate after expelling so much grief at the ceremonies . . . to heal. In the interim, Gia and the boys took advantage of their father's presence and forced him to take them wherever they wanted to go. They managed to visit the zoo, aquarium, and French Market thus far. Gia knew he was enjoying their time together, but he too was concerned about her mother. They never left the house for an adventure until *after* he tended to her. Every morning, he came by with fresh fruit, herbs, and vegetables, prepared her breakfast, and then woke her to eat. They would talk for a while, and then she would drift back to sleep. He would caress her back and kiss her sweetly on the cheek before leaving.

He returned at lunchtime and repeated the morning's routine. And Gia would watch them from a distance. There was no denying the love and admiration her parents had for each other. She hoped she and Amari would share the same. She smiled at the thought of him. Her father would approve of him. She was certain.

"GiGi, I'm goin' on my mornin' walk. You wanna come?" Toni wrapped her locks in a cotton cloth.

"Sure."

"Awrite. Go on and get dressed. I'll wait for ya outside."

DOMINIQUE SECURED the belt on her short, cotton robe as she stepped out of the bathroom into the bedroom. She tousled her hair, it bouncing, then settling at the small of her back. It needed to be pressed, but she'd been in a losing battle with NOLA's humidity since she stepped out of Louis Armstrong Airport. She made her way to the tall mahogany dresser adjacent to the bed and removed a cotton bra and panty set. Then she grabbed her jar of raw shea butter and sat on the chaise.

Someone knocked on the door.

"Come in."

Esai peeked in, smiling. "*Buenos dias, hermosa.*"

Dominique met his smile as she moisturized her legs and feet, careful not to let the robe rise. "Good mornin'."

He pushed the door open with his shoulder, then closed it with the heel of his foot.

"Ooo, pancakes! My favorite."

"Well, do not get too excited. They're not buttermilk; they're vegan." He sat beside her.

She frowned. "Ya kiddin', right?"

Esai laughed as he placed the tray down on the bed. "No. Just try them."

"I think I'll pass."

"No, you won't. You need to eat."

"I know I do. *Food.* I need *food*. Somethin' with sustenance."

"This *is* food. *Healthier food.*" He cut a piece for her, then held the fork to her lips.

Dominique puckered them . . . hesitant, then obliged. She chewed. Swallowed. "Not bad."

"See. I tell you," Esai nodded as he cut another piece. "Here. Have another bite."

She did. They shared a smile.

"Thank you for takin' care of me." Dominique's voice was sweet and genuine.

"It is my job," Esai said seriously. He brushed his thumb against her lips. Then held her cheek. He studied every beauty mark, the sparkle of her nose and eyebrow rings, the length of her lashes, and the specs around each iris. He leaned into her and kissed her tenderly. Dominique grabbed his hand and held it tight. She winced as she fell deep into the longing shared between them. Their tongues intertwined—dancing. Esai threw her arms around his neck, grabbed her at the waist, and guided her onto his lap. He rested his hands on her apple bottom, going back and forth between palming and squeezing it.

Dominique gripped the back of his head and sucked his bottom lip. He undid her belt and placed one breast into his mouth, tending to the erect nipple that fed his babies once upon a time. Then his lips made a trail of kisses to the other. He picked her up and walked to the side of the bed, laying her down across it. He hovered for a moment, taking in the splendor that was her body. Dominique pinched his beard lightly as he licked his lips. Then she watched him place her legs over his shoulders, kiss the inside of her thighs, and bury his face in her cove. She let out a soft moan.

An image of Antoine flashed before her. Then another. Dirt shifting. And another. A Cheshire smile. And another. Earth quaking. And another. His hands roaming her body. Then another. Trees falling onto wet, uneven ground. And another. Metal and leather crashing against ripe skin. Red stripes of dishonor. Left behind.

"Esai, stop."

"I'M GONNA GO TAKE A SHOWER." Gia popped a grape into her mouth.

"Awrite, love," Toni said over her shoulder.

Gia released her hair from the hair tie and ruffled it as she made her way down the hall. She opened the door to the guest room and jumped, completely thrown by the sight before her.

"Oh no!" She covered her eyes, turning her back immediately.

"Gia!" Dominique struggled to cover herself with a pillow.

Esai remained, unfazed by the disruption. Dominique attempted to scoot away from him, but he tightened his grip.

"Close the door, ladybug," he chuckled.

Gia happily obliged. She rushed back into the living room and placed her hands on the top of her head, then closed her eyes, squeezing them tight.

Toni turned the dishwasher on, then looked at Gia as she began to retreat to her room. "What's the matter, GiGi? You look like you just seen a ghost or somethin'."

She rubbed her forehead. "Worse. I, uh, I just walked in on my parents. You know..."

"Aww, yeah?"

"Mm-hmm."

Toni laughed. "Well, awrite. I ain't mad at 'em."

"TeeTee!"

"What?" Toni chuckled some more.

Mortified, Gia rubbed her forehead again. She knew she was probably scarred for life, and her aunt thought the whole situation was funny.

Dominique walked in, holding the lapel of her robe together. Her face and chest were flushed, evident signs of her arousal and embarrassment. "Hey."

"Hey!" Toni smirked, trying to maintain her composure.

"How was ya walk?"

"Oh, it was perfect. I was happy to have such wonderful company."

"That's good."

Toni grinned as she gave her a once-over. "Mm-hmm. How was ya *ride*?"

"Oh my God!" Gia cringed. She took off to the back.

"You can use my shower, GiGi!" Toni yelled.

A door slammed. Toni bent over. Hysterical.

"You terrible," Dominique shook her head.

"I know. I'm sorry."

"No, ya not," Dominique grinned.

"Ya right," Toni giggled. "But *you* . . . *You* are supposed to be fasting."

"I know. We didn't get far. I made him stop," Dominique confessed.

"Okay. Don't let all of Mama's hard work be in vain."

Footsteps moving along the porch's creaking wood caught their attention. Simone tapped on the screen door.

"Knock, knock."

"Hey, love. What you doin' here?" Toni gave her a cheek kiss.

"I came by to speak to Dominique."

Dominique rolled her eyes as she fixed herself a bowl of fruit salad.

"Oh, awrite. I'll leave you two then. Go take my shower." She tapped Dominique on the shoulder. "Play nice."

"Can we step outside for a moment?"

Dominique signaled for her to precede her. She leaned against one of the pillars and sighed. "What can I do you for?"

"That rest did you some good. You're as beautiful . . . as ever," Simone sneered disappointedly.

Dominique continued eating and watched her sister's insecurities surface.

"The streets are buzzing about you being back. Everyone from Father O'Malley to Big Chief Lightfoot."

"That's to be expected."

Simone forced a smile. "Must really be something being you."

"How's that?"

"Being the 'chosen one'. Stepping into Mama's shoes and being sought after the way you are. You're the closest thing next to God."

"She hasn't stepped down yet."

"But she will. And when she does, people are going to be expecting miracles, *healing,* and you're not going to disappoint."

Dominique put down the partially empty bowl and crossed her arms at her chest. "Did you come all this way to patronize me?"

"No. I want to tell you . . . that I spoke to Antoine. And he confirmed . . . you know."

"He confirmed what?"

"You know."

Dominique raised a brow. "I don't."

"He confirmed that, uh, that Gia's his."

"But you knew that. You've known it for seventeen years."

Dominique stabbed a chunk of watermelon with her fork, then popped it into her mouth. "So, what? You here to apologize?"

"No, I actually want to run a proposition by you."

"A proposition?"

"Yes." Simone unzipped her purse and retrieved her checkbook. "I am willing to buy Maison Favier and Au-Delà Du Voile from you if you agree to stay away. *For good*. You can't come back to visit Mama and Daddy, Toni, and the twins—no one."

Dominique slowly lowered her arms. "What?"

"At the reading, you made it quite clear that you have no intention of coming back here to stay because of your fabulous life up North. So, I want to make it easier for you."

"I never said such a thing. I only agreed with you about not havin' any regrets for leavin' the first time."

"Whatever the case may be, I'm here to help you make your final decision."

Simone clicked her pen.

"I think you better go."

"How much? I have a blank check here."

Dominique closed the space between them, their noses almost touching. "Knowin' who I am and what I'm capable of, you have the nerve to stand here and continue to disrespect me?"

Simone struggled to meet her eyes. So she didn't. "I mean no disrespect, Dominique. I don't."

"Oh no?"

"No. I could have had you arrested for attacking me."

"But instead, you sent *him* after me." Dominique rubbed her throat. It was burning.

"Well, he *is* the only one who knows how to tame you."

Dominique began to laugh in spite of herself. "Are you that deeply in love with him that—"

"Yes! I am! What happened between you two at Daddy's repast should have never happened. And it can't happen again.

I won't allow it. This is my chance to be happy finally, and I'm not going to let you ruin it."

"No matter if I'm here or back in Jersey, Antoine's feelings for me ain't gonna change. He doesn't love you, Simone."

"He does!"

"He doesn't! And he *never* will!"

"He does," she growled. "He just doesn't know it yet. Love doesn't always come right away. And I'm patient. I can wait for it."

"He's no good."

"For *you.*"

"For anyone. He's gonna hurt you—*bad.*"

Simone clicked her pen again, placed it inside her checkbook, and then zipped her handbag, adjusting it on her shoulder. "Think about my offer."

GIA LOOKED out of the back passenger-side window, studying the wrought iron gates of St. Louis Cemetery No. 1. The drive there had been a quiet one, except for jazz playing softly on WWROZ. Toni tried to make conversation with her and her mother, but both had been lost in their thoughts. Gia was still unnerved by her mother's encounter with her father. She wondered if he knew about Louis or even noticed the hickey on her neck that she tried to conceal with makeup. She knew Antoine had given it to her because she hadn't encountered any other men since they'd been down there. *But when and where?* Her mother despised that man, so why did she allow him to get close enough to her to leave his mark? As much as Gia wanted to believe her aunt, believe that her mother wasn't a loose woman, she just couldn't. Her actions weren't matching the woman's words. She wasn't even sure if she believed that her mother deserved a second chance with her father. In her eyes, she wasn't worthy of him.

A steady tide was rising within, the waters unsteady. It was only a matter of time before she and Dominique would get into another argument, and she'd throw everything in her face.

Dominique wrung her hands as Toni rounded the block in search of a parking space. She'd told her about the conversation with Simone, and Toni assured her that their love-stricken sister was bluffing. Dominique knew better than to believe that. Simone was desperate, and desperate people did desperate things. Suddenly, she felt unsure of herself. *Have I done the right thing by turning down Simone's offer? Should I have thrown Antoine's disregard of her love for him back in her face?* Simone had, yet again, gotten to her. There was no way she could pay her respects to her father under the duress of her mental and emotional states.

Toni turned off the car and unbuckled her seat belt. "Awrite," she smiled. She pressed the unlock button, then exited. Gia followed suit. She shifted the bouquet of roses in her arms and got out of the car. As she and Toni made their way onto the sidewalk, they noticed Dominique hadn't moved.

"Isn't she coming?"

Toni sighed. "Let me see what's goin' on. Stay here." She quickly rubbed Gia's shoulder before walking back to the car. She opened the passenger door and knelt down. "What's goin' on, suge?"

"You and Gia go on. I'm gonna—I'm gonna stay in the car and wait until y'all are done."

Toni looked back at Gia and sighed again. "You can do this, baby."

"No, I can't."

"Yes, you can. If there's any place to bury ya burdens, it's here."

Dominique began to tremble, tears cascading down her cheeks.

Toni grabbed her hand and rubbed her cheek with the back of her fingers.

"I'll be on one side of you. GiGi will be on the other."

"It's not that. I just . . . I can't," she hiccupped. She was angry as hell. Angry with Simone for upsetting her. Angry that she let Simone upset her. Angry still with her father for speaking Antoine's name, and the universe for listening to him.

"*We promised her.*"

"I know, but . . . please. I'm not ready." Dominique finally looked at her, her eyes begging.

Toni surrendered. She squeezed her hand, then pressed their heads together. "Awrite." She kissed her on the cheek, then rose to her feet and made her way back to Gia.

"Is she coming?"

"No. She needs more time."

Gia looked back at her, confused. It didn't make sense. Her mother was in and out of cemeteries every week. It was part of her job. *So why can't she step into this one and pay her respects to my grandfather?*

"But—"

"Grief has no expiration date, *cher.*"

DOMINIQUE GATHERED her maxi skirt as she moved from one side of her mother's storefront to the other. The geraniums in the window boxes were in desperate need of water, so she took her time and watered them. She'd walked all the way from the cemetery to her mother's shop. She'd thought about cutting through City Park, but she didn't want to be around anyone, so she ventured up Esplanade instead. The walk had been long but therapeutic. She managed to calm down on the way there.

"I thought I'd find you here." The voice was familiar and light.

Dominique closed her eyes and shook her head. She continued to water the plants. "How's that?" she threw over her shoulder.

"It's Sunday. You always did inventory and tended to ya mama's flowers on Sunday."

"Mmm."

"Is she inside?"

"No, but I wouldn't be surprised if she decided to stop by to check on me."

"Then I won't stay long."

Dominique turned around to face Antoine. "What can I do you for?"

He reached into his pocket and retrieved a toothpick. He placed it in his mouth as he took in her beauty. "I just left ya ex."

Dominique, unmoved, refilled the watering can and focused on the rosebushes. "Is that right?"

"Mm-hmm. He's a real stand-up guy."

"Yes, he is," she nodded.

"He wanted to beat my ass, ya know?" Antoine ran his tongue over his teeth.

"I do," Dominique nodded again, her back still turned to him.

"Yeah. But I apologized to him for the way things went down."

"You talked ya way out of it," she threw over her shoulder.

Antoine laughed guiltily. "If that's how you wanna put it."

"I do because that's what you did." Dominique gently removed a caterpillar from one of the window boxes and placed it on a petal.

"Well, we can agree to disagree on that." He watched her with the caterpillar, then remembered what he was there for.

"Anyway, I thought you'd like to know that he and I made some leeway. And we both think that the three of us should get together to figure this thing out with Gia. Decide the best way to approach her about it."

Dominique's eyebrows furrowed. "I really don't care what you two think *we* should do. Y'all ain't gonna make that call. I am. *Me. I* have the final say."

Antoine leaned against the gate. "Well, that ain't fair."

"Well, you leavin' me to raise her on my own ain't fair either, but here we are."

"You ain't raise her by yaself. You had that nigga to help you. And even though I'm not happy about it—"

Dominique slammed the watering can down on one of the steps. "You are in no position to have feelings about anything. You didn't want to be a father, *remember*? I recall you disappearin' right after Gia was conceived. Ya daddy couldn't find you, ya friends—nobody. Where you been for the last seventeen years, 'Toine?"

Antoine stared at her for a moment. "Houston."

"Houston?"

"Yeah. The last afternoon we spent together, I knew I'd gotten you pregnant. Somethin' inside told me so. And I just . . . I woke up the next mornin', got in my car, and drove to Houston. *That's* where I've been. Stayed wit' a couple of my mama's people. Called and told my daddy eventually."

He watched Dominique process his confession. She said nothing, remaining rooted at the bottom of the steps.

"You know I always loved planes, so I learned how to fix 'em. Been an aviation mechanic supervisor for Southwest for ten years now. I transferred back to Nawlins last October to care for my pops."

Dominique shook her head in disbelief. "Wow."

"I fucked up. I know. I was wrong for leavin' you like that. I hurt you . . . bad. And I'm sorry for that. I mean it. I don't-I don't know what else to say to you. I was a kid, ya know? What the fuck did I know?"

"So was I! Any good sense I had went right out the window after I started messin' with you again. I should have listened to my mama and left ya ass alone."

Antoine reached for her. Dominique flinched and stepped back.

"But you didn't. And even though the way we went about things was wrong, you can't deny the love we had for each other, Dom. I loved you. I still do. I ain't never stopped."

Dominique shook her head at a memory that was surfacing. She began to sting in places that she never let Esai or any other man touch. "My mama almost beat that girl outta me. I still have the scars. If it hadn't been for my sisters . . ."

"I'm sorry she did that to you."

Dominique looked back at him. His eyes were despondent. He extended his hand and caught a tear threatening to fall from her eye.

"Don't cry. You too beautiful to cry."

A cream-colored Oldsmobile tooted its horn as it pulled up and parked in front of the botanica. Dominique quickly wiped her eyes and focused on the attractive elderly woman behind the wheel. She was dressed in a sheer animal print poncho, curly burgundy wig, and glossed lips.

"Excuse me?"

"Yes, ma'am?" Dominique smiled.

"Are you Madam Favier's daughter?"

"Yes, ma'am. Her youngest chile."

"I knew it!" she slapped the wheel. "You look just like ya mama!"

Dominique blushed. "Thank you."

"You the one she's always talkin' 'bout. You live up North, right?"

"Yes, ma'am."

"Yeah. She misses you somethin' terrible. You can see it in her eyes any time she speaks about ya."

Dominique took in a deep breath, then slowly released it.

"She said you'd come back."

"Ma'am?"

"Ya mama. She said you'd come back after ya daddy was gone. Pick up where she plans on leavin' off." The woman looked off into the distance for a moment.

"Yes, ma'am," Dominique nodded, her voice quivering.

"Are you open today?"

Dominique cleared her throat. "No—No, ma'am. Tuesday–Saturday from 9:00 to 9:00.

"Aw, shit. Oh, excuse me."

Dominique and Antoine cracked subtle smiles. "You fine."

"I'll just come back Tuesday then."

"Well, what is it that you need? I may be able to help ya."

"Oh, I know ya can. Ya mama said so," she smiled wide.

Taken aback, Dominique looked over at Antoine, then back at the older woman. She moved past him out the gate and settled at the car. The lady opened the door. Dominique extended her hand for her to take. "Well, come on inside, so we can get you what you need."

The two moved toward the shop. Antoine helped to assist them up the stairs carefully. "I'll talk to you another time," he whispered to her back.

GIA PASSED Corey the bowl of popcorn as she snuggled with her brothers beneath the covers in their oversized recliners. Their aunt Jackie's theater room was cozy and reminiscent of a retro movie theater. The walls were heavily draped with red velvet curtains and gold tassels. And the room was fully equipped with three rows of seating, an overstocked concession stand, popcorn machine, and bar. The third generation of Faviers were thoroughly enjoying themselves. It was pouring outside, so it made sense to kick back and watch a couple of movies while the adults played games and drank upstairs.

Dominique tucked her legs beneath her as she laughed at her brother-in-law's failed attempt at pantomiming the music title on his card. Charades was one of the Favier sisters' favorite pastimes. Toni declared she was the best at the game. Dominique argued that she was the better player. And the twins swore neither one of them was any good or any real competition. The reason being—they always won because they always cheated. Tonight, however, the twins' winning streak would officially end because Jackie was partnered with Toni, Big GiGi was partnered with her husband, and Dominique was left with Esai. And because Esai's English wasn't the best, Dominique knew they didn't stand a chance against the rest of them.

The vibration of her cell phone pulled her attention away from the drunken sideshow that was her brother-in-law. She turned it over and read the name on the screen, then opened the message. A scowl blanketed her face. Esai noticed immediately.

"*Que pasa?*"

"Nothin'." Fuming, Dominique rose from the couch.

"Where are you going?"

"To the bathroom," she threw over her shoulder. But, instead, she made a beeline to the basement. Dominique trotted down the steps and rested at their feet. She waited for her eyes to adjust to the darkness before setting them on Gia.

"Gia," she whispered.

Gia turned around, looking over the recliner. "Yes?"

Dominique signaled for her to meet her. Gia did.

"Yes?"

"I just got a text from Amari's mama sayin' how sorry she is for our loss."

Gia nervously shifted from one foot to the other. "I-I was going to tell you."

"There shouldn't be nothin' to tell. You . . ." Dominique balled her hands into fists, then shook her head. "Why can't you do right? By me . . . by yaself?"

"I just needed someone to talk to."

"All this family around you, and you didn't think enough of anybody to turn to 'em?"

"Mommy—"

"I can't trust you. I *don't* trust you. Any faith I did have in you is all gone now. *Gone.*"

Gia bowed her head, then looked back up at her. "I'm-I'm sorry."

"Yeah. Yeah, you are. And since you don't want to respect me or my rules, you can't stay with me."

"What?"

"Tomorrow mornin', ya gettin' on the plane with ya daddy and ya brothers. I'm goin' back to Jersey alone."

"What about—"

"I need the rest of this summer to myself." Dominique turned her back and ascended the steps with Gia on her heels.

"What about work? How am I gonna pay my phone bill?"

Dominique shrugged her shoulders. "That's for you to figure out."

"You're treating me the same way Mamaw treated you, and I'm not even pregnant!"

"Not yet! Give yaself some time!"

Gia stopped in her tracks, thrown by her mother's admonishment. Corrine, who was at the kitchen sink, stopped what she was doing as well.

"How can you say that to me?! How?! Like I'm some piece of shit?!"

Corrine rushed to them. "Whoa, whoa. Hold on now. What's goin' on?"

"Mommy found out that I've been talking to Amari behind her back. And because of it, she's sending me to DR with my dad and brothers tomorrow."

"Dominique—"

"Mama, please."

The sound of crunching metal against the heavy rainfall outside caused them to pause. Hurried footsteps and the opening and closing of the front door echoed. A cacophony of muffled voices made a rhythm with the rolling thunder. The front door flew open. Simone appeared with Esai on one side of her and Devere on the other.

"Where is she?!"

Toni, Jackie, and Big GiGi ran over to her and sat her down on the bench in the foyer. Dominique, Gia, and Corrine turned the corner, unnerved by the pandemonium that erupted.

Simone was drenched. Blood was running down from her forehead. Jackie patted her dry with towels, trying to help her out of her wet clothes, but she was fighting against her.

"Simone, calm down! I need to get a good look at ya! Be still, now," Corrine demanded.

"I just got that damn car!" Devere paced back and forth.

"I know, baby. I know," Big GiGi struggled to help Corrine treat the cut on Simone's forehead. "Help me keep her still, Jackie."

"I'm tryin'."

"It's always some shit wit' her!" Devere hollered.

Dominique watched her brother-in-law storm up the stairs, then met Esai's eyes. "What happened?"

"She crashed into his car."

"Is she drunk?"

"That or high." Esai moved past her, making his way into the kitchen to prepare a pot of coffee. He noticed the frightened look on Gia's face and smiled nervously. "She's going to be okay, *princessa*."

"What did you say to him?!" Simone rose on unsteady legs. "What?"

Simone met Dominique face-to-face. "What did you say?!"

"I didn't say anything!"

"You're a liar," she jeered. "And a *whore*."

Corrine placed herself in between them and began to push Simone back gently. "Awrite, Simone. That's enough."

As if on cue, Jackie moved behind Simone and took her by her arms. "Let's go on upstairs and get you changed into some dry clothes."

"No!" Simone snatched her arm away. "You all treat her like she's the second comin', but she ain't shit! The way she hurt you, Mama! And Daddy! The way she's

been hiding the truth from this child like that goddamn hickey on her neck. This bitch ain't shit!"

"Simone!" the twins cried.

She looked back at them. Then her eyes shifted. Tears began to fall. "He broke up with me."

"Who, baby? Who she talkin' 'bout?" Corrine asked, looking each of them in the eye.

No one responded.

"Told me he's got no room for me. Just enough for you and Gia."

Corrine's mouth fell open. Her brows began to knit together as she met each of her daughters' gazes.

Gia uncrossed her arms and looked over at her mother. "What is she talking about?"

"You happy now? You satisfied?" Simone slurred.

The twins began to tug on her again. "Come on, Simone."

"Y'all knew about this?" Corrine eyed them all.

She was met with silence again.

"How long?" She turned back to Simone. "How long, girl?!"

"Nine months. Mama, I knew you and Daddy wouldn't approve, and that's why I didn't tell you. But I love him."

Without warning, Corrine's hand connected with Simone's face. Everyone flinched but Dominique.

"Mama, please, try to understand."

"Carry yo' ass upstairs! *Now!*" she trembled.

The twins led her to the stairs and disappeared.

"What was TeeTee Simone talking about?"

Dominique slowly looked over at Esai and Toni, then her mother. And finally, at Gia.

"GiGi, let's go have a seat in the livin' room and talk," Toni stressed.

"No, TeeTee. I'm fine right here." Gia shifted her weight from one leg to the other. "Why did she say you've been hiding the truth from me?"

Suddenly, Dominique's lips and throat were dry. "Because I have."

"Dominique," Corrine whispered. "Don't."

"The truth about what?"

Dominique closed her eyes, then shook her head painfully.

"Mommy."

Dominique remained.

"Look at me," Gia demanded.

"I . . . can't."

"Suge." Toni stood beside her and began to rub her back.

"Just tell me!"

Dominique released a heavy sigh. "Esai's not ya biological father. Mr. Brevard . . . *Antoine* . . . is." She finally reopened her eyes.

"What?" Gia looked from her grandmother to her aunt to Esai, then over at her mother. "You're kidding, right?"

"I wish I was."

"But, TeeTee, you said . . . I thought . . ."

"It wasn't my place to tell you, *cher.*"

Gia began to pace, her face flushed pink, hands balled into fists. "All this time. All this time!"

Dominique jumped, startled by Gia's tortured scream. "Gia —" she muttered just above a whisper.

"All my life, it's been 'respect yourself, Gia.' 'Keep your legs closed, Gia.' 'I'm not raising no liars and no thieves, Gia.' 'Do right by yourself, Gia.' And you've been lying to me for *seventeen fucking years*! What the fuck is wrong with you?!"

Esai moved toward her. "*Princessa*—"

"Don't call me that shit!"

"Gia!" Toni and Corrine cried.

"What?! This is some bullshit! Like, for real!" She turned back to face Esai. "How can you love her?! How?! How can y'all stand her with all the hypocritical shit that comes out of her mouth?!"

"Allow her to explain, GiGi," Toni stated coolly.

"What's there to explain? She's everything TeeTee Simone said she is!"

Dominique raised an eyebrow.

"Now, wait a minute," Corrine began.

"No, Mamaw. She has made me feel like I'm this, this . . . terrible person. Like, like I'm this . . . *ho* when *she's* the one who can't keep her fucking legs closed! What type of shit is that?! Huh?!" Gia glared back at her mother. "If I'm a ho', it's because I learned it from you!"

"Girl! I got ya ho!" Dominique lunged at her. Toni and Corrine grabbed her in an attempt to stop her. They began to wrestle. "You gon' disrespect me now?! Huh?! You gon' stand up here and disrespect me?!" She pushed past them and slapped Gia in the face. Then she grabbed her hair and continued to strike her. Gia, in turn, delivered wild, blind punches. Corrine, Toni, and Esai struggled to pull them apart. The boys ran upstairs and tried to intervene, to no avail.

"Let go of her, Dom! Let go!" Esai ordered.

"GiGi, let go! Yo' bleedin'! Yo' bleedin!'" Corrine stressed.

The two finally separated.

"Let me look at you."

Gia's nose was runny. A red river. And there was a cut above Dominique's eyebrow and scratches on her face and chest.

"You gon' side with a bitch who's got nothin' but hate in her heart for me?!"

"You should have told me!"

"I was protectin' you!"

"You were protecting yourself!"

Dominique lunged at her again. Esai blocked her, then tightly wrapped his arms around her.

"I had a right to know, Mommy!"

"To know what?! That he didn't *want* you?!"

"Dominique, stop," Toni pleaded.

"That you look just like him?! You act just like him?! And at times, I can't stand those parts of you?! That I *hate* 'em?! *That's* what you wanted me to tell you?!"

"Are you sure those are his parts? I don't know him, but I *know* you. You sure those aren't *your* parts that you hate so much?"

Dominique's top lip trembled with vehemence. "I curse the day I had you."

The wind was immediately knocked out of Gia. A breath that was shared and stolen from Toni and Corrine as well. They all stood stunned for a moment. Then Gia emerged from her state of shock and balled up the bloody tissue her grandmother placed in her nose.

"She didn't mean that, GiGi," Toni stressed.

"No, she didn't," Corrine followed. "Apolo—apologize to her, Dominique," her voice strained. "Apologize to this chile. *Now—right now.*"

Dominique remained impassive to her mother's desperate

plea. She rubbed her runny nose with the back of her hand. Her eyes never steered away from Gia's.

"I wanna-I wanna go. I'm ready to go. I can't stay here," Gia paced.

Corrine grabbed her by her face attempting to soothe her. "GiGi—"

"Mamaw, please?" A fresh flood of tears cascaded down her face.

"Okay, awright. We leavin'. Toni, go get my purse."

"Gia, listen . . ." Esai reached for her.

"Don't touch me!"

"Don't talk to him like that!" Dominique countered.

"He's *nothing* to me!"

"He has been ya *everything!*"

"Just like Antoine has been mine," Simone declared calmly from the kitchen threshold. She was still wearing her wet clothes. The water from her raincoat dripped onto the wooden floor. It began to form a puddle beneath her bare feet. "Gia's . . . supposed to be . . . mine." She slowly reached into her coat pocket, pulled out a Glock 43, pointed it in Dominique's direction . . . and fired.

6

Dominique ran her hand over the bandage covering the gunshot wound that pierced through her shoulder as her mother slipped her arm around her waist. They watched a nurse clean and re-dress Gia's thoracotomy incision. The scar would be nasty because the cut began under Gia's left breast and wrapped around her side, stopping beneath her shoulder. Simone's second bullet managed to catch Gia in her left lung, shredding its upper lobe and shattering four of her ribs. The surgeon had to remove the damaged part of that lung, but Dominique didn't care what he had to eradicate so long as her child survived.

Gia lay in her arms, bleeding out while they waited for the ambulance to arrive. Dominique begged for her to keep her eyes open, to forgive her for her cruel admission, and keep talking to her. And Gia did for a little while . . . until she didn't. Big GiGi performed CPR until the paramedics reached them and took over. The ride to the hospital felt like an eternity. The storm outside hadn't abated. Nor had the one within Dominique. Gia coded again, and all Dominique could think about was her last words to her child.

The nurse smiled at them as she balled up the soiled wound dressing and threw it in the trash. She placed the small mound of sheets and blankets back over Gia and gently tucked her in.

"She's a fighter."

Dominique's lips quivered.

"Yes, she is," Corrine cooed.

"She gon' be awrite. And so are y'all." The nurse smiled again.

Dominique tried to smile back, but she couldn't muster up one. It didn't feel right.

"Can I get y'all anything? Another blanket or pillow?"

"No. Thank you," mother and daughter replied.

"Awrite. I'll be back in thirty to check on y'all." The nurse quietly left.

Dominique watched Corrine make her way back to Gia's bedside and sit. She took her limp hand into hers, kissed it, then pressed it against her cheek.

It had been a long three days, but Gia was making strides. She would be taken off the ventilator tomorrow with hopes that she would be breathing on her own without complication. And although she was under heavy sedation for pain management, the moments when she did emerge from her long slumbers, she always opened her eyes and communicated with her hands.

Simone was arrested on DUI, cocaine possession, and attempted manslaughter charges in the first degree. She was currently sitting in the Orleans Parish Sheriff's Office awaiting her bail hearing. Corrine and the girls divided their time between Simone and Gia. They didn't bring her up in conversation, and Dominique appreciated them for it.

Esai and the boys flew back to DR at her request. She didn't believe Dominic and Mikey needed to see any more than they already had. Dominique was certain they were going to be scarred for life. The upside of the matter, Gia was somewhat stable, so there was no need to stick around and wait for a dramatic turn. Dominique wanted them to get back to as much normalcy as possible. She reassured Esai that she'd keep him updated daily. And she had, indeed, kept her word.

Antoine found out about the shooting after receiving a collect call from Simone at the parish jail. He'd rushed to the hospital to see mother and daughter but had been turned away by Toni.

Dominique readjusted the strap on her sling as she settled on the other side of Gia's bed and rubbed her forehead. She kissed it and noticed her lips were chapped, so she retrieved a miniature jar of shea butter from her purse and applied some to them. She yawned after that, wiping her heavy eyes.

"You need to get some sleep," Corrine said softly.

"I know," Dominique yawned again.

"Why don't you go on back to the house and get sum rest? I'll stay wit' her tonight."

Dominique placed the top back on the salve. "I can't keep my eyes closed long enough without seein' her . . ." She paused for a moment before placing the jar of ointment back into her purse. ". . . I'll get some sleep once she's outta here."

Dominique could feel her mother's eyes on her, watching her much like Gia.

"Yo' sister . . . She didn't mean it," Corrine said just above a whisper. "I know she didn't."

"Oh, I know. Both of those bullets were meant for me. This . . ." she pointed at Gia, ". . . was supposed to be me."

"She wasn't in her right frame of mind, Dominique."

"She never is when it concerns me," Dominique snapped.

Corrine shook her head. "Don't say that."

Dominique could feel her blood beginning to boil. And she was confident it was going to bubble over if they continued this conversation about her sister. "Why not? It's the truth. Simone has hated me all our lives, Mama. You know that. Daddy knew it. Toni and the twins . . . It was only a matter of time before she tried to take me out for good."

"Simone loves you, Dominique," Corrine began.

Dominique stared back at her as if she had two heads, then chortled.

"She does. She just . . . I don't know. That cocaine and alcohol in her system—"

"Gave her the courage to do what's she's wanted to do for a long time," Dominique sneered.

Corrine rubbed her forehead and sighed. "It's not her fault."

"Well, whose is it? Mine?" Dominique spat.

"No, I didn't say that."

"Then *whose*, Mama? I didn't ask to be born. That was you and Daddy's pleasure. And I surely didn't ask Antoine to weasel his way back into our lives. That was Simone's doin'." Dominique began to pace. "She sent him after me. Right after the fight. Straight to Toni's house. *Her.* Knowin' the history, knowin' the effect he has on me. And in her twisted mind, she thought he would put the fear of God in me, but the shit backfired on her," she smirked. "She sent him to *tame me.* That's what she said—*your* daughter. Tame me because he's the only one who knows how. Like I'm some wild fuckin' animal. Fuck that bitch!"

Dominique continued to pace under her mother's defeated gaze. She didn't understand how the woman could sit there and make excuses for her sister's actions. As far as she was concerned, what she'd done was unforgivable, and she hoped the prison time given to her would be the maximum punishment. Dominique wanted her to suffer as much as she had over the years Certainly as much as she and Gia were suffering right now. Dominique wanted Simone to rot in there, then burn in hell afterward.

"I ain't mean fo' you to get upset," Corrine murmured.

"And I didn't mean to overstay my welcome." Dominique

finally stopped pacing and ran her hands across her face. She looked over at Gia and shook her head.

"Yo' not an inconvenience, Dominique," Corrine admitted.

"No. Just a disappointment, right?" Dominique sneered.

Corrine tilted her head to the side, her brows knitted together. "We not gonna do this here. Not in front of this chile. She don't need this right now."

Dominique sucked her teeth. "She already knows how you feel about me, Mama. Don't make a difference whether we talk about it here or back at the house."

"Oh yes, it does. It makes a huge damn difference. This is not the time nor the place to talk about hurt feelings and blame."

They stared at each other, each waiting for the other to withdraw. The beeping of Gia's heart monitor forced Dominique to stand down first. It dissolved the tension between her and her mother.

"Have you thought about what you gonna do after she's discharged?" Corrine asked, breaking the silence between them.

"No," Dominique sighed.

"Well . . . I think you girls should stay wit' me until you good and healed. I can take better care of you here than I can up there in New Jersey."

"No disrespect, Mama, but I want nothin' more to do with Louisiana."

"And I completely understand, but this is still yo' home. And you can't run and hide anymore, Dominique. You did that fo' the last fourteen years. And it may have seemed like it worked fo' you—"

"It *did* work for me."

"Well, you know what? That's all over now." Corrine gently placed Gia's hand back down. "It was inevitable that yo' paths were gonna cross again, no matter how many times you may have told yo'self you were free of him. No matter how many times I told myself the same thing." She sat back in her chair and crossed her legs at the knee. "What happened the other night happened to all of us, not just you and this chile."

Dominique cut her eyes. "I know that."

"Then *act* like it." Corrine watched her move from the bed to the windowsill. She began to fold a blanket that was taking too much of its space. "Yes, we got some long days ahead of us. And, yes, some of 'em are gonna be dark. But as long as my eyes can open, I'm gonna help you and this baby get through this. *Let me* help you get through this."

Dominique continued to fold the coverlet, then focused on a sheet that needed the same attention. As much as she wanted to accept her mother's offer, she was having difficulty doing so. Too much had happened in too little time. Her head was spinning.

"Well, if you not gonna stay, then, at least, let Gia. We can arrange for her to have her physiotherapy at the house, we all can pitch in to take her to her post-op appointments, I can treat her wound . . . nurse her back to health. Get her back to herself again."

Dominique couldn't argue with her mother about that. There were no better hands to leave her in. She was a healer. Bona fide. She had dedicated her entire life to it and wore it as a badge of honor. Dominique had seen her save grown men from the brink of death, so she knew very well what her mother was capable of. But Louisiana had left a sour taste in her mouth. And more trauma. Gia would probably need intensive psychotherapy after all of this. The boys too. Maybe the entire family.

Dominique hated to admit it to herself, but she knew Gia would want to stay in New Orleans with her grandmother rather than go back home with her. Rolling emotions had spilled over. Hurtful words had been spoken aloud. Dominique wasn't sure if her and Gia's relationship would ever recover.

"I'll think about it." Dominique's shoulder began to hurt. She pulled a small pill bottle out of her pocketbook.

"What are those?"

"Percocets." Dominique popped the top.

"Mmm-mmm. Gimme that bottle," Corrine extended her arm.

"Mama, please. My shoulder's killin' me, okay? I'm only takin' half of one."

"Not today, you not. Hand it over."

Dominique cocked her head to the side and sighed. She handed the bottle over to her mother, then watched her shove it in her pocket. Then she retrieved a blue thermos from a tote bag.

"Already got one daughter on drugs. I don't need another," she huffed, passing the container to Dominique.

Dominique removed the top and sniffed the liquid inside. "What's this?"

"Turmeric milk. Now, drink."

Dominique hesitated before obliging.

A light knock on the door sounded. Neither she nor Corrine responded. The door squeaked open, and a young nurse appeared.

"Excuse me, Ms. Favier. There's a Mr. Brevard out here to see you. I didn't see his name on the visitation list—"

"Because it's not." Dominique met her mother's dark eyes. "I'll be out in a minute."

"Awrite. He's at the nurse's station."

"Thank you." She took one more sip of the warm beverage before piling the blanket and sheet in the corner of the windowsill. "I'll be right back."

"No. I'll go. You stay here," Corrine replied austerely. She stepped out of the room, closing the door behind her.

Antoine was standing with two bouquets and balloons in hand. He sucked his teeth and rolled his eyes at the sight of her.

"How *dare* you. How *dare* you come here and disrespect my chile."

"I have every right to be here, Corrine. They my family too."

"You have no family, just like you have no God. 'Cause if you did, you wouldn't be sneakin' 'round tryin' to destroy mine. They are *my* family. Flesh of my flesh, blood of my blood."

"Gia is just as much my flesh and blood as she is yours. Whether you like it or not."

"Only a little," Corrine said, placing her hand on her hip. "If you knew anything, you'd know that her matter, her material is *all* maternal. Each and every time she touches her skin, she's not only touchin' Dominique, but she's also touchin' me, my mother, my mother's mother . . . her mother all the way down to the *first* mother."

"Okay, great. Whatever. Can you let me by, please?" He tried to sidestep her, but she blocked him.

"No."

"You know . . . Love will always prevail, Corrine. *Always.*"

"Nigga, please. You don't know a damn thing about that. "

"Don't tell me what I know and don't know about love. I know exactly what love is."

"Oh, do you now?"

"Yeah, I do."

"Well, who taught you? 'Cause it sure hell wasn't yo' daddy. And yo' mama—"

"Leave my mama outta this."

They shared a disconcerting glance.

"May she continue to rest in peace," Corrine smirked.

Antoine shifted from one leg to the other, his eyes darkening. "I love Dominique. That's one thing that ain't changed after all these years."

Corrine let out a short, sharp laugh. "What you feel fo' my

chile ain't love. That's lust. And the fact that you don't know the difference makes you dangerous—that or stupid."

Antoine's corneas contracted. "Don't call me stupid."

"Or what? What you gonna do? Hmm?" Corrine crossed her arms at her chest.

Antoine clenched his jaws, then unclenched them.

"That's what I thought," Corrine sneered, then closed the gap between them. "I know you came to my husband's repast and left yo' mark on her. You not gonna get that opportunity again."

"Well, that'll be up to her, won't it?" he grinned slyly.

"Dominique ain't Simone. Simone always been weak. More of her daddy's chile than mine. But Dominique . . . She's *mine*. Strong. Resilient. Always been that way. She just didn't know it then. She was a girl, sheltered and naive. But she ain't that no more. She fully grown, and you bes' believe you ain't ready fo' her hell—or *mine*."

Antoine flicked his nose with his thumb, then submitted. "It's only a matter of time before you lose this battle, Corrine. You ain't gonna live forever."

"You weren't listenin'," she sneered. "But that's okay. You gon' learn one way or another."

Antoine gave her a once-over, then slowly walked away backward. Corrine remained. She never batted an eye.

GIA SHIELDED her eyes from the sun as Toni wheeled her up the walkway to Maison Favier. Corrine walked beside them, her arms full of flowers and gifts from her clients and devotees. Dominique strolled on the other side, holding a handful of balloons.

"Lawd, how we gonna get this chile up these steps?" Corrine asked as she set the gifts down on the bottom step.

"She's gotta walk," Dominique replied, locking the chair's wheels.

"You think you can make it, GiGi?" Toni asked.

"I'll try," Gia wheezed softly. She struggled to take painless breaths as she slowly rose from the chair. Corrine hurried up the stairs to unlock the front door as Dominique and Toni grabbed Gia's hands.

"Hold on to us," Dominique instructed. She interlocked Gia's arm with hers. Toni followed suit. They took a step. Then another. And another one after that.

"I'm getting a little dizzy," Gia confessed.

"Just a couple of more steps," Toni assured her.

They made their way onto the porch and led her to the cushioned bench set against the bay window. Gia slowly sat down and closed her eyes. Her lungs were on fire.

"You feel like you gotta faint?" Dominique asked as she sat down beside her.

Gia shook her head. She hadn't said much to her mother since that dreadful night. There wasn't much *to* say. She'd wished she'd never been born. And to top it off, the man who was biologically her father hadn't wanted her either. Gia almost felt like an orphan.

Toni ran back down the steps to retrieve the gifts.

"Don't worry about the chair. I'll get it," Dominique said.

"You can't carry this thing."

"Neither can you," Dominique smirked. "Just leave it."

"Awrite," Toni huffed as she ascended the stairs and made her way inside.

Dominique studied the setting sun, then Gia. Then she pulled back to God's painting in the sky.

"Mamaw wants you to stay down here with her for the rest of the summer so she can take care of you. And I'm okay with that if that's what you want."

"It is," Gia wheezed.

"Okay," Dominique said sadly. She looked back into the distance. "I know things aren't that good between us right now, but I want you to know that I didn't mean what I said, Gia. It was the biggest lie I've ever told. And if I could take it all back, I would."

"But you can't," Gia cut her eyes.

"No, I can't." Dominique bit her bottom lip. "I've never claimed to be the perfect mother. Strived to be, but . . . I always come up . . . short." She stared at Gia. "Truth is, you're the best thing that ever happened to me, baby. You and ya brothers are my everything. You saved my life. And if I had to do it all over again at seventeen, I would."

Silence settled between them.

"What time is your train?" Gia asked nonchalantly.

"Six."

Gia slowly looked over at her. "Then you better get going."

"Don't you need me to—?"

"No. Just go," Gia sniffled, refocusing on the sunset.

Toni shimmied out of the house with a smile, then placed her hands on her hips.

"How we doin' out here? You feelin' a li'l better, *cher*?"

"Yes."

"Good. Let's get you on in the house. Ya grandmama got the bed turned down for ya, the TV set to Netflix, and some new pajamas laid out for you to wear."

"Okay." Gia grabbed her aunt's hand, taking steady steps into the house. She never looked back. She'd made her decision to stay, to heal the way she wanted. And she felt good about it. It had been a long time since she'd made a decision without worrying about her mother's thoughts or feelings concerning it. She needed to feel safe. She needed to feel loved. She needed to know the truth surrounding her conception. And she was going to make sure she would under her grandmother's wing.

DOMINIQUE WALKED through Newark Penn Station's sliding doors into the city's cool night air. She closed her eyes and exhaled, taking in the sounds of speeding cars and blaring truck horns on the highway. She opened her eyes, looking to her left to see if her ride was there in waiting. And to her relief, it was. Rose got out of her heavily tinted SUV and approached her best friend with a broad smile and open arms.

"Heeey, boo!"

Dominique managed to crack a painful grin as they came into a full embrace.

Rose stepped back, looked her over, then past her. "Where's GiGi?"

Dominique's lips parted, but nothing came out. She shook her head, her brows furrowing as she fought back tears. Rose immediately connected the dots and pulled Dominique in for another hug. "Awww, sissy. It's okay. Everything's gonna be okay."

Dominique submitted . . . cried until her body rocked like waves. Rose held her tighter. She'd gotten what she wanted—to spend the rest of the summer alone. But she regretted it now. The future was so uncertain, and there was no one to blame but herself.

PART II

JULY

7

G ia stood under the shower's rushing water with closed eyes and tilted head. The water pressure was just right. Not too hard, not too soft. Staying in New Orleans with her grandmother had been the best decision she could have made. Her grandmother doted on her hand and foot, prepared every meal from scratch, and allowed her to indulge in necessary periods of rest and reflection in peace. She gave her more than enough space, and Gia appreciated her for it. She didn't know where she got the strength to carry on. After all that happened last month, Gia wasn't sure if her grandmother should have been praised or pitied for her vigor.

"GiGi, baby, yo' mama just called," Corrine said as she walked in with a towel. "She said she tried to reach you on yo' cell, but—"

"She did."

Corrine processed her tone and delivery. They were desolate. "You gonna have to talk to her sooner or later, baby."

"I know."

Corrine made a mental note to revisit this conversation later. "Awrite, then. I think you 'bout ready to come out." She walked over to the shower and unfolded the towel. Then opened it afterward. "You didn't saturate that wound too much, did you?"

"No, ma'am." Gia turned off the shower, opened the door, and stepped into the warmth of the oversized towel. She began to carefully pat herself dry as she met her grandmother at the sink. It was covered with medical supplies and small wooden bowls of colorful herbs.

"Good girl. The therapist is gonna be here at noon. I want you to eat somethin' before she gets here, awrite?"

"Okay."

"I already made yo' breakfast. Yo' favorite . . . pancakes wit' a side of shrimp and grits, brabant potatoes, scrambled eggs, biscuits, and some fruit salad."

Gia grinned. "Mamaw, I can't eat all of that."

"I know. I just wanted you to have options. Eat what you can," she smiled back.

"Okay."

Corrine leaned against the sink's edge as she put on her eyeglasses. "Awrite. What you gonna do is tie the towel around yo' waist."

Gia rubbed her forehead in apprehension.

"What's the matter?" Corrine removed her glasses, hooking them onto the neck of her T-shirt. "I know you not gettin' all shy on me now," she grinned.

"It's not that," Gia whispered, her eyes averted.

Corrine reached for her and held her at her hips. "Then what, baby? Tell me."

Gia's eyes shifted from the sink to the floor. "I can't."

"You can't *what*, baby?"

Gia looked up, meeting her grandmother's warm gaze. Her worry lines were visible. "I can't . . . look at myself. I can't look at the . . ."

Corrine inhaled deeply, then exhaled. She realized, at that

moment, this was the first time they were cleaning and dressing Gia's incision in the bathroom. Since her release from the hospital, she'd been treating the wound while Gia lay in bed. There were no mirrors in her bedroom.

Corrine slowly rose from the sink and positioned herself behind Gia. She carefully wrapped her arms around her, then peeled the towel from her grasp. She tied it around her waist after that.

Gia began to cry.

"Open yo' eyes, baby," Corrine said tenderly. She rested her hands on her granddaughter's shoulders.

Gia shook her head.

"Come on. It's awrite. I'm here."

Gia opened her eyes and studied their reflections in the mirror.

"Tell me what you see."

"Us," she hiccupped.

"And?"

"Ugliness."

"Where? Tell me where," Corrine stroked her hair.

"Everywhere. My complexion. My shape. My hair. Where I was . . . shot. Where the doctors cut me open."

Corrine pressed her lips in to compose herself. She had no idea Gia's perception of herself was so distorted. "Tell me what's so ugly about you."

"I don't look like my mother. I look like the man she hates," Gia sniffled. "My mother's the most beautiful woman I've ever seen. And I . . . I don't measure up."

"But you do, Gia. You possess yo' mama's beauty and so much more," Corrine smiled. "You are the best of her. Her goodness. Her grace. Her joy. Her peace. Her savin' grace. And you are worth more than the price of this world. Just because you a little flawed now does not depreciate yo' value."

"Can you . . . can you make it disappear?"

"No, I can't. And I wouldn't want to," Corrine took one hand, placing it over Gia's heart and the other over her surgical incision. "'cause the scar that's gonna be left behind is gonna serve as memory, no matter how painful. It will be a visceral connection to the day yo' life was spared so that you could live it differently . . . live it better," Corrine gently added pressure to the spots her hands lay upon. "You *survived*, baby. Healin' begins in that feat."

~

Dominique touched up the makeup on the young decedent beneath her fingertips. She was a seventeen-year-old girl who was a front passenger in her friend's car. They were driving back home from the shore when a drunk driver hit them head-on. All four girls perished in the crash. Favier-Payne got the call to pick up two of the four friends. Even though Dominique hated the cases that involved babies, children, and teenagers, she was the better director to serve their families. Rose would get too emotionally involved and would need to take time off to reset. They were the hardest to deal with. Not just because of the parents' grief, but having to care for an innocent, fragile life that was taken too soon. It felt unnatural preparing their bodies. As if the birth-death order was very wrong.

The young lady under her touch reminded her of Gia. Her skin was fair, and her hair dark. Her upper lip protruded some. But she wasn't Gia, and for that, she was grateful. Her child had been given another chance to live, to see another day. She hadn't spoken to Gia since her discharge day, and it weighed heavily on her. Her child had said very little, then got up and walked away without looking back. There were no hugs or kisses, tears or smiles of joy. Just pain . . . and resentment . . . and guilt. Dominique called her once a day, but Gia never answered. So she sent a follow-up text message, but she never replied. Dominique would then be forced to call her mother, and she would give her updates about Gia throughout the day.

The past two weeks felt like an eternity. She and Gia had never gone this long without speaking. Then again, neither one had gotten shot before, and a huge family secret hadn't been compulsorily revealed. She missed her baby girl. So much so, she threw herself into her work immediately after returning from Louisiana. She needed to keep busy so that thoughts of Gia and Esai, Antoine and Simone, her mother and father could be kept at bay. There was no time to sit and marinate in all that happened, to feel the roller coaster of emotions that needed to be acknowledged. Dominique had to press on because if she didn't, she would surely suffer in ways she would not be able to recover from.

Dominique pulled her walkie-talkie from her hip and pressed its TALK button. "Danny."

"Yes, Ms. Favier?" Danny replied with a heavy Cuban accent.

"Is Chapel Two ready?"

"Yes, ma'am."

"Okay. Send Justin down to put her on the elevator."

"Yes, ma'am."

Dominique placed the color palette back into her makeup case and laid her brush atop it. She gave the young lady one last check, then put her hand on top of hers. "Awrite, sweet angel. You look as good as new."

A young man with perfectly cornrowed hair appeared in the doorway. "I'm here, Ms. Favier."

Dominique, still looking down at the young lady, nodded. "She's ready. I'll be up in five." She moved out of Justin's way so he could wheel the casket to the elevator.

"Ms. Favier," Kelly's voice chimed from the intercom.

Dominique moved toward the wall and pressed the receiving intercom button. "Yes, Kelly?"

"There's another zaddy here to see you."

Dominique shook her head and smiled in spite of herself. Kelly was a mess. Young, intelligent, hardworking, and driven. She wanted to be a funeral director, and Dominique knew she'd excel. There wasn't a family who didn't rave about her personable nature. She was doing very well in her mortuary classes, and Dominique had begun to train her in the prep room. She had to because this part of her life was coming to an end. Her mother needed her, and she *had* to answer the call.

She composed herself before pressing the button again. "Kelly, not today. Who is it?"

"I'm sorry, I'm sorry," she giggled. "What's your name again, sir?"

A short moment of silence followed.

"Mr. Brevard. Mr. Brevard is here to see you."

The blood from Dominique's face drained.

GIA READJUSTED her face mask as she sat in the reading nook of her grandmother's shop and watched her educate a customer about which herbs to use for spiritual strength. Corrine had urged her to wear the mask in public to prevent infection, so she did as she was told. Her grandmother was dressed in a white kaftan and matching tignon. Her wrists and neck were bejeweled in red jasper. Gia thought she looked majestic. She didn't know much about voodoo or hoodoo but was hoping her grandmother would teach her a thing or two while staying with her.

The customer wound up purchasing $108 worth of herbs. Gia thought that was pretty good, considering each herb was sold at two ounces for six dollars. She watched her grandmother instruct one of her employees to bag up the contents individually, then place them in the shop's signature tote bag.

The miniature bags were made of organza fabric and tied with a satin ribbon. They were the same bags and ribbons her mother used for her *gris-gris* bags . . . her mother. She didn't miss her but wondered what she was doing. An absent-minded, random thought. It was a quarter after one. Gia guessed she was either on a service or overseeing an inspection, maybe having a quick lunch, or FaceTiming her brothers and Esai to see how they were doing. She hoped it was one of those things and not entertaining Louis. Then again, what did she care?

"GiGi, I'm goin' out back for a while to tend to my garden," Corrine said, readjusting one of her bracelets.

"Can I come?"

"Of course. Some fresh air'll do you some good," Corrine smiled.

Corrine reached for her. Gia took her hands without hesitation. She pulled her up gently and led her to the backyard. Corrine flicked the switch on the wall next to the door, and the garden came alive. String lights and fairy lights were strewn over the pergola and covering the tall wooden fence, giving the garden a look of enchantment.

Gia cringed in pain as she sat down on the couch beneath the lit pergola. She watched her grandmother fill her watering can, then wet her thirsty flowers.

A cool breeze blew in, rustling her grandmother's kaftan.

"The breath of the ancestors," Corrine uttered, her back turned to Gia.

"That breeze?"

"Yup. They know yo' here, where you belong. They happy."

"How do you know?"

"When's the last time you felt a short, sudden breeze like that? Since you been down here?"

"The night I saw you performing that head washing ritual on my mother."

"You were standin' behind the screen door," Corrine reflected.

"You saw me?" Gia asked, her eyes wide.

Corrine turned around and smiled. "No. I felt you." She turned back around and resumed watering her flowers. "Did yo' mama know you followed her here?"

"No. But I told her the next day."

"That was very dangerous, GiGi."

"I know, Mamaw. Mommy already ripped into me about it. But in my defense, I only followed her and TeeTee because I didn't know where they were. They didn't leave a note or a text. I thought Mommy had another seizure or something."

"Okay. I believe you." Corrine began to hum. It was a melody Gia remembered from her childhood.

"They told me that you're a voodoo priestess."

"Fo' true," Corrine nodded without missing a beat.

"And Mommy's your successor."

"She is," Corrine nodded again.

"Does that mean I'm hers?"

"If you're chosen to be. Yo' position hasn't been revealed to me yet."

Gia breathed a sigh of relief. She wasn't ready to be thrust into such an unknown world. However, that thought was quickly intercepted. "We're gonna have to move back down here, aren't we? For her to do whatever it is she has to do for you?"

"Fo' voodoo. Fo' the community, our people. Not fo' me."

"When is that supposed to happen? Her taking your place?"

"When I retire," Corrine threw over her shoulder.

"Is that soon?" Gia asked in hesitation.

"No," Corrine nodded, locking eyes with her. "But when the day comes, I want you to be here to witness it." Corrine refilled her can. "Listen, baby, I know you have a life back in New Jersey. I'm aware of that. And I'm also aware that you'll be graduatin' next year, startin' a new chapter in yo' life. And I want nothin' more than fo' you to live it to the fullest. But yo' mama . . . as far as she goes . . . her life is here. It was interrupted, but it is here. And she has to come to terms wit' that. She can only *truly* walk in her purpose *here.*"

"Do you want her back here . . . to stay?" Gia waited patiently.

"The ancestors do. Don't matter what I want."

"But it does, Mamaw. If you told her you wanted her back here, she'd consider it, I think."

"I don't think so, baby."

"I do. She misses you, Mamaw. Don't you miss her?"

Corrine took in a long, deep breath, then released it. Gia had hit a nerve, and she knew it. Her mother and grandmother's relationship was poor, and she was beginning to attribute her volatile relationship with her mother as a result of it. If she could help them heal, maybe it would spill over onto her and Dominique.

"I know she's sorry for hurting you and Papaw. She doesn't say it, but I see it every time she gets off the phone with you. After every visit, every argument, she cries, Mamaw. How can you love me so much but hate—?"

"I don't hate yo' mama. I don't hate her. I don't hate any of my children. I just hate the poor decisions she's made over the years." Corrine's thoughts drifted. "The men. All those men."

"You hold them against her. Then she turns around and does the same to me. It isn't right. How are we supposed to keep your legacy alive when we're all fucked up?"

Corrine rose abruptly from pulling a weed. "Gia Corrine."

"I'm sorry, but we are. Mommy hasn't taught me anything about that voodoo stuff. She doesn't even talk about it. She barely talks about you because she can't. That's fucked up, right?"

Corrine's heart skipped a beat, then became heavy. At that

moment, she realized Dominique had not only denounced the practice upon leaving NOLA but denounced her as well. She'd considered them one force. And Corrine wasn't sure which condemnation hurt more.

"You got one more time, you hear?" Corrine pulled another weed before disposing of them. "That *stuff* . . . is yo' heritage, yo' bloodline, and it is to be respected, even if you don't understand it right now."

"Yes, ma'am."

Silence crept between them.

"Will you teach me?" Gia asked quietly.

A warm smile grew along Corrine's face. There was still hope. *Gia was the hope.* "Of course, I will." She refilled the watering can a second time. "But you need to understand that voodoo isn't somethin' you just do, baby. It's a way of life. A lifelong commitment."

"Yes, ma'am," Gia nodded as she watched her grandmother move toward the other side of the garden.

"Yo' mama . . . I initiated her on her sixteenth birthday." Corrine smiled at the memory. "You should have seen her, GiGi. *She was somethin'.* And the crowd . . . she had them at her fingertips."

Gia watched her slowly fall out of the memory.

"She was born wit' a veil over her face just like you. Did you know that?" Corrine continued.

"No, ma'am."

"Mm-hmm. That's how I knew she was goin' to be the one to continue my work after my ascension. She's somethin' special, yo' mama. She just doesn't know it."

"The men do. They tell her so."

Corrine stiffened, then continued to pull more weeds. "I bet they do," she said softly. "But I ain't talkin' 'bout that part of her, beloved. I ain't talkin' 'bout the tricks she's learned over the years to keep them comin' back to her fo' more. We all possess

that power. The ugliest woman possesses that power. I'm talkin'
'bout her *magic*. Her God-given gift to *heal*."

"TeeTee Toni said she hasn't slept with any of them."

"Yo' aunt will say anything to protect her sisters. Especially
that one."

"So, you don't believe her?"

"Did you believe her when she told you that?"

"No."

"Then you have yo' answer." Corrine sat down beside Gia.
"They don't *see* her, Gia. They never will. Her beauty . . . It has
always been a burden fo' her to bear. A heavy one at that. But
her sensuality . . . That was somethin' that came too soon, too
early. Yo' daddy pulled it out of her before I could teach her
about it. How to get a handle on it. How to carry it properly. To
understand it fully. He lit a fire in her that we been tryin'a put
out fo' the past eighteen years." Corrine looked out into the
garden and sighed. "I want better fo' you, GiGi. Yo' cross will be
heavy too if you don't learn from her mistakes."

Gia fidgeted with her mask as she processed her grandmother's fair warning.

She didn't want to repeat her mother's mistakes. In fact, she
didn't want to be anything like her mother, but she fell victim to
temptation every time it offered its hand, just like her mama.

"Tell me somethin'. And don't lie to me."

Gia met her gaze, her eyes worried. "Yes, ma'am."

"How long you and yo' mama been fightin' each other like
that? Scrappin' like that don't just happen. That kinda scrappin'
got a history."

"A couple of years," Gia said shamefully.

Corrine's eyebrows furrowed. "How long is a couple of
years?"

"Three."

"Since you were fourteen?"

"Yes, ma'am."

Corrine nodded slowly, her gears turning. "Mmm. Tell me somethin' else. Why did you defy her when she told you to stop speakin' to Amari?"

"TeeTee's the one who gave me my phone back so I could talk to him."

"Well, she's wrong too. Yo' mama took that phone fo' a reason, GiGi. And I'm sure it was a good one."

"I just needed someone to talk to, Mamaw. He's more than just my ex. He's my best friend. We were best friends long before we became a couple."

"Okay. Now . . . Tell me why yo' mama forbade you from speakin' to him in the first place."

Gia rubbed her forehead and weighed the pros and cons of telling her grandmother the truth. After lying to her about her mother's seizures, she didn't want to do it again.

"You havin' sex, Gia Corrine?"

Taken aback by the question, Gia scratched her scalp and thought about surrendering. But if she did, she knew her grandmother would blame her mother for her promiscuity. And it wasn't her mama's fault. It was a personal decision.

Just as Gia fixed her lips to tell her grandmother the altered version of her breakup, her grandmother's cell phone rang. Corrine removed it from her pocket and looked at its screen.

DOMINIQUE SLAMMED HER OFFICE DOOR.

"First, you follow me to my sister's house, then to my daddy's funeral, my mama's shop after that, and now to my place of business thousands of miles away from home? What the hell is wrong with you?!"

"I tried to see you at the hospital, but ya mama and sisters wouldn't let me. So, I decided to take matters into my own hands."

"Leave. *NOW.*"

"I will *after* you talk to me."

"I ain't got nothin' to say to you. Why can't you accept that?"

"Because I don't know how." Antoine shifted the flowers and box of chocolates from one hand to the other. "Look, I ain't come all the way up here to make a scene. I just wanted to see about ya."

"Okay, well, you seen me. Now go."

"These are for you and Gia."

"I'm not gonna tell you again."

"Just listen to me. Just listen for a minute." He shifted from one leg to the other. "I didn't know Simone was gonna fly off the handle like that."

"I told you at the repast how she felt about you, but you blew it off."

"You right. I did. But, shit . . . I didn't know she owned a gun. I didn't even know she knew how to use one."

"We all do. My daddy made sure of that."

Antoine bit his lip. "How's Gia?"

"Alive."

"I mean, is she critical or . . . stable? I've been prayin' for her. For both of you."

Dominique crossed her arms. "What God you serve? Huh? What God do you serve, 'cause I ain't never known you to pray to nothin'."

"I prayed all the time before my mama died. Can't say I had a reason to get back to it until now."

Dominique remained unmoved by his admission.

"People change, Dom."

"Yes, they do. They do. But *you* . . . You sumthin' different. *You* like to play on people's emotions, start shit, then sit back and act like you ain't have nothin' to do with it. *You* should have left things alone after I whooped Simone's ass. You should have left *me* alone. That was family business. None of yours."

"I needed to see ya."

"For what? You thought sleepin' with my sister was gonna get a rise outta me? Well, it didn't. Y'all niggas deserve each other. You were lucky to have me."

"Can I see Gia?"

"Hell no."

"Please?"

"She ain't up here. And don't go lookin' for her back home either, 'cause you ain't gonna find her."

Dominique's desk phone buzzed. She pressed the speaker button. "Yes, Kelly?"

"Mr. Louis is here to see you."

Dominique looked past Antoine through the window behind him. Louis was standing at the concierge desk with a container of food in hand.

Antoine followed her gaze, turning around to get a look at Louis. He turned back to face her.

"Thank you, Kelly."

Antoine ran his hand over his goatee, the gears in his head turning. "Who's that?"

"None of ya business."

Antoine studied the scorned woman before him. He removed a business card from his pocket, then placed the gifts down on one of the chairs. He grabbed a pen from Dominique's desk and began to write on the back of it.

"Here's my cell. I'm stayin' at the Hampton Inn in Newark by the river. I'll be there until the end of the week. If I don't hear from you by Wednesday, I'm gonna stop by here again."

"Do it, and I'ma have ya ass escorted out by the police."

"Come on, Dom. You know I ain't scared of no police."

~

GIA HELD her wound as she pulled herself out of another nightmare. Recurring dreams from that infamous night of mayhem rode her like a demon on her back.

She often found herself waking in cold sweats or fits of hysteria, struggling to breathe. Her grandmother would have to wipe her down with a wet cloth or talk her through the episode until she could regulate her breathing again. Gia could no longer sleep alone or find comfort in her grandparents' pillows. She could only fall asleep now in her grandmother's arms.

The gunshots from her aunt's gun resounded in her ears as she dragged her feet into her grandmother's master bathroom. The walk from the bed to the sink was short, but it had taken a lot out of her. Her wound dressing was soaked with blood and needed to be changed. She didn't know how it became so saturated and feared a staple or two had become undone. Gia began to panic. She didn't know where her grandmother kept her nursing kit or the other items needed to dress her wound. She opened and closed every cabinet but found nothing. She made her way out of the bathroom and into the hallway in search of her grandmother. It was a quarter after ten, way past her grandmother's bedtime. But Gia heard her voice amidst others in the distance and followed them.

As she made her way down the hallway, she passed a room where the door was slightly ajar. Gia hadn't had the opportunity to explore the house due to her inability to walk long distances without the support of her grandmother or losing her breath. The smell of lavender wafted through the opening, piquing Gia's curiosity. She gently pushed the door open and entered. Her fingers scaled the wall in search of a light switch. Finding it, she flipped it on and took in the sight before her.

A three-tiered wooden table sat against the distant wall draped with a white cloth. Oversized throw pillows rested at its legs. Framed photographs of her maternal great-grandparents, great-aunt, grandfather, and a miniature wooden statue of the infamous Marie Laveau sat erect in their placements. Bottles of Florida Water, red wine, rum, a single glass of clean water, two white candles, fresh flowers and fruit, satin hair ribbons, a pack of cigars, and a pair of pink knitted baby booties filled the spaces surrounding the pictures.

The figurine of her foremother sat on the top tier of the altar. A large abalone shell lay beside her with a bundle of sage in it. On the opposite side, a bundle of incense and palo santo. Gia moved closer to the wooden structure and studied each photo, especially her dearly departed grandfather's. She removed him from the middle tier and ran her fingers along his handsome, smiling face. A painful grin met his just before she placed him back.

Then the baby booties sitting beneath her grandfather caught her eye. Gia knew, without a doubt, who they were meant for. But she didn't know how her grandmother knew about the baby. *Did my mother tell her?* She went to reach for them, but a steady stream of blood running from her wound caused her to pause and refocus on her initial task. Gia caught the crimson stream with her fingertips as she quietly backed out of the room. She left the door ajar as she'd seen it and made her way toward the kitchen to alert her grandmother.

Corrine sat at the kitchen island, rubbing her forehead. Toni and the twins surrounded her, waiting for her to gather her thoughts. "We gonna have to pull her medical records and get 'em to Warren."

"You sure?" Toni asked.

"Yeah. She ain't built fo' prison."

Toni shook her head in dismay. "Okay. You have copies somewhere?"

"In yo' father's office you'll find a file wit' yo' sister's name on it in his desk. Bottom left drawer."

"Awrite." Toni excused herself.

Jackie smirked in disgust as she swirled her wine in its

glass. "If she just hadn't hooked up wit' Antoine's nasty ass nine months ago, we wouldn't be in this mess right now."

"I agree," Big GiGi nodded.

"Say his name again, and I'll slap you blind," Corrine hissed.

"Sorry, Mama."

"Y'all sittin' up here talkin' 'bout what yo' sister started up nine months ago, but what did you do about it? Hmm? Outside of tellin' her she was wrong fo' entertainin' that nigga, what did you do? I'll tell you what you did . . . nothin'! You didn't do a goddamn thing!"

Toni reappeared with the file in hand. "I got 'em."

"I wanted to tell you, but—" Jackie countered.

"So did I, but Toni—" Big GiGi followed.

"Toni? Toni didn't swear neither one of you to secrecy. If y'all wanted to tell her so bad, then you should have."

Corrine shook her head. "But they didn't, and neither did you, and here we are. Y'all tell me everything else, why not that? Huh?! Yo' baby sister and yo' only niece almost lost their lives! Do you understand that?! We almost buried yo' sister and her chile right after yo' Daddy! It didn't have to be! None of it!" Corrine rubbed her burning throat as she paced the kitchen floor. "Gia's not sleepin' through the night. She's havin' these awful nightmares, and-and yo' sister's not sleepin' at all. She bound to have another seizure if she don't get the proper rest."

"They're gonna be okay, Mama," Big GiGi stressed. "It's just gonna take some time."

"GiGi's right, Mama. They're gonna be just fine. You got your hands on Gia, and we're in constant contact with Dominique. Rose is keeping a close eye on her too," Jackie reassured her.

"That's all well and good, but she needs to be *here*. Wit' us. Wit' *me*." Corrine shook her head in dismay. "Did y'all know she wasn't practicin'? That she hasn't since she left? Or that Gia knows nothin'?"

The girls nodded.

"Maybe it was her way of starting over . . . starting anew," Big GiGi guessed.

"Well, it was the wrong way," Corrine snapped.

"Trauma will do that to ya, though. Force you to reinvent yaself for survival. But you know that better than anyone, Mama," Toni added.

Corrine stared at Toni for a long time. There was so much weight in that word: *Trauma.* So much weight in the truth.

"This is a mess. *We are a mess.*" She came to a slow stop, then leaned against the island.

"Well, the healing's gonna have to begin with you and Domi, Mama," Jackie said into her wineglass. "You're gonna have to extend the olive branch to her."

"I tried. At the hospital."

"Before or after you defended Simone?" Jackie sipped.

Corrine stared back at her anticipating daughter. "I didn't mean . . . it was a thought, a feelin'," Corrine sighed.

"I'm not trying to reprimand you, Mama. Honest, I'm not. I'm just trying to make you understand that *you* are the reason why you and Domi's relationship is so bad. You tear her down and disingenuously build her up in the same breath. You throw her past in her face every chance you get. You don't hug or kiss her when you see her . . . Do I need to go on? Okay, so she defied you and got pregnant. It was a *mistake.* And she learned from it, right? We *all* learned from it. Then she moved away, and you denounced *that.* But she made somethin' of herself. So, why not celebrate it? *Celebrate her?* I mean, when was the last time you told her you were proud of her? Better yet, when was the last time you told her you loved her?" Jackie waited for a response. She received nothing. "It isn't right, Mama. You're better than this."

"You sound like Gia," Corrine groaned.

"Well, she's right," Jackie smirked. "And if you're not gonna listen to me or Toni or GiGi, then listen to Gia. She's gotta lotta sense."

Toni and Big GiGi nodded in agreement.

"No disrespect to Daddy or his memory, but I think he's the one to blame for Mama and Domi's poor relationship. Her little teenage rebellion would have never happened if he'd just respected Mama's wishes," Big GiGi mumbled.

"What?" Toni asked with genuine confusion.

"Think about it. He was adamant about her dating 'you know who'. Even after Mama broke them up, Daddy wouldn't let it go. The way they would fight about it . . . Toni, you don't remember?"

"Yeah, I do," Toni nodded. "Woke up many a night to them hollerin' and screamin' at each other."

"Exactly my point," Big GiGi nodded.

"Do you blame him, Mama?" Toni turned her attention to Corrine.

"Yes, I blame him the most," Corrine nodded slowly. "Even on his deathbed, I still blamed him. And I think he knew it even though we didn't speak about it," she reflected. "Yo' daddy didn't understand that there's just as much evil in this world as there is good. And evil comes in all forms." She straightened her back. "He wanted yo' sister to be that boy's savin' grace like I'd been his. But I told 'im that type of evil was too much for her to do anything wit'. And I didn't want her gettin' wrapped up in its darkness." Corrine looked at each of her girls in the eye. "I was tryin' to protect her. I need y'all to know that. I was tryin' to protect her."

"Then that's what you say to her when you extend that olive branch, Mama. That's how you start the conversation. Do not project your anger with Daddy onto Domi anymore. It's time to let it go and leave it with him because Domi's suffered long enough," Jackie said matter-of-factly.

Corrine remained silent. She couldn't argue with Jackie, even if she wanted to. It was time to lay her anger, pride, and the past to rest. "How many years did Warren say Simone can get fo' the . . . What is it, Toni?" Corrine began.

"Heat of passion attempted manslaughter charge."

"Yeah, that."

"Twenty if she doesn't plead guilty or temporary insanity."

"She will. I'll see to it. Make sure Warren gets that file first thing in the mornin'."

Toni nodded. "I will, Mama."

"Thank you."

Silence filled the space. The girls watched Corrine's mind drift. Her eyes following a thought or emotion not yet spoken. "You know, ever since that night, I've been thinkin' . . . maybe this is all my fault. Maybe, maybe I should have done more."

Toni grimaced with confusion as the twins took sips of their wine. "Like what?"

"Now, *you* talkin' crazy," Jackie followed.

"Naw, naw, I mean it."

"What could you have possibly done to prevent Domi and Gia from gettin' shot?" Big GiGi asked as she refilled her twin's glass.

"I don't know. She ain't been right since Dominique was born. She never took to her the way you other girls did. Every time you turned around, they were fightin' and carryin' on."

"But we all had our share of fights around the house, Mama," Big GiGi hiccupped.

"Yeah, but not like the ones between those two. Remember when Simone pushed Dominique down the stairs?"

The twins nodded. "Yes, ma'am."

"Dominique was only five. Just a baby. She broke her little hand tryin' to catch herself from that fall. Or the time she was walkin' along the back of the couch, actin' like she was a tightrope walker, and Simone snatched her foot from up under her. She went headfirst into the glass coffee table."

"Who could forget?" Toni cringed.

"Yeah, that was pretty bad. How many stitches did she have to get?" Big GiGi followed.

"Fifteen," Corrine replied with her eyes closed, remembering.

"She looked like a baby bride of Frankenstein walkin' around here," Jackie sniffled.

"Jackie," Toni warned.

"She did. I felt so bad for her, but she was so good about it. So brave."

Corrine wiped her wet eyes. "Yes, she was."

"No disrespect, Mama, but you and Daddy should'a had Simone's crazy ass committed."

"They did," Toni confirmed.

Jackie put down her glass, preparing herself for the details. "When?"

"Right after the table incident. You don't remember?" Jackie shook her head. "They left here early one Saturday morning and drove to New Iberia to seek counsel from a manbo, but Daddy cut the visit short. He was totally against it. Didn't believe anything she said. Right, Mama?"

"That's right," Corrine nodded.

"Well, what did she say?" Big GiGi asked.

Corrine sighed. "She said Simone had the spirit of a bitter ancestor who hadn't fulfilled her purpose in the previous life. That her life had been cut short because of her ill ways. So she returned in this life to right all her wrongs. But . . ."

The girls watched their mother's words get lost. Toni, as if on cue, continued the story for her.

"So they drove back a couple of days later and put her in the behavioral health center on Magazine Street. She was there for months."

Jackie looked from Corrine to Toni, then scratched the back of her head in

discomfort. "Really?"

"Mm-hmm. That's how yo' father and I found out she was bipolar."

"Damn, Mama. I'm sorry. I must have repressed it."

"It's awrite," Corrine smiled small.

"Look, Mama, no matter what you may think or feel, you did ya best with all of us. You can't blame yaself for Simone's bad behavior," Toni professed.

"Toni's right, Mama. Simone's a grown-ass woman. And she just so happens to be rotten. Rotten to the core, and that ain't your fault or Daddy's fault. It's just the way she is. So, please don't beat yaself up over it. You can't carry that."

"Naw, you can't. And we ain't gonna let you," Big GiGi added.

The girls gathered around her, each rubbing her back and taking turns kissing her on the cheek.

Gia appeared in the entryway, marinating in the exposed truth about her aunt. This family was more dysfunctional than she had thought. She was happy to see her grandmother hurt for her mother, but she wished she'd protected her better— then *and* now. As she watched her aunts envelop her, Gia thought her grandmother looked small sitting in the midst of them. She didn't want to interrupt, but her wound needed tending. Finally, she took a step into the kitchen, immediately capturing her grandmother's attention.

Corrine smiled at the sight of her, wiping her wet cheeks in the process. "GiGi, what you doin' up?" She rose from her stool and made her way over to her. "What's the matter?"

Gia revealed the stained gauze beneath her crimson-colored hand. "My wound. I think I may have hit it or something while I was asleep."

"Damn, that's a lot of blood," Jackie cringed.

"It's time fo' y'all to go," Corrine snapped.

"See what you did, Jackie," Big GiGi smirked.

"I didn't mean anything by it."

Corrine rolled her eyes. "Come on, baby. Let's get you cleaned up."

DOMINIQUE WATCHED Louis rub the back of his neck, struggling to grasp the loss of a child he hadn't known existed. Their lunch date had been cut short due to Antoine's impromptu drop-in. He had thrown Dominique off, and she'd asked Louis to come by the house later that evening to make up for it. She brought him up to date about her father's passing, the shooting, and her decision to move back home. Louis listened intently, placing his feelings aside. He responded with an occasional nod or stroke of his goatee. The news about the baby hadn't been planned.

"I didn't know how to tell you."

Louis looked over at her and shook his head. The look of shock overshadowed any other emotion he may have been feeling. "I don't know what to say." He took her hand into his and began to rub it. "Are you okay?"

Dominique breathed a little easier, grateful that he didn't insult her by questioning if he had truly been the father or berate her for waiting so long to tell him. "Yeah. Today, I am."

Dominique was no stranger to grief. She was surrounded by it daily. Knew it well. Grief came in waves like thoughts and memories. One never knew when the tides would come, but when they did, they crashed violently ashore.

"Good." Louis kissed her hand, then held it tighter. "I'm

sorry you had to go through that alone. I'm sorry you had to go through it at all."

"What doesn't kill you, right?" Dominique smiled sadly.

"Right. Come here." He pulled her into him and held her close. "We had some good times, didn't we?"

"Yeah, we did," Dominique smiled as tears cascaded down her face.

"You deserved better. You know that, right?" He looked down at her and caressed her cheek. "I wasn't good enough for you, Dom."

"Louis—"

"It's true. I knew it the moment I laid eyes on you, but I thought I could get away with acting like I was on your level. Shit didn't work," he chuckled. "You deserved more than what I gave you, baby. And for that, I'm sorry."

Dominique stared back into his eyes and stroked his chestnut-brown face. She noticed his long eyelashes had begun to gray like his hair. "I'm goin' to miss you," she hiccupped.

"I'm gonna miss you more, baby."

Dominique pulled Louis down toward her and pressed her full lips against his. She didn't need or want anything else from him. Their relationship had run its course—a bittersweet yet necessary ending to a decade-long affair.

8

"Amari, please don't be upset. I'm okay." Gia rubbed her forehead as she sat on the edge of her bed.

"Nah, babe. It's fucked up, yo. You could'a been gone forever. Somebody should'a called me. One of your aunts or somebody. I should'a been there wit' you."

"I know, babe, but please don't take it personally. There was so much going on at the time that it just didn't cross anyone's mind."

"Shit ain't right, man. I deserved to know. I'm your boyfriend," he sniffled. "Wait. Does anyone even know we're together?"

Gia remained silent.

"Gia?"

"Well . . . no. Not really. I mean, I didn't have time to talk to my mom like we discussed, but one of my aunts knows," she sighed.

"So you didn't think that was something you needed to tell me?" he jeered.

"Amari, I just got outta the hospital, okay? And I'm not even talking to my mother right now." Gia sucked her teeth. "The last thing I need is you bitchin' about me not telling her about us. You're worried about the wrong shit right now."

"What are you talkin' about? I'm worried about *your* ass right now! You're the one who got shot! Why do you always have to be so damn difficult?"

"I'm not trying to be difficult. I'm just . . . I'm just having a hard time right now," she moaned. "I'm all fucked up. I can't talk, I can't walk, I can't stand up . . . I can't do shit without losing my breath or getting dizzy. My grandmother has to help me do everything."

"Well, damn. What type of gun was it?"

"I don't know, but I'm missing half of my left lung." Gia shook her head.

"What?!" Amari yelled, his voice cracking.

"Yeah. My mom got shot first, and that bullet hit her in her shoulder. The second bullet hit me by accident and caught me in my left lung."

"Are you serious?" Amari cried almost hysterically.

"Yeah," Gia sighed. "Amari, please don't cry. I'm gonna be okay."

"Nah, fuck that! Who the fuck shot you, yo?" he seethed.

"Amari—"

"You're coming home, Gia. I'm going to pay for the flight."

Gia smiled sadly at the sweet and futile gesture. "I can't fly, babe."

"Then I'll get you a train ticket."

"I have to stay. Besides, I don't have anyone to take care of me up there."

"What the fuck do you mean you don't have anyone to take care of you up here? You have me and your mother. That's enough."

"I don't want to be up there." Gia shook her head, her eyes closed. "And I don't want to stay with my mother. I don't want her help, and I know for a fact your mother isn't going to have me up in her house."

"So now you don't want your mother's help? She's just as much a victim as you."

"Fuck her. She . . . I don't even want to talk about her."

"That's fucked up, Gia." Amari sucked his teeth. "You and her should be closer than ever now, especially after all of this. You're survivors."

"She had a choice to leave sooner, right after my Papaw's funeral. But she didn't. She stayed. And because she stayed, *this* is what happened," Gia hissed. "Amari, look, you don't know the venomous shit that came out her mouth that night. I don't wanna have anything to do with her. Maybe later, in the future or something, but not now. I don't have anything to say to her."

"Did she apologize? Maybe she was just really angry and didn't mean it."

"Oh no, she meant it. And her bootleg-ass apology. She's always judging me like she was any better, making me question every little decision I've made. Like I'm some trick-ass bitch in the street."

"Gia, don't say that. Your mother loves you."

"Gia," Corrine's voice chimed through the intercom.

Gia slowly rose from the bed and pressed the button on the wall unit. "Yes?"

"Yo' cold drink is ready, baby."

"Okay, I'm coming." She released the button. "I gotta go, babe. I'll call you later."

"You promise?"

"Yes. I promise," she smiled sadly.

"Okay. I love you," Amari sniffled.

"I love you too." Gia disconnected the call, then placed her phone down on the end table. She made her way to the kitchen, where her grandmother was pouring a concoction from a blender into a cup.

Corrine looked up, noticing the sadness on Gia's face. She placed the cup on the island and pushed it toward her. A plate of hot food, fork, and napkin followed.

"Everything awrite?"

"Mm-hmm," Gia lied. "Everything is fine."

"You sure?" Corrine asked while pouring a glass for herself.

"Yes, ma'am. How's your morning?" Gia asked, attempting to change the subject.

"Oh, it's awrite," Corrine sipped.

"That's good," Gia smiled small as she poked her fork into her pancake.

"Yeah. But you know, it'll be much better after you tell me what's wrong."

"Nothing's wrong, Mamaw. Just my wound stings a little. It's been hurting since last night."

"I'll take a look at it after breakfast." Corrine continued to study her. "You sure that's it?"

Gia smiled. "Mamaw, is there something you wanna ask me?"

"All depends," Corrine smirked.

"On what?"

"If you got the answer I'm lookin' fo'."

"Well, that all depends on what you're gonna ask," Gia replied nervously.

"I think you already know," Corrine crossed her arms.

"Ma'am?"

"Don't play me for a fool, GiGi. What's the matter?"

Gia sighed heavily. "I just had a conversation with Amari about Dominique."

"*Yo' mama*," Corrine replied sternly.

"Yes. *Her*."

"And?"

"And it just hit a nerve. I didn't tell him what she said to me. He just knows it was bad, and she apologized. But he thinks that just because she apologized, it makes things better, and it doesn't. He's always talking about peace and making peace and all this other stuff. But I don't want to make peace. I want to be upset right now. And he doesn't see how I could possibly be upset with her after what happened. But, Mamaw, none of that matters to me. What she said to me matters. It's the *only* thing that matters."

"GiGi . . . words sometimes cut deeper than the blade of the sharpest knife," Corrine began. "Yo' mama's tongue is sharper than that. And she needed to hurt you wit' it to stop you from tellin' the truth, *her* truth. They are one. Interchangeable," Corrine shook her head. "You read her like an open book, beloved. And she wasn't ready." Corrine took another sip of her concoction. "The hurt yo' feelin' right now will pass. I promise you. And it's okay to hold her accountable. That's what a good daughter does. A *woman* does the same. But a woman also knows not to allow herself to be consumed by the pain inflicted upon her by someone else. Feel it. Be present in it. But don't let it hold you hostage. Do not become a prisoner of it because you will *not* survive. You hear me?" Corrine caressed Gia's cheek.

"Yes, ma'am."

Corrine grinned. "Good."

Gia jiggled her cup. "What's this?"

"Turmeric milk."

"But I thought you said it was cold. This is warm."

"You makin' fun of me, li'l girl? Of the way we refer to beverages down here?" she smirked.

"Of course not," Gia grinned back. "I love the way you talk, Mamaw."

"Mm-hmm. Drink."

Gia picked up the glass and held it under her nose. She took a sniff and cringed.

"I swear, you and that daughter of mine are two of the same," she shook her head. "You gonna like it. I put a little honey in it to sweeten it up fo' you. And you have almond milk instead of whole. I know how that whole milk don't agree wit' you. Now, drink."

"What is it supposed to do?"

"It's gonna help heal you from the inside out."

Gia put the glass to her lips and drank. The warm liquid slid down her throat like silk. She was pleasantly surprised by the taste. "Mmm, it is good. It tastes like a latte."

"I'm glad you like it. Keep drinkin'."

Gia chuckled as she obeyed her grandmother's order. "What are we doing today?"

"*You* are goin' to rest while I take care of some business concernin' yo' aunt Simone. Then I'm goin' to make groceries afterward."

"Can you wash my hair and grease my scalp after you're done with everything?"

"I surely can."

"Thank you."

"Of course, baby."

The phone rang. Corrine removed it from its cradle and read the name on the screen. "It's yo' mama."

"I'm going back to my room," Gia sulked as she took the cup of milk and plate of food in hand.

"Okay. Be careful now." Corrine pursed her lips as she watched Gia slowly shuffle out of the room and down the long hallway. Then she pressed the TALK and SPEAKER buttons. "Well, good mornin'."

"Mornin', Mama," Dominique said. "You busy?"

"No. I'm just preparin' GiGi's meals fo' the day. What you doin' up so early?"

"Had a home removal."

"Oh no. You didn't pick up the body yo'self, did you? Yo' shoulder's still—"

"No, no. I let my guys do all the heavy liftin'."

"Good. You drinkin' yo' turmeric milk like I told you?"

"Twice a day."

"Good girl. And what about the lavender? How's it workin' fo' you?"

"I haven't used it yet," Dominique confessed.

Corrine frowned. "You need to if you want to sleep, Dominique. You gonna crash and burn, and I do not want to get that call when you do. I can't just up and leave Gia to see about you all the way up there."

"I'll put some on my pillow tonight, okay? Just for you."

"Thank you," Corrine sighed in relief.

"Is she awake?"

"No, not yet. But when she is, I will let her know you called like I always do."

"Okay," Dominique groaned.

"Don't sound so disappointed."

"Well, it's hard not to, Mama. My daughter refuses to speak to me. I mean, my God, it's been two weeks already."

"That ain't really nothin' compared to these last six months we didn't speak or the eight months that passed between us eighteen years ago."

"Well, that was ya call, Mama. Not mine. I wanted to talk to you."

Dominique thought against falling into her mother's trap of blame, but she had time today. The desire to play it cool, play nice so she could continue receiving updates about her child, went right out the window.

"Dominique, don't start yo' shit this mornin'. I mean it. It's too early."

"If not now, then when, Mama? Huh? When would you prefer to discuss the day you threw me outta the house pregnant with the same child you carin' for?"

Corrine wiped her brow, then stared icily down at the phone. "Dominique!"

"Mama, I needed you! *I needed you!*" Dominique screamed through tears.

"And I needed *you!*" Corrine hollered back. "You had a purpose to fulfill! A *legacy* to uphold! And you threw it all away! All of it! When you went behind my back and laid down wit' that no-good piece of shit! I wanted more fo' you, girl! Me and yo' daddy!" She took a breath. "You—you have no idea what I had to go through, what I had to *endure* in order fo' you and yo' sisters to live a life of privilege. What I *sacrificed* in the name of love. The *price I paid* fo' *you* to live *easy!* But you didn't want what we were givin'. And I warned you, Dominique. I *warned* you. I told you to leave that nigga alone, and you didn't listen. I told you if you disobeyed me, you were goin' to have to find some other place to live," she slammed down the knife. "I didn't put you out on da goddamn street! You put yo'self there!"

"I was seventeen!"

"And doin' woman things! You laid down like a woman, so you had to get up like one!"

"I made a mistake, Mama! It was a *mistake!*"

"And this chile is showin' you just how much of a mistake it was, ain't she?" Corrine smirked. "Sins of the mother. I told you when she was born, she'd bring you to yo' knees just like her daddy. And she has." Corrine shook her head. "You should'a listened to me, Dominique. You brought this all on yo'self."

"When are you gonna take accountability for some of this shit? Huh? Did you ever think that maybe Gia's the way she is because you refused to teach me how to be a mother? A *good* mother to her?! How the fuck could I be any kind of mother to her when you stopped bein' mine a long time ago?!"

"You gotta be a daughter first to understand what it means to be a mother! And you failed at that!" Corrine barked.

"You *let* me fail! And not even Daddy, Toni, or the twins could help me," Dominique whimpered.

"Nobody told you to carry yo' ass all the way to New Jersey

wit' this chile! You could have continued raisin' her down here!
You could have raised all the kids down here! You *should* have!
And I told you, if you left here, yo' life would be hard. The
ancestors would be displeased, and you'd pay fo' it. But you and
Esai wanted to get as far away from here as possible! So, hey!"

"He had to for work! What was I supposed to do? I was his
wife!" Dominique countered.

"All that workin' and what good did it do fo' yo' marriage?
He was workin' just as much, if not more, when y'all were down
here, Dominique! What made you think things were goin' to be
different up there?!" Corrine hollered as she began wrapping
the platters of uneaten food. "And to make matters worse, the
nigga never had any money!"

"You know why!" Dominique countered.

"And that was wrong! His parents were and still are grown
and able! And so are his brothers! If they couldn't sustain they
li'l family business, they should'a sold it! Yo' trust money was
fo' *you*—not him and his people! Esai should'a been pourin'
into you instead of drainin' you!"

"He paid me back, Mama!"

"Through his wallet or his pants?" Corrine smirked.

Dominique choked back a fresh set of tears.

"He took yo' money, and he abandoned you and those
babies! I tried to work wit' you! To come see you and the kids
every summer. I did what I could fo' you from here. If you felt it
wasn't enough, you should have brought yo' ass home after the
first time he left you and my grandbabies by yo'selves!"

"I was tryin' to be the woman you wanted me to be,"
Dominique hiccupped.

"No, you were tryin' to be a *woman*. What I wanted had
nothin' to do wit' that," Corrine countered. "What *I* wanted was
fo' you to stay. I tried to make peace wit' you after the accident. I
asked you to come back home, and what did you say?"

"I said I couldn't."

"You said you couldn't."

"That didn't mean I didn't *want* to, Mama. It meant I was *afraid of you*. You beat the shit outta me. How could you expect me to come back home after that? How could you expect me not to live in fear of bein' thrown out again if I did somethin' else you didn't agree with?"

Dominique was met with silence. Corrine reeled at the island.

"How the hell am I supposed to take over the shop when the blood is so bad between us? Hmm? How am I supposed to fill ya shoes when you would rather see me barefoot than give them to me?"

"I never have and never will find joy in someone else's pain. Even when that someone is you," Corrine countered. "And my retirement, well . . . It's happenin' whether or not I'm ready fo' it. But that's none of yo' concern. Yo' focus needs to be on answerin' the ancestors' call. It's what they want of you. And what they want *fo'* you."

"And what do *you* want, Mama?" Dominique asked in a hushed tone.

"What do I want?" Corrine whispered. "I wanna turn back the hands of time."

"You can't," Dominique replied softly.

"No, I can't," Corrine agreed as she plopped down on one of the stools. "I'm tired. You hear me, Dominique? I'm tired, and we can't go on like this. We can't. I *won't*. No more. *No more.*"

Dominique sniffled again as she wiped her wet eyes, her exhaustion matching her mother's. "How much longer you think? For Gia?"

"As long as she needs," Corrine smirked. "You said some terrible things to that chile. And you need to understand this ain't gonna be no quick fix. Her soul's been rocked to its core. Let the poison you spewed at her run its course."

Dominique said nothing. Her breathing quieted. There was

no point in trying to explain herself, to get her mother to understand where she was mentally and emotionally when she and Gia came to blows.

"Until then, try to find some comfort in knowin' that I'm givin' her all of yo' messages."

"Awrite. Well, I, uh, I gotta go."

"Okay. I have to finish gettin' these meals prepped, then get ready to run some errands after. I'll talk to you later."

"Okay. Bye."

"Bye."

DOMINIQUE FLUNG the phone across her desk and buried her face into her hands. She hated having to go to her mother for news about Gia. She was the one who was supposed to be caring for her daughter, not her mother. She was supposed to be the one Gia sought for protection and peace, not her mother. Corrine hadn't been that for her. Not after she'd gotten pregnant. *So why is Gia more deserving?*

Dominique was jealous. She wasn't proud of it, but she could admit it. Gia and her mother were close. Closer than close. They had always been. Their relationship was special, like that of many between grandchild and grandparent. One Dominique never had with her own. Her grandmother, Corrine's mother, was already an ancestor by the time she was born. She didn't know a grandmother's unconditional love. Only her mother's—until it became conditional.

Rose appeared in her doorway and lightly knocked on the open door with a handful of catalogs in hand. "Hey, boo."

Dominique looked up as her hands slid down her face. "Hey, girl."

"Everything okay? Gia all right?"

Rose made herself comfortable in one of the guest chairs, then placed the catalogs on Dominique's desk.

"I guess so."

"You guess so?"

"Yeah. I guess so. I still can't get a hold of her."

"For real?"

Dominique nodded in disgust.

"What about your mom? You get in touch with her?"

"Yeah. I just got off the phone with her."

"What she say?"

"She said Gia would talk to me when she's ready. That I need to relax and find comfort in knowin' that she's givin' her all of my messages."

"Dang. She can't intercede?"

"She doesn't want to. And to tell you the truth, I think she's enjoyin' every minute of this shit. Gia not speakin' to me just further proves to her that I'm not a good mother. It's somethin' she's always believed."

"Really?"

"Mm-hmm."

"She told you that?"

"In her own way, yeah."

"Dang. But no one's perfect, you know? There's no such thing as a perfect mother."

"I know that *now*," Dominique smirked. "Oh, and to make matters worse, she tried to say that these two weeks Gia and I haven't spoken is a walk in the park compared to the eight months she and I didn't speak."

"Eight months?"

"Yup. Eight months. After she kicked me out of the house, she didn't want to see or speak to me. My sisters tried to get her to, even my daddy, but she wouldn't budge. She didn't come around until Esai and I got into a car accident comin' home from his aunt's house. He fell asleep at the wheel. I was eight months pregnant with Gia when it happened."

"Oh my God. I remember you telling me that you two stopped speaking for some time, but I had no idea it was for eight months. I know she had to be sick to her stomach when she got that call."

"Who knows? I don't really remember much from that night. I just remember wakin' up in the hospital and seein' my parents' faces. My mama was holdin' my hand, prayin', and my daddy was sittin' at the foot of my bed rubbin' my legs. They told me that Esai had hit a tree. And if we hadn't been wearin' our seat belts, we wouldn't have made it. He walked away with a broken arm, me with a concussion, and Gia unharmed."

"But God! She let you come home then?"

"She insisted, but I couldn't do it. I couldn't go back there. The damage had already been done, ya know? And I had turned eighteen already, so she really couldn't make me."

"I hear you. But I know you had to be scared to death. I know I was when I was pregnant with Melissa, and I was twenty-eight!"

"You sure were!"

They shared a laugh.

"I don't care if you're eighteen or twenty-eight. Being pregnant is just as much scary as it is joyful." Rose sat back. "Makes you wonder."

"About?"

"If she would have continued not speaking to you had the accident never happened."

"Most likely. My mama's very stubborn. A no-nonsense woman. It was and still is her way or no way. You break the rules, you pay the price. That's it."

"Dang. I don't even know her, and I'm scared of her."

They shared another laugh.

"But, listen, all jokes aside . . . You guys are going to have to talk about that dark time in your lives sooner or later, especially since you're going to take over her business."

"We just did."

"That was *you* in here screaming?" Rose asked, her brows raised. "I thought that somebody outside."

"Nope. That was me."

"You can't afford to get upset like that, boo," Rose sulked. "We need you well. Seizure free."

"I know, but she takes me there every single time. Never fails. Her and . . . Gia," Dominique said quietly.

Rose's face was blanketed with sadness. "When are you going back to see her?"

"The end of the month."

"Okay. Are you going to talk to your mom about the shop while you're there?"

"There's nothin' to talk about. I'm takin' it over."

Silence found itself between them.

"I can't believe you're leaving."

"Me either. This time next year, Kelly will be sittin' in this chair. Who would'a thought?" Dominique smiled proudly.

"Not me," Rose grinned.

"I'm proud of her. She's worked hard, ya know? She deserves this and so much more."

"Yeah, she does."

"I truly believe she's what these families need," Dominique added.

"Yeah, but she's not you."

"Thank God for that," Dominique chuckled as Rose forced a sad smile. "Seriously, though, my mama used to tell us, 'A lady always knows when to leave.'"

"Well, I can't argue with that." Rose stood up and stretched. "You know what?"

"What?"

"I think your mom could have left her shop to any of your

sisters. She could have left it to your oldest sister, especially. But she didn't. She left it to you. And that's gotta mean something, right?"

GIA SAT under her grandmother's bottle tree in the backyard staring at her cell phone. When she asked her grandmother what the bottles represented, she explained that their ancestors believed that the bottles trapped evil spirits. They would remain in them until morning, then be destroyed by the morning's sun. Gia went on to ask her about the cobalt-blue color, to which her grandmother expressed that it is believed to have healing powers. Gia accepted her responses without question. Even though she was still very much uninformed about voodoo and their family's place in it, she was grateful to her grandmother for answering any question she had. She never made her feel any more stupid than she already felt.

Gia fidgeted with her phone, debating whether to call her father. He'd left just as many voice and text messages as her mother over the last two weeks. When she thought about how she spoke to him the night of the shooting, it made her stomach turn. She'd never lashed out at him like that before. He'd become a casualty in the ongoing war between her and her mother. An innocent bystander who wanted nothing more than for her to be okay. Esai Polanco had taken the responsibility of fathering a child that wasn't his. Gave her his last name and loved her as if she'd been created from the same union her brothers had been born of. Reared from the love and passion she watched her parents display openly. He'd done nothing but love and spoil her, protect and provide for her.

Gia pressed his name on her Favorites list and waited for his voice to fill her ear.

"*Alo?*"

Gia smiled. She loved his heavy accent. "*Hola, Papi.*"

"Gia?"

"*Sí. Soy yo.*"

"*Todo bien contigo?* You okay?"

She could hear the panic in his voice. "Yes, I'm fine. There's nothing wrong."

"Okay, good. Good. I left you messages. Did you get them? *Las conseguiste?*"

"*Sí.* I haven't listened to all of them, but . . . I just wanted to —I just wanted to call you . . . to apologize for disrespecting you. For hurting you last month."

"Oh, *princessa.* I'm sorry. I mean—"

"You can call me that, *Papi.* Please . . . call me that," Gia's voice quivered.

"Of course. *Cualquier cosa por ti, mi vida.*"

Gia smiled, letting out a small sigh of relief. She hadn't ruined her relationship with him.

"You are getting stronger and stronger each day I am hearing from your mother."

"Yes."

"That's good. I can sleep a little better now," he smiled. "*Un poco más fácil.*"

"Yes, you can."

"I know your mother has not been sleeping well either. Have you spoken to her yet?"

"No. I'm not ready to talk to her. I can't right now."

"Oh no. She is very worried about you, Gia. Don't punish her with your silence. She is suffering enough with the recalls of you dying in her arms."

"I understand that, *Papi,* but she said some messed up stuff to me that night. I'm just . . . I'm not ready yet. Can we talk about something else? How are Dominic and Mikey?"

"They are good. *Muy bien.* They miss you."

"I miss them too. When are you bringing them back?"

"The end of August."

Gia hesitated before finding the courage to continue. "Are you going to stay? I mean . . . are you still going to ask her to marry you?"

Gia was met with a pause.

"If it is okay with you."

Gia bit the inside of her cheek. "You deserve better, *Papi.*"

"She *is* my better, *princessa*," he replied matter-of-factly. "And it is my hope that you will understand one day that everyone . . . *everyone* deserves to be loved."

DOMINIQUE PUSHED through the metal turnstile, stepping into Turtle Back Zoo's main area. It had been years since she'd last been there. The boys were toddlers, and Gia, a little girl. The sights and sounds brought back memories and a smile to her face. It soon faded upon spotting Antoine leaning against a pillar in the amphitheater. He was dressed in a black tank top, madras shorts, and matching black Nikes. A diamond Cuban link chain sparkled around his neck. His wrist donned a matching bracelet. Antoine's hair and goatee were freshly trimmed, both oiled and gleaming under the sun's light. His tattoo-covered muscular arms flexed as he waited and watched the crowd for her.

Dominique hated to admit, but Antoine looked good. In fact, he was *fine*. Always had been. But his cunningness overshadowed any hint of beauty he may have possessed on the inside. That thought alone caused her to frown. She'd accepted his invitation against her better judgment. Had she not been outnumbered by Esai and her father, she wouldn't have shown up at all. Their support of Antoine's reintroduction into Gia's life trumped her objections. She needed this outing to be short and sweet. It was hot, her head was still spinning from the conversation with her mother that morning, and her shoulder was killing her.

Dominique took in a deep breath, then released it as she approached Antoine. He immediately smiled at the sight of her.

"Hey, you."

"Hey, yaself," Dominique countered dryly.

"You lookin' good, girl. Like a snow leopard."

Dominique shook her head and laughed in spite of herself. She may have overdone it with the white cotton crop top, matching white pedal pushers, and Air Force 1s, but she wanted to dress as cool as possible.

"You so stupid."

"Love makes you that way, ya know?"

Dominique's smile faded. She looked away, trying to focus on something other than him and his last comment. "So...why here?"

"I wanted you to feel comfortable. That, and I know how much you love animals."

"That I do," she nodded.

"See there. I ain't forget," he smiled, his dimples deepening. They were identical to Gia's. "And, ya know, I heard they gotta carousel here too."

"They do."

"You wanna go for a ride while we're here?"

"Naw, I think we just need to stick to talkin'. That's the only reason why I'm here."

"You right," Antoine buried his hands in his pockets. "Can we, at least, walk around and see the exhibits?"

"That's fine."

"Cool."

Dominique took a step first, heading toward the sea animals.

"Thank you for meetin' me."

"Ya welcome."

They stopped at the sea turtle recovery center.

"I can't believe the last time we met at the zoo, Gia was a toddler."

"Yeah," Dominique said quietly.

"She was the most beautiful thing I'd ever seen. I couldn't believe we really created somethin' so perfect."

Dominique bit down on her bottom lip as she went back in time, placing herself in Antoine's recollection. "When I asked you where you'd been for three years, you told me it didn't matter. But it did. You were only four hours away. And never once did you think enough of our daughter or me to close the time and distance between us."

"I couldn't do nothin' for you at nineteen, Dom. Not nineteen or twenty, twenty-one, not even twenty-two. So, no . . . It didn't matter."

"Ya wrong. It would have made a world of difference." Dominique began to walk again. Two sea otters swimming in sync caught her eye. She settled at their tank and watched them glide beneath the water's gentle waves.

"She still got that li'l ballerina bunny rabbit I gave her?"

"No. Esai got rid of it after I told him about our meetin'."

Antoine's upper lip curled. "Oh."

Dominique caught a flash of anger in his eyes, then looked away. "You can't blame 'im for bein' angry, for bein' hurt behind that. I was his wife and I didn't speak to him before makin' a decision like that." She pressed her lips in. "*He* was her daddy —him—*not you*. And I disrespected him. I made him question my position in his life just so that I could prove to myself that I didn't love you anymore. That bringin' Gia to meet you would make you regret leavin'."

"Well, it worked. And I don't think you were wrong for it."

"Of course you don't. You didn't have anything to lose."

"You right. I'd already lost it." Antoine folded his arms across his broad chest.

"I guess I just wanted to see if I could turn things around that day. Make things right between us."

"Yeah, well, you failed."

"Sho' nuff." Antoine cracked another smile. "I know exactly where I went wrong. I didn't ask you if you still loved me. If I had, maybe things would have turned out different." He placed a loose curl back in place, then twirled another strand around his index finger. "When I saw ya moms at the hospital, I tried to tell her I still loved you, but she didn't believe me."

Dominique rolled her eyes. "How could she? You'd been sleepin' with my sister."

"She blames me for you and Gia gettin' shot." He sighed.

"Yes, she does," Dominique nodded slowly.

"Do you?" Antoine waited patiently.

Dominique thought about his question. Dissected it. "Partially. This wasn't the first time she tried to kill me. She just had a good reason this time."

"Damn. I'm sorry, love."

"Don't be," Dominique smirked as Antoine watched her mood shift.

"Ya know, I don't think there's anything harder than tryin' to get back in you and ya moms' good graces," he chuckled.

"You were never in her good graces."

"True dat. It reminds me of the mornin' after we broke curfew. I came by the house to apologize to her and ya pops. He wasn't home, so I was left to explain myself to her. But she ain't wanna hear it. She just called me a whole buncha names and said some other real foul shit."

Dominique, taken aback by the news, shifted her ponytail, throwing it over the opposite shoulder. "What did she say?"

"I don't remember verbatim."

Dominique knew he was lying. He always avoided eye contact when he lied.

"Why didn't you tell me?" she asked sincerely.

"Hurt too much, I guess," he shrugged. "And I . . . I started to believe her after a while."

Dominique held her head and stared back at him in embarrassment. "Is that why you left? Because of what she said to you?"

Antoine pressed his lips together as he shrunk under her gaze.

Dominique cringed. She couldn't believe he'd kept something so significant to himself all these years. It blew her mind.

"It might sound fucked up, but I really thought goin' against her wishes was the best way to prove to myself, and you, that what we had was real. That it was good and we deserved it. That her thoughts and feelings about me were wrong. They were all wrong," Antoine confessed. "I know this, uh, this is hard for you."

"Do you now?"

"You know what I mean."

"Naw, I can't say that I do. I don't know much of anything anymore."

Dominique looked over at him. She had his undivided attention. He was completely engaged, waiting for her to indulge him with her uncertainties. "You should have said somethin', 'Toine." She shook her head. "I can't put all the blame on my mama."

"I know. I'm sorry. I'm . . . sorry," he exhaled.

"I'm still against you meetin' Gia. You already know that. But she's gonna wanna speak to you once she gets herself together. I know that much is true. Esai approves of it. And my daddy would approve of it too if he were here. It was somethin' that he wanted for her. I just don't know why."

"I reached out to ya pops after we met at the zoo and told

'im I wanted to right my wrongs. I wanted to apologize to him personally for disrespecting him and dishonoring you as the mother of my child. He told me to come to his office, and we'd speak about it. So I did. He listened as I told him what my intentions were and asked him for his forgiveness. I know I wasn't in no position to ask him for it, but he gave it to me." Antoine pinched his nose as he choked back tears. "I always thought highly of ya pops, ya know? He was my daddy's best friend, and he always stepped up whenever my daddy fell short. I, uh, opened up a savings account at his bank for Gia and put money in it twice a month from that day on."

"What?"

"Yeah. She's got a li'l over $72,000 in there," Antoine nodded.

Dominique's mouth fell open. "Oh my God."

"What? What's wrong?" Antoine asked in anticipation of another nosebleed.

"My daddy . . ." Dominique began. ". . . when I spoke to him at the hospital, he told me there was somethin' waitin' for me at the bank. I didn't know what he was talkin' 'bout, and I'd forgotten all about it . . . until now."

Antoine relaxed a bit, leaning back on the wall beside the otter tank. "It's the least I could do for her," he grinned.

"She'll be grateful," Dominique nodded, her eyes soft.

Time seemed to have stopped. Old feelings began to reemerge. Dominique could hear her heart beat in her ears. Love's steady rhythm with inflections of temptation. Her eyes were transfixed on his moist lips and dimples.

"So . . . How about that carousel ride?" Antoine asked with wide, hopeful eyes.

～

GIA LOADED THE DISHWASHER, then wiped the excess water from around the sink before placing the dishcloth on the brim of it. She looked through the window above the sink and saw her grandmother moving about in her shed at the back of the yard. She hadn't spoken much during dinner. Gia knew the shouting match between her and her mother that morning had affected her mood for the rest of the day. Gia had listened from the bedroom. Sitting on the edge of the bed, nervous and forlorn, she took in her grandmother's frustration and her mother's heartache. Her grandmother hadn't apologized for forcing her mother into womanhood before her time, and her mother hadn't forgiven her for doing so, each too deep in their own misery to acknowledge the other.

Gia didn't know what to do. Her mother was hurting badly, but so was she. *How can I help her if I can't even help myself?* And what about her grandmother? She was hurting just as much as them, if not more. But she was also the one who had all the answers. *How am I supposed to help her when her entire life is based on helping others?* Gia inhaled, then exhaled as she mustered up the courage to approach her grandmother. She opened the back door and made her way down the wooden deck's steps and along the lit gravel path to the shack. She peered into the window of the shed and studied the woman who'd taken on the job of saving her from herself. LaBelle's song *"Isn't It A Shame"* blasted from two miniature speakers hoisted in the corners of the workspace. Gia watched her grandmother sway from side to side as Patti groaned melodically against the band's break-down. Gia gently opened the door and stepped in. The workstation was bright white. Its walls were accented with floating shelves filled with metal pots, wax, wicks, glass containers, mason jars, essential oils, colored dyes, and skewers. An oversized wooden island sat in the center of the space with one stool at its base.

Her grandmother's hands were covered with wax, her cheeks wet with tears.

She wiped her runny nose with a hand towel thrown over her shoulder. Gia watched her fall deeper under Patti, Nona, and Sarah's spell, then finally submit. Her grandmother plopped down onto the stool and rested her head against praying hands. Her sonorous cries caused Gia to shiver. And before she knew it, Gia was crying along with her. Gia moved slowly toward the broken woman. She placed her hands gently on her back, then lay her head there. She closed her eyes and wrapped her arms around her. Her grandmother grabbed her hands without hesitation and held onto them. Tight. Gia squeezed back. And it was at that moment when she realized *she* was her grandmother's aid. The woman who helped and healed the helpless didn't need words or gifts or pity. She needed someone to breathe life back into her. It had been sucked out of her somewhere along the way.

Gia knew what she had to do now. She just needed to regain enough strength to put her plan in motion.

DOMINIQUE AND ANTOINE sat on a bench along the Hampton Inn's river walk overlooking the Hudson River, an urban landscape heightened by a starlit sky. An abstract painting brushed with contemporary strokes. Gas lights created perfect circles of light between each bench. An iron fence separated the city's concrete from the water.

Dominique and Antoine spent the entire afternoon at the zoo, then partook of lunch at McLoone's Boathouse next door. Antoine, not wanting the day to end, convinced her to go roller skating at Branch Brook Park Skating Rink. So they did. And they enjoyed themselves immensely. Dominique needed to use the restroom toward the end of the outing but wasn't comfortable using the public lavatory at the rink. So Antoine offered his at the hotel. She declined at first. Then obliged with reservation, locking the door behind her. Even though he'd respectfully stayed outside of the room and waited for her in the hall, she didn't want to take any chances.

Dominique winced in pain as she rotated her shoulder.

"You got somethin' for the pain?" Antoine asked with genuine concern.

"Just turmeric milk." She shook her head. "My mama took my meds. Didn't want me gettin' hooked on 'em like . . ." Dominique pressed her lips together at the thought of Simone.

"Yeah, I can understand that," Antoine nodded. Then a short pause. "I didn't get her hooked on coke, if that's what ya thinkin'. She was already doin' that shit way before I came along. At least, that's what she told me," he shrugged.

Dominique brushed off any emerging thoughts of her sister. "I wasn't thinkin' anything," she confessed quietly.

Antoine looked over at her, searching for the lie he couldn't find. "You know any voodoo spells? Maybe one of them'll help," he mocked.

Dominique peered back at him, not amused. "I walked away from voodoo the day my mama threw me out."

Antoine sat back, astonished. "Good for you. I never told you, but I always felt like she forced that shit on you."

Dominique sucked her teeth. "She didn't. I was born into it. And *I* decided to continue to practice."

"But ya pops was Catholic," Antoine stated in confusion.

"Yeah, and so is she." Dominique shifted in annoyance.

"Really?" Antoine's eyebrows rose.

"Yes," Dominique smirked. "But like her mama and her mama before her, she masks her *Lwas* behind imposed Catholicism to protect and continue her practice. She's doin' the same thing the slaves did."

"Oh," Antoine replied.

Dominique tilted her head slightly. "Mm-hmm. You judgin' my mama, but you last stepped into a church . . .?"

"Ya pop's funeral."

"More reason for you to keep ya thoughts to yaself," Dominique smirked. "My daddy loved my mama for who she was. For *what* she was. What she *is*. He may not have understood that part of her or the practice as a whole, but he loved her and accepted it nonetheless."

"I just figured with ya pain and all, a spell or two might help."

"You were being an asshole, and it was uncalled for," Dominique jeered.

Antoine nodded, "You right. You right. I'm sorry."

A loud silence fell between them.

"Ya pops wasn't alone, ya know? I never understood that part of you either."

"And instead of trying to learn about it, you disrespected it every chance you got," Dominique said.

"I was a knucklehead, ya know?" he shrugged.

"What's ya excuse now?" Dominique continued to rub her shoulder.

"Damn, Dom. I said I was sorry."

Dominique shook her head as an awkward silence began to creep in again.

"If you don't have any medicine, and you don't know any spells for ya pain . . . how about some herb? I got some in my suitcase upstairs."

"You do?"

"Never leave home without it," he grinned. "I got some sour, purple haze, Jack Herer. . . uhhh . . . red hot, alien dawg . . ."

"Alien dawg?" Dominique frowned. "What the hell is that?"

"Some shit that'll knock the pain right outta ya shoulder," he chuckled.

"Sounds like it'll knock my soul outta my body too," she smirked.

"Naw," Antoine smiled wide. "That one is actually used the most for pain . . . depression, migraines . . . all of that."

"You gotta suitcase full of it?" she eyed him in disbelief.

"Yeah. I gotta connect out in Cali. Wanna try some?"

"Naw, that shit may be laced with somethin'. I'm awrite," she said, rubbing her shoulder.

"I wouldn't do that to you. All my shit's clean," he replied seriously.

"Well, that's good, but I'll pass. I'm fastin'."

"Awrite," Antoine scratched his chin. "What about essential oils? I got some of them upstairs too."

"Ya just a travelin' apothecary, huh?" Dominique chortled.

"Naw," Antoine met her laughter. "The weed and oils just help me sleep. My sleep pattern gets fucked up sometimes behind my work schedule."

"Oh, okay."

"After everything that's happened, I know ya not sleepin' well. You can't be. I know *I'm* not," Antoine said, staring into the dark waters.

"I'm fine, Antoine," Dominique sighed.

"A'ight, but I still think you need *somethin'*, Dom. You can't just let yaself suffer like this. Besides, you the one who introduced me to oils in the first place. Taught me about 'em and all their benefits and shit. You learned a nigga good," he smiled.

Dominique met his with her own. "I already have a bottle at home."

"Just one?"

"*Yes, just one,*" she smirked.

"What kind? Wait . . . Let me guess. See if I remember." Antoine cut his eyes at her. "Lavender."

Dominique shook her head in disbelief again.

"I knew it! Lavender was always your favorite," he beamed.

"And I bet it smells good too. But it ain't got nothin' on my *French* Lavender."

"No, I'm sure it doesn't," Dominique chuckled.

"Well, see ya gonna *have to* take a bottle for yaself now," he teased. "It's got geranium and Moroccan chamomile oil in it. It's da shit," he nodded. "You just spray it on ya pillow, take a deep breath in, and drift off to sleep."

Sleep. Dominique needed it more than anyone. She missed it. The security of its arms enveloping her in its loving embrace. She was tempted. And she was tired. If she had to choose between falling under inertia's spell and that of Antoine's, sleep would undoubtedly be the victor. And so it was.

9

Gia closed the cash register and handed a female customer her change before placing her items in a recycled tote bag. She smiled as she stuffed the receipt in the bag and slid it across the counter. The woman returned a warm smile, thanking her as she shimmied away and out the door. Gia gently patted her rib, attempting to stop the itching that seemed to plague her multiple times a day. Her health was on the up-and-up now. She could walk and talk without losing her breath and needing her grandmother's assistance. Her respiratory therapy sessions were down to twice a week instead of four. She was breathing without pain and discomfort. And her incision was no longer adorned with staples.

Even though Gia had a long way to go with embracing the imminent scarring, her grandmother worked on it daily to ease her discomfort and beautify it to the best of her ability.

Gia had been frequenting the shop with her grandmother more often and asked if she could be of some assistance to her. Initially, Corrine objected to her request out of fear Gia would contract an infection from any germs carried by the customers. But Gia's doctor reassured her that she wouldn't so long as she continued to wear her face mask in public. So she did. And Gia spent her afternoons in the shop taking inventory, filling orders, watering her grandmother's garden, and reading the myriad of books about voodoo.

"You better get from behind that counter," Toni warned as she floated through the front door. She turned the double-sided signage on it to CLOSED before making her way through. "And put ya mask back on."

Gia sucked her teeth as she dug into her pocket and retrieved her mask. She hooked it onto her ears and adjusted it so that her nose and mouth were securely covered. Then she made her way around the counter and leaned against it, waiting for her aunt to return from the back and give her further instructions. Toni reappeared with a pair of tongs and a paper bag in gloved hands. Her face twisted with repulsion.

"I don't smell any Lysol," she threw over her shoulder.

Gia retrieved the can of disinfectant from off the counter and sprayed it.

She watched her aunt lay the tongs and bag down at the base of the boa constrictor's encasement, then unlock the lid on one end. She dipped the tongs into the bag, pulled out a dead rat, and quickly dropped it into the aquarium. As she relocked the cover, she and Gia watched the snake slither out of one of its many hides, strike the dead rodent, and constrict around it before swallowing it whole.

"I hate feedin' this damn thing," Toni huffed as she balled up the bag and snatched off the medical gloves.

"I'll do it next time if you want," Gia said lightly. "I'm not afraid."

"Well, that's good to know, but I can't let you do anything without ya grandmama's permission," Toni eyed her. "Bad enough you sneakin' behind this counter every chance you get and havin' contact with the customers."

Gia sucked her teeth.

"Keep it up," Toni continued. "She gonna drop in when you least expect it and catch you, then drag ya ass outta here."

"I just wanna help, " Gia pouted.

Toni moved past her and settled behind the cashier's counter. "You wanna help? Okay, I'll tell you how you can help. Do as ya told. That's how you can help. Got it?"

"Got it," Gia nodded.

Toni removed a box from one of the bottom shelves behind her and handed it to Gia. "Put these T-shirts on the table over there, please."

Gia took the box and made her way toward the empty two-tiered table across the room. "Do you want me to put each size in its own pile or stack them in size order?"

"Stack 'em. We have more than enough to fill the entire table," Toni confirmed.

"Okay," Gia said as she began to remove the tops from the box. They were black, with *Au-Delà Du Voile* written in a fancy white script. "These are nice."

"Aren't they?" Toni smiled. "Ya grandmama always had exceptional taste. A stickler for quality, ya know?"

"Yeah," Gia agreed. "Do we have other colors?"

"Why, yes, we do. We've got white and her signature cobalt blue over there waitin' for you."

The two shared a laugh.

"What do you want for lunch today?" Toni asked as she removed a pile of menus from a drawer. "What do you have a taste for?"

"Umm . . . How about barbecue?" Gia replied without breaking her concentration.

"Barbecue it is." Toni found the menu of her favorite barbecue spot, Mia's Eatery, and perused it for their order.

"TeeTee?"

"Yes, ma'am?" Toni responded without looking up.

"Do you know how I can get in touch with Mr. Brevard?"

Gia had been thinking about him a great deal since her mother and grandmother's fight. If he was the problem, then she needed to make it her business to absolve him from whatever hell he'd been living in and forced upon them. She wanted peace for her mother and grandmother. Understanding and acceptance between her and her mother. Nothing more, nothing less.

Toni looked up from the restaurant circular, then slowly placed it down on the counter. "I can't say that I do, GiGi."

"I can't ask Mamaw for obvious reasons. But I thought you might—"

"Even if I did, I wouldn't give you his information without speakin' to your mama first. I'm already in the doghouse with her *and* ya grandmama for givin' you your phone," Toni sighed. "If you want to contact him, I suggest you go through your mama. I'm sure she has all his information. Talk to her about it and see what she says."

"We're still not . . . speaking," Gia confessed, her eyes averted.

"No. You mean, *you're still not speaking to her,*" Toni said matter-of-factly.

"Yeah," Gia replied timidly.

"Well, I suggest you start if this is somethin' you truly believe is worth pursuin'," Toni said as she reopened the menu.

"'Kay," Gia whispered as she proceeded to sort the T-shirts.

"Oh . . . and GiGi?" Toni flipped a page in the menu.

"Yes, ma'am?" Gia looked up warily.

"When you *do* decide to call her . . . you make sure you ask her how *she's* been. Because for the last month, she's had to ask ya grandmama that question *every day* about you."

～

DOMINIQUE STIRRED as the moaning of a lawn mower rose and fell beneath her bedroom window. She slowly rolled onto her back and opened her eyes. She blinked, then wiped them with the back of her hands. The room was bright, cooled by the low setting of the AC. Dominique reached over and retrieved her phone. The time read 2:15 p.m. She cursed herself as she scrolled through the home screen and surveyed the missed phone calls from Toni, Esai, and Antoine. She'd began applying the lavender spray her mother gave her onto her pillow at night. She wasn't sure if she'd overslept because she sprayed too much or she'd been that tired.

She texted Toni and Esai back. A short message to Gia followed. There was no emergency. The two were just checking on her. Dominique thought about returning Antoine's call but decided to force herself out of bed instead and see who was cutting her grass.

She watched Amari rub his brow as he ran the machine back and forth across the front lawn. She noticed her hedges had been trimmed and flower boxes tended to as well. She wanted to hold on to the disappointment she had toward him, but Amari pulled at her heartstrings. She wasn't sure if he was aware of the shooting, but she decided this was as good as a time as any to tell him.

Dominique showered and dressed for the remainder of the day. She made a tall glass of iced tea for Amari, then walked outside. Amari, bare chest with his T-shirt wrapped around his head, was placing the lawn mower and hedge trimmers back into the shed.

"You really should start thinkin' about that landscapin' business like we discussed."

Startled, Amari jumped up, placing his hands nervously in his pockets. He was drenched in sweat. "You scared me."

"I didn't mean to," Dominique said quietly.

"I know you told me not to come by, but I didn't feel right

about leaving the house unsupervised. So I came by every day while y'all were gone to make sure it was good." Amari wiped his sweaty palms on his shorts. "I maintained the grass and shrubs for you too. Kept you and Gia's cars clean."

"Thank you. You did a beautiful job, as usual."

Amari smiled small. Dominique studied him. Watched him become a little boy before her.

"Here. I know ya thirsty."

"Thank you."

"Of course. Come on in the house and get somethin' to eat when ya done." Dominique removed the hot plate of leftover crab cakes from the microwave, added a helping of potato salad and roasted vegetables, then set it down before Amari. He added some ketchup to the dish, then dove in. Dominique watched him inhale one crab cake, then the other. She wondered when he'd last eaten. His mother struggled to feed him and his brothers at times, so she would send hot pans of food over or give Amari money to take care of the groceries. Even though Amari had a job of his own, he didn't make enough to cover food.

"Don't forget to eat ya vegetables," she cooed.

"Okay," he replied, his mouth full.

Dominique prepared herself a plate and began to eat. "How's ya mom?"

Amari shook his head. "Not too good. She was laid off last week."

"I'm sorry to hear that."

"Yeah. I spoke to my manager about picking up more shifts, but he said he had all the coverage he needed right now."

Dominique groaned in disgust. "Remind me of what she does."

"Office stuff."

"She was an administrative assistant."

"Unh-hunh," he nodded as he took a big gulp of the cold drink.

"Okay. Well, you tell her to come down to the funeral home tomorrow mornin'. We'll see what we can do for her." Dominique took another bite of her food.

"Really, Ms. Favier?"

"Mm-hmm," she nodded.

"Oh my God. Thank you!" Amari stood and outstretched his arms across the island.

"Ya welcome, love." Dominique completed their hug, then kissed him on the forehead.

"I love you so much, yo."

Dominique chuckled. "I love you back, baby."

"I'm always tellin' Gia how amazing you are. How you always give and never take. You're always lookin' out for other people," he said as he stuffed a forkful of potato salad in his mouth. "I know how much you love her. She doesn't see it, though."

"That's my daughter, all right." Dominique sucked in some air, then let it out. "Have you spoken to her recently?"

"Yes," Amari paused for a moment. "She told me about the shooting. Are you okay? I mean . . . yeah, are you . . . okay?"

"Today I am."

"That's good," he took another bite out of his meal. "She won't tell me how it all went down or who shot y'all." He looked to her for an answer. Dominique didn't give it. "She told me y'all aren't talkin' either."

Dominique shook her head. "No, we aren't."

"Is it because we were sneaking around behind your back? I know it may not mean much now, but I told her to tell you after she called me the first time."

"It isn't your fault, so don't take yaself through any unnecessary changes, okay? Gia and I have been at each other's throats for some time now. Long before you came into the picture."

"I know, but . . . It shouldn't be like that."

"Well, it is," Dominique shrugged. "I hurt her pretty bad this time, 'Mari. I didn't mean to, but I did. And she decided, for the both of us, that we not speak. Not until she's ready. And I have to respect that."

"I get that, but y'all should be closer now. I told her that. What happened should have brought y'all together."

"Well, it didn't, love."

"I'll keep trying to get through to her, Ms. Favier. She needs you. Y'all need each other, even if she doesn't think so."

"I appreciate you for wantin' to help, baby, but it's best just to leave her be. Gia is very stubborn. Once her mind is made up, there's no way to change it. She'll come around when she's ready," Dominique said matter-of-factly, even though she wasn't so sure.

"She's pushin' you away, Ms. Favier. She does the same thing to me."

"Does she?" Dominique grimaced, embarrassed by how Gia treats him.

"Yup."

Dominique rested her hands on the edge of the island. "Tell me, what do you do about it?"

"I push back," he shrugged. "You have to when someone is worth fighting for. And she's worth it, isn't she?"

"More than she knows."

"Just leavin' evidence all over the place," Corrine huffed as she scrubbed dried droplets of Gia's blood off the floor. "The next time you go snoopin' around this house, you make sure you clean up behind yo'self."

Gia was sure she'd caught all of the blood that dripped

down her side the night she found the altar room. "Sorry, Mamaw. I was just curious," she brooded.

"Yeah, well, curiosity killed the cat. You ever hear that before?" Corrine asked as she looked up at her.

"Yes, ma'am."

"Mm-hmm." Corrine slowly rose to her feet, tossing the miniature sponge into the basin of bubbly water. Then she dried her hands with a towel. She looked over at Gia and noticed how transfixed she was on her altar. "Would you like to help me clean it?"

"Yes, please!" Gia smiled, her eyes grateful.

Corrine returned the smile. "Awrite. Take this rag and dabble a little Florida Water on it, then wipe each tier down wit' intention."

"'Kay," Gia replied as she followed through. "Each object represents something, right?"

"That's right. They're offerings to the ancestors. Each ancestor has a specific item solely dedicated to them."

"The baby booties too?" Gia asked with an unnatural innocence.

Corrine, locking eyes with her, nodded slowly. "Yes, the baby booties too."

Gia could hear a twinge of sadness in her voice. "Which ancestor are they for? I don't see a picture with them."

"Yo' sister didn't live long enough to take any," Corrine replied, her head tilted to one side. Her eyes unwavering. "But somethin' tells me you already knew they were for her."

Gia stopped wiping. "I wasn't sure. I didn't think she told anyone."

Corrine began to place the offerings back on the altar, starting at the bottom tier. "I had a dream, Gia. I dreamt of a baby girl drowning in a basin of blood. And I woke up from that dream in tears. Careful not to wake yo' Papaw from his nap, I slipped outta bed and came in here. Got down on my knees and began to pray. I thought about which one of my daughters was gonna lose God's most precious gift to a woman. Which one of them was gonna be unprepared for the searing pain she was gonna endure in the mornin'. I knew it couldn't be Toni because she'd already gone through menopause. Jackie had her tubes tied years ago, and GiGi had a hysterectomy not too long after. So that only left Simone and yo' mama," she paused. "When I called Simone, she told me she'd just begun her cycle. So then I knew it was yo' mama," Corrine reflected. "I called her and told her about the dream, just like I had Simone. Asked her if she was expectin'. And she said, '*Not anymore*'. She'd lost her while I was havin' my dream." Corrine cleared her throat as she choked back tears. "We tethered, me and yo' mama. Bound by blood and burdens."

Gia gave her grandmother a moment to compose herself before responding.

"She didn't mourn. Just worked."

"Oh, she mourned, GiGi. Late at night, when you and yo' brothers' were asleep, she mourned. And she named her."

"She did?"

"Mm-hmm," Corrine went on as she began to stock the middle tier. "A nameless child has no identity and no fightin' chance to be remembered on this side of the veil or the other."

"What is it? Her name?" Gia asked cautiously.

"Antonia. She named her Antonia for yo' aunt," Corrine smiled small.

"The best name ever," Gia smiled back.

"Beautiful, isn't it?" Corrine's chest poked out some. "So we honor her just as we do Papaw, my mama and daddy, their parents, my sister Charlotte, Manman Marie, and all those whose names we don't know."

"Okay." Gia handed her grandmother the booties and watched her place them down carefully. "Mamaw?"

"Yes, beloved?"

"Would it be wrong to learn about my father's side too? I mean, my real father's side?"

Corrine slowed a bit as she processed the question, then met her steady pace again. "No, I suppose it wouldn't. They a part of you too, right?"

"Right," Gia nodded. "Do you know anything about them?"

"Well, yo' paternal grandfather's name is René Brevard. He was a prominent jazz pianist and educator in New Orleans fo' thirty-five years, and then he retired. Now, he owns and operates a local bar and lounge called The Black Cat. His first wife, yo' grandmama, her name was Naomi Dunaway-Brevard, and she was a socialite who really didn't do much but socialize . . . and drink. She was an alcoholic who eventually drank herself to death," she said disgustedly. "I don't know what else you wanna know. There's not much else to tell."

"My grandfather's alive?"

"Mm-hmm," Corrine replied with her back to her.

"Does he still live in New Orleans?"

"Mm-hmm."

"Does he know about me?"

"Mm-hmm. Papaw told him all about you. Kept him informed over the years," Corrine threw over her shoulder. "Do you remember the man who sat wit' me at the funeral?"

"Yes."

"That was him."

Gia played the images of her grandfather's homegoing back in her mind. "Oh, wow. Okay." She gathered some strength for the next question. "Can I meet him?"

Corrine sighed, expecting that question. "Is that what you want?"

"Yes, ma'am."

"Well, then I'm sure we can arrange somethin'."

"Thank you, Mamaw!" Gia carefully threw her arms around her grandmother's neck.

"Yo' welcome, love."

Silence crept into the quaint space.

"Mamaw?"

"Yes, baby?" Corrine asked as she straightened Duke's photograph.

"Can I meet my father too?"

Corrine wiped the frame down as she thought about what she was going to say next. "From what yo' mama told me, you already met 'im."

"Yeah . . . kinda, but—"

Corrine faced Gia. "So you saw what effect he had on her?"

"Yes, but—"

"And you want the same?" Her arms crossed.

"No, Mamaw."

"But that's what's goin' to happen, GiGi. He's gonna hurt you just like he hurt her, and yo' gonna have a helluva time tryin' to recover from it. Yo' mama *still* hasn't recovered from it."

"Mamaw—"

"He's dangerous, Gia!" Corrine growled, causing Gia to jump. Her grandmother never raised her voice at her—ever.

"How?" Gia asked, confused.

"His lust for yo' mama knows no bounds, that's how! He will do anything, and I mean *anything,* to get close to her! To destroy her and everything she's worked so hard fo'!" Corrine rubbed her chest. Flushed, she took in a breath, then released it. "To destroy me!"

"What does that even mean?"

"It means grudges are sometimes held onto tighter than lovers' hands."

Gia knew her grandmother despised the man, but she thought she was being a little overdramatic. Did she herself believe Antoine wanted to destroy her mother (whatever *that* meant)? No. Seduce her? Absolutely.

"I don't understand. I just wanna—"

"He ain't shit like his mama wasn't shit," Corrine fumed. She threw her rag, snatched the basin off the floor, and made her way to the door.

"But—" Gia began, her mouth agape.

"I forbid it, Gia! You hear me?! I forbid it!" She turned the knob on the door. "And if you go behind my back and find a way to meet him, the price you gonna pay will be a heavy one."

10

Dominique and Amari stepped out of Louis Armstrong International Airport, ready for the day's adventure. Amari set their carry-ons beside him, retrieved his cell phone from his fanny pack, and turned it on. Dominique checked the time on her watch. Toni was running late. She figured she'd gotten stuck in rush-hour traffic. She removed her sunglasses from the strap of her pocketbook and put them on. The sun was high and beaming directly down on them. It was going to be another sweltering day.

"I didn't know New Orleans had palm trees," Amari said, looking up in excitement.

"Oh yeah. She has plenty," Dominique grinned.

"Reminds me of Puerto Rico. The streets are lined with them."

"Canal Street is lined with them too. We'll drive through so you can see," Dominique promised.

"Okay!"

Just as Dominique reached into her purse to retrieve her phone, a black Mercedes G-Wagon pulled up. Its tooting horn brought a smile to her face.

"Daaamn!" Amari exclaimed in awe, admiring the pristine jeep.

"Hey, now!" Toni yelled through the open passenger window.

"Hey!" Dominique and Amari replied in unison.

Toni put the car in park, then turned the hazard lights on. She got out and met them with open arms. "You lookin' better. Much better." She looked Dominique over as they parted from their hug. "How's ya shoulder?"

"Hurtin' like hell," Dominique sighed.

"No worries. I got some Tylenol in the car," she winked.

"Thank you," Dominique smiled.

"Mm-hmm," Toni said as she sized up Amari.

"Toni, this is . . ."

". . . the infamous Amari," Toni teased.

"Yes, ma'am. It's a pleasure to meet you finally. Gia talks about you all the time." He extended his hand.

"Likewise. And we hug in this family, baby."

"Yes, ma'am."

The two embraced as Dominique looked on with delight.

"Uh-huh. I can see why my niece stays in trouble behind you," Toni muttered with a mischievous grin. Amari blushed.

"Toni," Dominique warned.

"Awrite, awrite. Let's get outta here." Toni popped the trunk and made room for Amari to place the bags inside. They settled in the jeep after that and set off toward the highway.

"Ms. Favier?" Amari said, buckling his seat belt.

"Yes, 'Mari?" Dominique threw over her shoulder.

"Can we stop somewhere and get flowers for Gia?"

"I don't see why not. Toni, do you mind?"

"No, I don't mind at all," Toni smiled from ear to ear.

"We'll stop somewhere in town for ya, love."

"Okay. Thank you." Amari relaxed a bit.

"Ya welcome. And call ya mama," Dominique eyed him. "Let her know we landed safely."

"Yes, ma'am." He retrieved his phone and placed his EarPods in his ear.

"GiGi's gotta prize here," Toni whispered.

"Yes, she does," Dominique nodded.

"He's fine as wine too, ain't he? A pretty somethin'," Toni said, taking a peek at him through the rearview mirror.

"Toni, hush."

"Well, he is. She got good taste like her mama."

"Oh no. She's got way better taste than me. She hit the jackpot with this one."

"I'll say." Toni pulled onto the highway. "Mama's gonna be fit to be tied when she sees him."

"Yeah, but she'll save face for Gia. Besides, he's only here for the weekend, and he ain't stayin' over there. He's gonna be at ya house."

"Doesn't matter. She's enjoyin' havin' that child all to herself."

"Well, she's gonna have to share her this weekend." Dominique took a brief look over her shoulder at Amari. "He's good to her and good *for* her. She'll get over it. She ain't gotta choice."

GIA SAT on her grandmother's porch swiping through photos of engagement rings that Esai sent her the previous evening. She hearted a ring from Tiffany's, then texted him about how much her mother would love the emerald-cut center stone surrounded by a halo of diamonds. Gia put her phone in her back shorts pocket and began plucking Tarot cards from a deck. Then she placed them down on the bench cushion as she took in the early-morning air. It smelled of after rain, which she absolutely loved. Dewdrops glistened from the trees along the street, giving them a diamondlike effect. A horn played a lost lover's tune in the distance. It dragged and cried. Thoughts of her parents came to mind. Two imperfect people who found each other at the perfect time. Two imperfect people who believed they were perfect for each other. Her father was going to propose to her mother once he returned with her brothers at the end of August. He'd asked her to help him plan the special day's events, to which Gia agreed with much reservation. *What can I do?* Her father's mind was made up. His love for her mother was unconditional, and Gia had no other choice but to accept it.

A Mercedes G-Wagon pulled up, parking behind a Buick in waiting. Gia plucked another card before looking up and smiling. Her favorite aunt had arrived to pick her up and go to the shop.

Toni put the jeep in park and looked over at her sister. "Listen, I need to tell you somethin' before we get out."

"What?" Dominique met her eyes.

"The other day, GiGi told Mama she wanted to meet Antoine and it didn't go well. Mama lost her cool."

Dominique frowned, "She didn't put her hands on her, did she?"

"No, no. She just hollered at her and forbade her from seein' him."

"Damn, you tellin' me this *now*?" Dominique shook her head in disbelief. "You know I'm not good at savin' face, Toni."

"Well, today's a good day to start practicin'," Toni shrugged. "And while ya perfectin' that, I also want you to promise me . . . Promise me ya gonna be peaceful," Toni raised her pinky finger.

"I promise," Dominique intertwined her pinky with Toni's.

Toni exited the car and waved at Gia. "Hey, *cher!*"

"Hey, TeeTee!" Gia waved back as she made her way down the steps.

"The shirt looks good on you!" Toni approached the trunk and opened it. She retrieved a piece of luggage, then another.

"Thank you!" Gia beamed.

"Where's Mamaw?" Toni looked past her.

"In the house with a client."

"Okay." Toni rounded the car and walked to the driver's side of the Buick parked before hers. The man inside explained he was waiting for his mother, to which she acknowledged, "You ready to go?" She asked Gia as she turned her attention back to her.

"Yeah!" Gia's smile grew wider.

"Good. We got some extra help today," Toni grinned mischievously.

"We do?"

"Mm-hmm," Toni slapped the back of the truck hard.

The back passenger door opened, and Amari stepped out with a bouquet in hand.

"No," Gia covered her mouth in disbelief. "No. What is going on?"

"Hey, babe," Amari smiled with his arms opened wide.

Gia stared back and forth between Toni and Amari, flushed with excitement.

Amari closed the space between them and hugged her gently, careful not to hurt her.

"TeeTee?"

"Not me," Toni grinned as the front passenger door opened.

Dominique smiled small as her eyes met Gia's. Dominique thought she looked good. Healthier. She'd gotten her color back and some of her weight. She was pleased.

"I thought you could use a little company," Dominique grinned.

"I don't know what to say," Gia said just above a whisper.

"'*Thank you, Mommy*' is a good start," Toni said.

Gia blushed with embarrassment. "Thank you, Mommy."

"Ya welcome," Dominique nodded as she watched Gia fidget in discomfort. "Where's ya grandmama?"

"Inside with a client."

"She's back to doin' divinations at the house?" Dominique asked Toni in confusion.

Toni nodded, "Only for the elders."

The heavy wooden door of the house opened. Corrine emerged, her hand clasped with her aged client's. She looked toward the street and saw the foursome engaged in conversation. Her brows furrowed. She and the client descended the stairs, catching the group's attention. Amari jogged over to assist. The man in the waiting car followed.

"Let me help you," Amari smiled nervously.

"Thank you, baby," the elder smiled, her mouth full of chewing tobacco.

"This yo' grandbaby, madame?"

"No, ma'am. My granddaughter's friend," Corrine eyed him.

"Oh, how nice. Hey, Billy," she smiled at her son.

"Hey, Mama."

Corrine cut her eyes at Toni and Dominique as she assisted the elder into her son's car. "Now, you make sure she drinks this cherry juice for the next two weeks to get rid of that gout," Corrine instructed seriously. "She's got a jar of an earth clay and herbal blend that'll draw out da toxins in her body too. Make sure her home health aide rubs her down wit' it twice a day."

"Yes, ma'am," Billy nodded.

"I'll see you next month, Madame Johnson." Corrine winked at her.

"God willin' and da creek don't rise," she smiled.

"Y'all drive safely," Corrine waved as she backed away from the car.Billy tooted the horn and slowly pulled off.

Corrine placed her hands on her hips and bit the inside of her cheek. "Well, this is an unexpected surprise."

"Hey, Mama. I thought it would be nice for Amari to come down and visit Gia for the weekend," Dominique began. "After all that's happened, I figured it would be nice for them to see each other."

Corrine looked over at Gia, whose eyes were pleading with her. "Well, I suppose yo' right."

"Thank you, Mamaw!" Gia squealed as she hugged her tightly.

Dominique clenched her jaw, scorned by the response she wanted from her child.

"I assume he'll be stayin' wit' you, Toni?" Corrine's brow raised.

"Yes, ma'am," Toni replied.

"Good. And where are you stayin', Dominique?" Corrine asked, looking her over. She was covertly pleased with her daughter's healthy appearance.

Dominique shrugged and said drily, "Wherever you want me, Mama."

"Here. I want you to stay here."

"Okay," Dominique forced a smile.

Toni grinned small at her mother's peacemaking attempt, then interlocked her arm with Dominique's.

"Have y'all had breakfast?"

"No, ma'am," Dominique and Amari replied in unison.

"Well, then, let's get those stomachs filled. How about some shrimp and grits?" Corrine led them back to the house.

"I never had shrimp and grits before," Amari rubbed his stomach.

"No?" Corrine raised an eyebrow.

"No, ma'am," he shook his head.

"Well, then, today's yo' lucky day. I make the best shrimp and grits this side of the Mississippi."

"She does." Gia nodded.

"I'll make that wit' a side of bacon and eggs and biscuits and gravy. How's that sound?"

"Sounds amazing, Mrs. Favier," Amari smiled wide.

"Good," Corrine smiled as she allowed Amari to escort her up the porch steps. "You know, Gia's not too bad in the kitchen, either," Corrine winked at her and Dominique.

UNDER HER MOTHER'S DIRECTIVE, Dominique stood at the kitchen counter preparing a *gris-gris* bag for the client she was advising in the dining room. Moments like this reminded her of the days she assisted her mother with readings and helped her prepare for her divinations. She always stayed hidden in another room, careful not to disrespect the sanctity of the experience or disturb the ancestors as they spoke through her mother. Even though Dominique had stepped away from voodoo, she still managed to apply certain things she'd been taught to her funeral business. The *gris-gris* bags, specifically.

Corrine walked in, interrupting her thoughts.

"Are the bags ready?"

"Yes, ma'am. I also wrote down the instructions for her just in case she forgets what you told her." Dominique handed her the scroll tied with a blue ribbon.

"Always thinkin' one step ahead. Thank you," Corrine smiled.

"Ya welcome."

Dominique began to clear the island, placing leftover herbs back into their jars.

"Awrite, she's all taken care of." Corrine walked back in, moving straight to the faucet to wash her hands.

"How many more appointments do you have?"

"Just two. One at 3:30 and the other at 5:00."

"Okay."

"Thank you again for helpin' me this afternoon." She dried her hands with a towel.

"Ya welcome."

"Want me to fix you some lunch? I've got some leftover chicken creole from last night."

"I can fix myself somethin' to eat, Mama. You don't have to do it." Dominique retrieved a wet dishrag from the sink and wiped the counter.

"I want to."

Dominique held her hands up in surrender.

"I'm glad yo' stayin' wit' me and Gia. It's important that yo' here to help her heal. The physical's comin' along nicely, but the mental and spiritual need a lot mo' work."

"Well, I'm sure you goin' off on her didn't helpin' any," Dominique raised a brow.

"I know, I know. And I apologized to her for it." Corrine applied balm to her hands. "It's one thing for her to meet René, but his son . . . can't happen."

"It's what she wants. And if it doesn't happen this year, she'll make sure it does when she turns eighteen next year. We really won't have no say then."

"He's gonna hurt that girl." Corrine shook her head.

"Maybe. Maybe not."

Corrine slowly lifted her head and glared back at Dominique. "I beg ya pardon?"

Dominique rubbed the back of her neck.

"You givin' him the benefit of the doubt?" Corrine continued.

Dominique remained silent.

"You been in contact wit' him, ain't you?"

Dominique shifted a bit.

"He's started workin' on you."

Dominique hesitated. "He followed me to Jersey."

"He did *what*?" Corrine spat, resting her hands on the edge of the island.

"He showed up at the parlor," Dominique sighed.

Corrine slowly grabbed her throat and began to rub it.

"Nothin' happened," Dominique continued. "We just talked. He told me some things."

"What kind of things?" Corrine's voice flippant.

"He told me that he and Daddy stayed in touch these last fourteen years. Did you know that?"

"No, I didn't."

"Yeah. He, uh, he also opened an account for Gia at the bank. She's got over $72,000 in there."

"Mmm." Corrine pursed her lips. "Money don't make up fo' abandonment."

"No, it doesn't." Dominique paused. "He also told me he came by here to apologize to you the day after we broke curfew. Is that true?"

"It is," Corrine nodded without hesitation.

"Why didn't you tell me?"

"Because there was nothin' to tell. As far as I was concerned, he didn't exist." Corrine moved away from the counter and retrieved the leftover dinner from the refrigerator.

"But he did, Mama. What did you say to him?" Dominique watched her closely.

"Now, you know better than to question me," Corrine threw over her shoulder.

"Well, I am," Dominique replied firmly.

Corrine turned around to face her daughter. Dominique was rooted and ready. She wanted an answer.

"Do you know how many years ago that was?" Corrine smirked.

"Eighteen, but ya memory has always been long. What did you say, Mama?"

Corrine snatched the foil off the glass baking dish. "Why do you need to know? Why is it important to you *now?*"

"Because he wouldn't tell me. And I need to know he left me and Gia on his own accord and not because of *you.*"

Corrine stopped in her tracks and peered back at Dominique. She was offended.

"I need to know he didn't use me to get back at you. *What did you say, Mama?*"

Corrine pursed her lips. "I told him he was broken, and you were not in the *'build-a-nigga'* business. I told him he had no respect. Not fo' you or me or ya daddy. And even though he had ya daddy fooled and wrapped around his finger, I knew better. I could see right through him. I told him no daughter of mine, especially my baby girl, was goin' to have anything else to do wit' the likes of him. A no-count-fo'-nothin' nigga who was not fit to breathe the same air as my child. Instead, he should have been swallowed like the liquor his mama loved so much."

"Oh my God," Dominique deflated on her bar stool.

Corrine shrugged her shoulders. "You wanted me to tell you."

"How could you? He didn't deserve all that, Mama. He didn't. You went too far," Dominique shook her head.

"No, baby girl, I met him right in the middle."

The back screen door opened and slammed shut. Toni walked in, wrapping her locks in a scarf. "Hey, y'all! I'm back to pick up the candles. They ready?" She was met with stony silence and suffocating tension. She looked at her sister, then her mother. "What happened now?"

"Ask ya mother." Fuming, Dominique slid off the bar stool, cut her eyes at Corrine, then stormed out.

"Where you goin'?!" Corrine called to her back.

Dominique kept her stride. Corrine cursed herself as she slammed the platter down and followed her.

"What the hell happened?" Toni ran behind her mother.

Corrine caught Dominique by the wrist just as her hand touched the knob on the front door. "Where you goin'? Huh?"

"Mama, let go of me." Dominique's eyes glossed over.

"You runnin' outta here to go see him? You gonna go runnin' back into his arms?" Corrine squeezed tighter.

"Mama, please!" Dominique hollered, trying to wriggle her way out of her mother's grasp.

"Shame me again? Break my heart?" Corrine screamed.

"Mama, please!" Dominique whined through angry tears.

"Mama, let her go!" Toni grabbed her sister with one hand and pried her mother's fingers from Dominique's arm with the other.

Corrine positioned herself in front of the door. "No! Not this time! I'm not gonna make the same mistake twice!" She cupped Dominique's face, willing her eyes to meet hers. "He's gonna be the death of you. You hear me?" Corrine's voice quivered. "*He's gonna be the death of you.* And I won't be able to save you."

Breathless, her body quaking, Dominique gripped her mother's hands and smiled dismally as tears cascaded down her face. Corrine's eyes flickered, a flash of helplessness blinding her momentarily.

"Don't leave this house." Corrine's warning sounded more like a plea. "Don't leave," she whispered.

Dominique kissed her mother's palm, then peeled her hands from her face.

She flung the front door open and flew down the steps. Her mother and sister, stunned by the great escape, watched her jump into Dreux's old pickup truck and drive off.

GIA AND AMARI sat on a sheet in the middle of her grandmother's garden dabbling in an assortment of pralines and beignets. They'd spent the entire morning at the shop, then explored the

French Quarter throughout the afternoon. In spite of Amari's impromptu visit, Gia was expected to honor the curfew her grandmother had in place for her. So there she and Amari sat, gazing in each other's eyes among rosebushes and honeysuckle.

"I'm kinda nervous, to be honest with you." Gia wiped her mouth with a napkin.

"Why?"

"I don't know," she shrugged. "I guess because he knows more about me than I do him."

Amari nodded. "Yeah, I can see that being nerve-racking. But I bet you he's gonna be just as nervous as you or more."

"You think so?" Gia's eyes looked hopeful.

"Yeah. His son didn't step up like he should have, and he'll probably be really embarrassed about it."

"I didn't think about that," Gia said to herself.

Amari wiped his mouth with a napkin. "Yup. You want me to go with you?"

"Yes," Gia said without hesitation.

"Okay." He stuffed his mouth with a beignet.

Gia cringed. "You're gonna choke."

"No, I'm not. I'm good."

Gia watched him pop another one into his mouth. "I told you you'd like them."

"Yeah, yeah!" Amari grinned. "But you know what? If I had to pick my favorite, it would have to be the pralines. The coconut ones."

"Nooo, the chocolate ones are way better!"

"Coconut all day, baby!"

"Get out of here!" Gia squealed as she gently shoved him. Amari responded with a playful shove of his own.

"Ouch!" Gia grabbed the place where her lung used to be.

Amari reached for her. "Oh my God. I'm sorry. I'm sorry. Are you all right?"

Gia burst into laughter. Amari, confused, stared back at her.

"I'm fine! I'm just playing!"

Amari sucked his teeth. "That's not funny, babe."

"You should have seen your face," Gia continued to laugh. Tears began to roll down her cheeks.

"Man." Amari rose from the blanket and made his way into the house. Gia followed, struggling to compose herself.

"You want something to drink? I need some water or somethin' to flush all dis sugar out of my system."

Gia walked up behind him and wrapped her arms around his lithe waist.

"I'm sorry, baby. Don't be mad at me, okay?"

Amari stared down at her. His brows furrowed. "That wasn't funny."

"I know. I just . . . I wanted to relieve some of the tension. You haven't really hugged me or anything today. It's like you're too scared to touch me."

"Because I am." He laughed nervously.

"Well, don't be." She smiled. "I'm much better than I was. Honest. I'm not sore anymore. I can breathe. It's like I'm brand-new."

"Okay," he replied distrustfully.

"Can I have a kiss?" Gia poked her bottom lip out and batted her eyes.

Amari shook his head in disbelief. "Yeah. I guess so." He leaned down and gave her a tender kiss on the forehead. She, in turn, gave him a quizzical glance. "If you think I'm kissin' you on the lips in *this* house, with your Mamaw walkin' around, you're crazy," he said seriously.

Gia chuckled. "Oh my God."

Corrine stormed in with her cell phone to her ear. Amari and Gia quickly separated.

"GiGi, have you heard from your mama?" There was panic in her voice.

"No, ma'am. Why? What's the matter?"

Corrine scrolled through her phone in search of something she wasn't even quite sure of. "She's not pickin' up her phone."

"She probably has it on silent mode," Gia said, completely unaware of the afternoon's argument between the two women.

"I don't know. It's not like her to ignore my calls. Yo' aunts been callin' her too, and she didn't pick up fo' them either."

Gia watched worry lines grow along her grandmother's forehead.

"You want me to try?" she asked as she pulled her phone out of her back pocket.

"Yes, please." Corrine paced the kitchen floor as she looked on.

Gia dialed her mother's number. "It went straight to voicemail."

"Shit." Corrine placed her hands on her hips and began to think.

Gia looked over at Amari. He was attempting to get in touch with her.

"I'm sure she's all right, Mamaw."

"She ever pull a stunt like this back in New Jersey?"

"No, ma'am."

Corrine sighed in dismay as she rubbed the back of her neck. "I'm goin' out to look for her." She made her way into the foyer with the kids on her heels.

"At this hour?"

"*Yes, at this hour.*" Corrine gathered her keys, pocketbook, and jacket.

"Do you want us to—" Gia began.

"No. You two stay here in case she calls or comes back befo' I do."

"Okay," Gia said, unsure of how she should feel.

"I love you." Corrine kissed her on the cheek, then headed out.

"Love you too," Gia whispered to her back.

She and Amari stood under the porch light, watching her grandmother get into her Cadillac and speed off down the street.

Amari placed folded hands atop his head. "Should we be worried?"

"I don't know," Gia shrugged. "Maybe. I don't know."

"We should pray."

"What?" She looked up at him with a twinge of annoyance.

"We should pray."

Gia bit down on her bottom lip. "I'm sure she's fine."

"Yeah, but . . . what if she isn't?"

Gia watched dread blanket Amari's face.

"You didn't say much to her when we surprised you this morning. You barely looked her way. And you didn't say anything to her at breakfast or before we left to go to the shop either. Now—"

"She's fine!" Gia snapped as she backpedaled into the house. "Wherever she is, she's fine. You and my Mamaw need to chill the fuck out. My mother knows this city like the back of her hand."

Amari studied her for a moment, then quietly said, "But she's been gone since two, Gia. It's a quarter after ten now."

"I know what time it is, Amari," she hissed again.

"Then pray with me."

"You pray. I'm gonna go out and look for her." Gia snatched up the plates of dessert and the sheet from the ground.

"But your Mamaw told us to stay here."

"I know she did, but I think I may know where she is. And as long as we get back here before my Mamaw does, we'll be fine."

~

DOMINIQUE SAT on the rocks at the bottom of one of the terraced landings of the Moonwalk in Riverwalk Park. The Mississippi River's waters were still and dark. She wet her feet in its mouth as she thought of her African ancestors who'd made the journey over. She was sitting at the location of one of the largest ports and slave markets in the country. History, in all its painful glory, wrapped itself around her ankles.

She'd parked her car somewhere on Decatur Street, then bought a bouquet from a floral shop on Dumaine before walking to Washington Artillery Park. At her back, Jackson Square was abuzz with tourists and artists. She could hear Professor Longhair's *"Tipitina"* playing from the calliope onboard the *Natchez* at the dock. She closed her eyes and allowed the stutter-stepping rhythm to rock her.

Dominique had been at the banks all day. Walking at times. Standing still. And now sitting. Tears stained her face as she watched a tour guide lead a group to an African drumming circle that was preparing to perform. She knew the lead drummer, Adole. He was her mother's master drummer. He was looking in her direction, but she hoped he couldn't see her through the darkness. She wasn't in the mood for conversation. She just wanted to be alone. She needed to think.

Her life had been hard. And it may have been different, a little easier had Antoine told her what her mother said after it happened. *Is he perfect?* No. *But who is?* He'd always been complicated. A product of a wealthy family who did their best to protect him from the world outside of the safe one they'd created for him. But Antoine had been curious by the outside world and all its chaos. Tempted to be a part of it by any means necessary. No one knew what he was searching for or what drew him to it. Why he couldn't stay on the straight and narrow path, but he was masterful in keeping the two worlds separate.

She knew he missed his mother. Maybe he'd been searching for comfort or answers about why she was taken so early in his life. Why he'd been forced to live the rest of it without her. Antoine wasn't perfect by any means, but he didn't deserve to be spoken down to the way he had been. She'd lain down with him and had his child—a child who reminded her daily that she was just as much his as she was hers.

Slow and steady footsteps approached her.

"Dom? You a'ight?" Antoine approached her with caution, then crouched down beside her.

Dominique didn't acknowledge him. She remained silent.

"My pops called and told me you were missin'. You got everybody shook, love. Ya moms and sisters are out lookin' for you . . ."

Dominique peered at the street lamps brightening along the bricked promenade. "How'd you find me?" Her voice quivered.

"You always came down here when you needed some time to yourself."

Dominique nodded slowly. "She told me what she said to you." She looked over at him with pity. "I'm sorry."

"You don't need to apologize. It's water under the bridge. Besides, it never changed the way I felt about you."

"We can't be together. You abandoned me—our daughter. You slept with my sister. Filled her up with lies. We can never . . . be." Dominique looked over at him again and watched him become uncomfortable under her gaze.

"I don't know if I can accept that," he peered back at her.

Dominique shrugged. "You gon' have to."

Antoine ran his tongue across his teeth. "What about Gia?"

"If she wants a relationship with you, she's free to have one. But you and me . . . we begin and end with her."

Antoine caressed her wet cheek with the back of his hand. "I never meant to hurt you, love. Or her." His phone rang, pulling his attention away from her. His father's name lit up against a black background.

"Answer it," Dominique sniffled as she rose to her feet.

"What do you want me to tell 'im?"

"I'm safe."

Dominique continued to study the water and noticed it had begun to pulsate, moving in measure with a beat Adole had started to play. She looked past Antoine and saw the master drummer staring in their direction. He could see her. His eyes found hers, and he nodded. An ancient rhythm, the *bamboula*, fell beneath his calloused hands, awakening something in Dominique she thought had died years ago. He was invoking the power of God and enticing her to enter a realm where there were no boundaries between herself and the vast spaciousness of being.

Dominique rose to her feet, climbed back onto the concrete landing and began to walk in the direction of the drummers and crowd. Antoine followed suit, making sure he retrieved her belongings first. Dominique excused herself as she moved through the bodies and settled in front of them. Adole smiled widely at the sight of her. He began to caress his drum harder and watch its holy vibration begin to permeate her body.

Dominique closed her eyes and gently threw her head back as her feet began to lead her into the circle's center. She gathered her long red maxi skirt at her thighs and stomped her foot in response to Adole's call. Her body rolled as she created thunder beneath her. The other drummers met Adole's pulse and created a symphonic heartbeat. She twirled and dipped, contracted and gyrated. Her torso muscles isolated themselves from the rest of her body. Undulations of her hips and abdomen made it difficult for an onlooker to conceive how she did it. Her hips moved in staccato—rocking, lifting, and twisting to the percussive sounds. Antoine watched, his mouth agape. Dominique had him and the entire crowd entranced. She'd seduced them all with her moves and hadn't even noticed. She was elsewhere mentally and spiritually. On a higher plane of understanding and peace. She'd transcended this world and into the one beyond the veil. The faces surrounding her were not of the crowd but that of her ancestors. They watched her dance. Smiled with approval. Then directed her.

To the water.

DEFEATED, Gia and Amari stood outside of St. Louis Cathedral. They'd scoured the entire French Quarter in search of her mother. Gia thought she might have been at the ancestors' tree in Congo Square, but there was no trace of her there when they arrived. Gia wasn't sure where else to look. Her mother's phone was still turned off and her aunts and grandmother had no luck finding her yet.

Gia began to kick herself. She'd completely dismissed her mother for the past two months. She was consumed in her own pain and enjoyed making the woman suffer behind it. But never did she think in a million years she would be punished like this for it. She knew a few kids at her school who were motherless. Sickness or violence had claimed their lives. And Gia had seen the toll it took on them. She didn't want that for herself, nor would she wish it on her worst enemy. She looked in one direction, then the other, before deciding to walk through Jackson Square.

"We should get back to your Mamaw's," Amari said as he rubbed Gia's back.

"We can't. We have to find her," Gia replied as she watched some people run up the stairs toward Washington Artillery Park.

"Where else is there to look? We've been everywhere." Amari rubbed his head.

"Up there," Gia pointed. "Something's going on." She

waited for a horse and buggy to pass before making her way toward the tower of concrete steps.

"Can you do this many steps?" Amari asked, scratching his incoming chin hair.

"Yeah. Let's go."

The two climbed the two-flight stairway and saw a gathering of people watching the water. Some were hysterical, while others were dazed by the commotion. Gia and Amari jogged down to the Moonwalk to get a better look. A handful of men were scattered in the river, treading and watching hopelessly for something or someone to surface. They couldn't go any further than where they were. It was too dark. As the young couple moved closer to the water's edge, Gia heard a woman say, *"She didn't come back up."* Then someone else screamed, *"Oh my God! Where is she?!"* Gia didn't want to think the worst. A pang in her stomach was growing, which she hoped it was a result of her nervousness and not confirmation. But then she recognized Antoine among the men in the water. He was calling out to her mother, his voice booming. Distressed. And she found herself making a mad dash toward him.

"Mommy? Mommy!" Gia hollered before Amari grabbed her by the waist and held her.

"Gia, Gia. What are you doing? You can't go in there," he said.

"I have to!" Gia wrestled with him.

"Gia, stop!" Amari yelled, struggling to restrain her.

"Mommy!" she cried. "Mommy!"

Several female crowd members enveloped Amari in an attempt to assist him with Gia. She began to hyperventilate, her breaths short and violent. They sat her down on one of the promenade's benches and fanned her, urging her to take slow, deep breaths and try to drink the water that was available to her. She couldn't catch her breath long enough to speak or take what was being offered. Everyone's voices were muffled. Gia watched the water and willed her mother to resurface . . . but she didn't. A familiar voice resounded from the throng of spectators, momentarily drawing her out of her mania.

"Lawd, no!" Corrine charged through the crowd straight to the water with Toni and the twins right behind her. "Dominique!" she screamed. "Dominique!" She immediately caught sight of Antoine as he dragged himself out of the river and attacked him. "What did you do?!" She threw a wild punch. "What did you do?!" Then another.

"I didn't—I didn't do anything!" Antoine growled. He was telling the truth.

Dominique had stopped dancing, slowly approached him, and took the bouquet of roses out of his hand. Then she turned toward the water and gazed at it for a moment before taking her place before it. Finally, she freed the flowers from the cellophane and dropped them in the river one by one.

Antoine walked up beside her and placed his hand gently on the small of her back. He asked her if she was okay, but she didn't respond. Instead, she looked over at him, her eyes distant. He ran his hand along her spine and rested it on the nape of her neck. He caressed her cheek with the other, then leaned in to kiss her. She didn't protest. Their tongues danced as he pulled her into him, closing the years he'd dreamt and yearned for her.

She reached down and rubbed his throbbing nature. Squeezed it in an attempt to harden it to the point of aching bliss. She tugged on his bottom lip with her teeth—then bit down on it hard. Antoine cursed aloud and pulled back. He grabbed his lip. Blood was drawn. His fingertips were painted red. He asked her why she'd bitten him. Dominique looked up at him and replied, *"Avoir peur,"* before diving into the river.

Gia watched her grandmother's desperate blows connect with her father's raised arms. He struggled to protect his face while trying to regain his strength. Amari ran over to help Toni and the twins redirect their mother's ferocity. After a short exchange between Amari and Toni, he led her over to Gia. She sat down beside the distraught girl and held her. An onlooker offered her an unopened bottle of water, which she accepted without hesitation. She opened it, poured some onto her hand, and wiped Gia's face with it. Then begged her to drink some. But Gia refused. She just kept her eyes on the water and her grandmother.

Corrine was down on her knees with her arms outstretched toward the water, begging it to release her child. She knew the sea better than anyone, understanding that it was just as temperamental as any woman. What was spread out before her was an unyielding force of nature. But, for whatever reason, her child felt comfortable enough to entrust it with her life. Those who had been left behind were at its/her mercy.

A chant found its place on Corrine's tongue. A prayer followed—both shifting
between Kouri-Vini, French, and Yoruba. Adole, who had been among the other men in the water, picked up his drum and carried it over to Corrine's location. He tied his floor-length locks into a messy bun as he planted himself beside her. He positioned his drum between his legs, closed his eyes, and began to play. Ripples in the water flowed from the promenade along an unseen trail toward its belly. The harder Adole played, the bigger the waves grew. The louder Corrine prayed, the more violent the water became. Antoine was back in the river with the other men, trying to swim against the tide. Heads submerged, then reemerged. There was still no sign of Dominique.

Gia watched a handful of NOPD's finest make their presence known and try to move the crowd back to Washington Artillery Park. The twins were explaining the situation to one officer while Amari spoke to another. Her aunt Toni squeezed her tighter as they sat on the edge of the bench, watching the pandemonium evolve into something greater. Gia looked to the river once again. A whirlpool had formed at its belly. She stood up, grabbed her aunt's hand, and lead her to her grandmother at its mouth. Something was surfacing.

"Mamaw," Gia whispered. "Mamaw, look."

Corrine lowered her head and settled her eyes on the rotating water in the distance. Adole continued to play, his body drenched in sweat.

"*Allez,*" she groaned low. "*Allez!*"

A head emerged. Then arms. A torso and legs. Dominique lay on her back with her arms spread wide. Eyes closed. Still. The current moved her in the direction of Antoine and the other men. But as her body came into full view, they noticed she was floating *above* the water, its surface unbroken. One of the men cursed himself and backstroked away. Antoine looked back at the remaining spectators on the promenade to see if they too were seeing the phenomenon before him. Gia and his eyes locked. She stood in disbelief as her grandmother looked on as well, breathing heavily on all fours.

"Grab her!" Corrine shouted breathlessly.

Antoine did as he was told. He gently grabbed Dominique beneath her arms and pulled her down. He wrapped one arm securely around her chest and swam back to shore with the other arm. The drummers, police officers, and Favier women met them at the landing she'd dived from and pulled her onto it. Gia took one look at her mother's lifeless body and became hysterical all over again. Her sonorous cries reverberated along the shoreline, bouncing off the steps and onto the square.

"Get her out of here!" Antoine barked at Amari.

Amari scooped Gia into his arms and made his way back to Washington Artillery Park.

Corrine and the girls surrounded Dominique, falling to their knees and laying their hands on as many parts of her body as they could. Corrine put her ear to Dominique's chest and listened for her heartbeat. There was nothing. Corrine took Dominique's wet face into her hands and wiped it before tilting her head back. She pinched her daughter's nose shut, then covered her mouth with her own. Corrine expelled a breath. Then another. And another. She set her hands over the center of Dominique's chest, then pushed down. Straight and hard. Expelled another breath. Then another. And another. Still . . . There was nothing.

PART III

AUGUST

11

Gia gently moved the sheer curtain aside and watched her grandmother back out of the driveway, then drive off down the street. She wondered where she was off to so early in the morning. Stillness seemed to have become a thing of the past for her . . . for any of them since her mother's drowning. Her mother's status was still unknown to her only. Her grandmother forbade her from visiting her at the hospital, and she wasn't allowed to ask any questions. When she did, no one answered.

The last five days had been a whirlwind. Each morning and evening was filled with a steady flow of visitors. Colleagues and community members all came to gift her with flowers and nutritious offerings. The foyer and great rooms were filled with floral arrangements. They reminded Gia of the floral room at her mother's funeral parlor back home. Members of her grandmother's spiritual haus manned the home, taking shifts to tend to her grandmother's needs. Since the night on the river, her grandmother had spent most of her time in Dominique's childhood bedroom. Gia was forbidden to go anywhere near it. Two haus members guarded it day and night, leaving her to wonder what was happening behind the door. Whatever she wanted or needed had to be requested through one of the other servicing haus members. They, in turn, would honor her requests. The shop was closed until further notice, and Amari had since returned home, so Gia spent her time in the backyard reading and looking up at her mother's bedroom window. She didn't know what she expected to see, but she found herself watching it, nonetheless.

Gia retrieved her robe and wrapped herself in it. She stepped into the hallway, instantly hit with the pungent aroma of Florida Water filtering through her mother's bedroom door. She immediately noticed it was void of safeguards. Gia rubbed her forehead nervously before approaching it. She placed her ear to the cool wood, straining to hear any sound of life behind it. There was nothing. Hesitant once again, she slowly reached for the knob. Just as her fingertips touched it, two women draped in white appeared at the top of the stairwell. Gia quickly moved away from the door, nodded, and smiled at them, then made her way down to the first floor. She hoped they weren't going to tell her grandmother about her failed attempt.

More women in white were milling around, chatting, and following whatever directives had been given to them by her grandmother. She greeted each of them before settling in the kitchen. Her aunts, Toni and Jackie, stood at the island preparing dishes and delving deeper into a conversation Gia wished she could be a part of. But they were speaking Louisiana Creole. And her grandmother's daughters only spoke it when they didn't want anyone else to know what was being said. Like their culture, the language of their foremothers was sacred. They too were draped in white from head to toe.

"Morning," Gia said lightly.

Toni and Jackie looked her way and smiled warmly.

"Mornin', Sleepin' Beauty," Jackie teased as she pinched Gia's chin.

"Mornin', *cher*," Toni followed, taking Gia into her arms and hugging her. "How'd you sleep?"

Gia shrugged her shoulders. "All right, I guess."

"Just all right?" Jackie asked.

"Yeah. It's been kinda hard with all of Mamaw's godchildren . . .?"

"Yes, godchildren," Toni nodded.

". . . with all of them here. All the whispering and walking at night," Gia confessed.

"Well, we can understand that," Toni confirmed. "It's been pretty busy around here."

"And these old wooden floors talk every time anybody takes a step," Jackie chimed in.

"That's the truth. But Jackie and I can assure you that ya safe. And it won't be long now before this is all over." Toni smiled.

"Okay," Gia replied uncertainly.

"You hungry?" Jackie asked.

"A little," Gia grinned.

"Good. You can join us on the porch for breakfast." Jackie smiled.

"Okay, but what about Mamaw? Shouldn't we wait until she comes back to eat?" Gia frowned.

"We're allowed to eat without her, GiGi," Toni chuckled.

"Oh." Gia blushed in embarrassment.

"Yeah. She'll be back as soon as she's finished makin' her deliveries," Jackie continued.

"Oh, okay," Gia replied.

"But she did tell us that she wanted you to change the cushion and pillows on the porch swing," Jackie continued.

"All right," Gia said quietly.

Jackie retrieved two paisley print pillows from the circular dining table in the breakfast nook and handed them to Gia. Then taking the seat cushion, Toni retrieved a light throw blanket from one of the chairs, a full plate of food, and led them to the foyer. She opened the front door and stepped out of Gia's way. Gia walked onto the porch and gasped. Confusion and fright washed over her. Taken aback by surprise, she squeezed the pillow tightly at the sight of her mother.

Dominique sat with her legs tucked beneath her, staring back at her child with adoration. She wasn't the lifeless, ghastly figure she'd been at the riverfront. Instead, her skin and hair were celestially aglow. Gia thought she looked almost angelic in her long, sky-blue nightgown.

Toni gave Dominique the plate of food along with a fork and napkin. She took the pillow from Gia and smiled widely. "You can change the pillows later." Then she winked at Dominique before retreating into the house with Jackie behind her.

Gia bowed her head and twiddled her fingers as she stood under her mother's gaze. She wanted to shower her with hugs and kisses, but she'd been so cruel to her and didn't know how she'd respond. The woman before her wasn't the same woman who died and had been disrespected. Instead, this woman exuded peace and a quiet power that many possessed but few embraced.

"Hi," Dominique said.

"Hi," Gia replied just above a whisper, still fidgeting.

"Come," Dominique patted the seat cushion. "Sit with me." Gia remained.

"Don't be afraid, baby. There's nothing to be afraid of."

Gia hesitantly obliged. She stared at her mother intently as tears welled in her eyes. There were no remnants of the drowning. Only hints of dark circles beneath her eyes. An indicator of lost sleep. She raised her hand, gently touching her mother's face. "You're alive. When did you . . .? I didn't know . . . you were here. I thought you were . . ." Dominique pushed a curl back from Gia's face. "I've asked for you. Every day since . . . no one would tell me . . ." Gia hiccupped. ". . . anything." She rested her fingertips on her mother's lips. "You were dead. I s-saw you."

"I was. But I had to die in order to live." She stroked Gia's wet, flushed face. Dominique grinned as she kissed the palm of Gia's hand, closed her eyes, and held it to her cheek.

Gia folded under her mother's tender kiss. She threw her arms around her neck and held on tight. "I'm so sorry, Mommy. I didn't mean anything I said. I didn't mean to-to ignore you when you got here. I love you . . . so much. I really do."

Dominique caressed her daughter's back and buried her fingers in her Afro. She massaged her scalp and rocked her child as she allowed her cries to run their course. "I know. I know. And I love you more, *mon coeur*," Dominique whispered. "All is forgiven."

Gia squeezed her tighter. "I forgive you . . . too," she sniffled.

"Thank you." Dominique smiled small. She cupped Gia's face and wiped her tears. Then kissed her lovingly on the lips.

"Does Mamaw know you're . . . up?" Gia asked, holding her mother's hand.

"No. And if she saw me sittin' out here instead of upstairs in bed, she'd kill me," Dominique chuckled. "So, please, don't tell her."

"I won't."

A slowly passing car pulled their attention to the street. Two middle-aged Black women snickered as their eyes locked with Dominique's. One of them pointed at her as disbelief blanketed her face. Gia looked over at her mother, whose gaze was penetrating through the invisible veil of judgment and fear that separated her from them. She didn't blink. She didn't speak or move. Her mother's eyes simply followed them until they disappeared down the street.

Dominique took in a deep breath, then released it. "That's

gonna happen for a while." She looked over at Gia and smiled before turning attention to her breakfast.

"Mommy?"

"Yes, love?"

"What happened . . . to you? What happened at the river?" Gia asked, her eyes hooded with worry. "That night, people were saying—"

"I'd committed suicide."

Gia nodded. "Yeah. Is it true?" She braced herself.

"No. It's not true." Dominique thought about her words carefully. "And I wish I could tell you I had a seizure and fell in, but that didn't happen either. Instead, I dove back into a world I swore I'd never return to."

"What does that mean?" Gia asked confused.

Dominique studied Gia's curious eyes and thought deeply about what she'd experienced. She didn't know how to put it into words. She'd been taught by her mother that music, specifically, carries hallowed meaning and the spirit of the soul. It is a medium that calls down and internalizes spiritual energy for divine celebration, healing, and communication with the spiritual world. And she just happened to be chosen as a physical channel that night.

"It means . . . I surrendered. It means that I am not the same. I am finally the woman I was meant to be. I've reached a level of consciousness that so many others will never achieve." She smiled. "Ya mama saw some things on the other side, GiGi. Things that would break ya heart. Things that would scare you half to death. Things you could wrap ya mind around—others you couldn't. There was beauty and ugliness. Joy and pain." Dominique took a moment to compose herself. "I saw Papaw over there."

"You did?" Gia asked in a hushed tone.

"Mm-hmm," Dominique nodded, sniffling. "He wanted me to stay."

THE BLACK CAT was located in three rooms of a renovated 1800s storefront located in the Faubourg Marigny district, just outside the French Quarter. The bricked walls of the dining room, bar, and music room were decorated with a mixture of contemporary art, black-and-white photographs of the great jazz legends, and posters of musical acts, past and present.

Corrine and Gia stepped into the dimly lit bar in search of René, quickly finding him onstage playing a tune on the piano. His rendition of Dr. John's *"Sweet Home New Orleans"* was a joyous, improvisational feeling of rhythm that caused Corrine to bop her head and tap her foot. All that was missing was a drummer, organist, and horn player. René sang with a murkiness that was reminiscent of the swamp. The New Orleans overtones added flavor and a punch that could knock a person down if she weren't prepared for it.

Gia watched the piano man fall deeper into a trance, and her grandmother enjoy every bit of the impromptu performance. Then as he began to approach the bridge, his voice cracked, breaking him out of his reverie. His eyes found Gia and Corrine standing beneath the EXIT sign at the entrance.

"Why you messin' up that man's song like that?" Corrine giggled.

"Messin' it up? I played it perfectly," René smirked.

Corrine shook her head. "You did no such thing. That song has to be played in B flat."

René raised his brows in playful disbelief. "You think you can do better?"

"I know I can," Corrine said matter-of-factly.

"Well, have at it." René scooted off the bench, making room for her.

Corrine waved her hand dismissively. "Another time. I don't wanna embarrass you in front of this chile."

"Mamaw, you can play?" Gia asked, crossing her arms.

"I can do a li'l somethin'," she smirked.

Gia looked at her quizzically. "I didn't know that."

René let out a raspy chuckle as he made his way offstage. "She can do more than a little somethin'. Your grandmother had the most anointed, and if I may add, *prettiest,* fingers to ever grace a Steinway. She wasn't too bad on the organ either."

"That is so dope," Gia smiled. "You gotta play something for me now."

"No, no. I haven't touched a piano in years. It'll be a mess," Corrine replied quickly, trying to brush it off.

"Please, Mamaw?" Gia pouted.

"This is not what we came here fo'." Corrine eyed her, trying to fight against the guilt trip Gia was placing on her.

"How can you deny that beautiful face?" René grinned.

Corrine sucked her teeth.

"She did say please," he chuckled again as he extended his hand for her to accept. "Go to church, Cori," he urged.

Corrine accepted his hand hesitantly, then settled behind the Yamaha keyboard. Center stage. She closed her eyes and began crafting a rich and roaming introduction to Aretha Franklin's rendition of Simon & Garfunkel's *"Bridge Over Troubled Water"*. With a rumbling bass, she hammered the chords and softened melodic lines with the precision of a classically trained pianist. Her sensual right-hand chords ramped up an emotion in her that she couldn't explain. It was a nostalgic performance given by a heavy spirit. A humble declaration of love for her only granddaughter. When she was through, she opened her eyes and found Gia in a state of astonishment. René was standing beside her with his chest poked out like a proud father.

"The world truly missed out." He extended his hand once again.

Corrine received it, making her way offstage. "I had a family to raise and a community of women to serve. Playin' just wasn't my callin'."

Gia didn't believe that for one second. She saw how entranced the woman had been. She wondered if marrying her grandfather had something to do with her early "retirement." *Was he against her playing? Had she no support from her family?* She was a baby boomer. Her generation's impact on society redefined the ideas of gender, family, and sexuality. *So why didn't she go out into the world and nurture her talent? Share her gift with the world?* Gia pondered what else she didn't know about her beloved grandmother.

"Maybe in the next lifetime," René grinned.

"Maybe." Corrine met his grin with her own.

"Give me a hug, girl." The two embraced. "You're lookin' lovely as ever."

"Thank you, love." She rested her hands on Gia's shoulders. "As promised. This is yo' granddaughter, Gia."

René smiled wider. "My granddaughter. I love the way that sounds." He extended his hand. "It's a pleasure to finally . . . to *officially* meet you, Gia. Thank you for comin', my dear."

"Thank you for having me," Gia smiled back, shaking his hand firmly. She thought he was a nice-looking man. Distinguished looking. His wavy salt-and-pepper hair was laid down. And his matching goatee was trimmed meticulously against his mahogany-brown skin. He was tall and broad-shouldered. His eyeglasses matched the short-sleeved pants set he was wearing, and his gap-toothed smile was warm. His accent was just as heavy as her grandmother's, if not more. He was a silver fox for sure. She thought Antoine favored him.

"Of course. Of course." René led them to a table. "Can I get you two anything? A cold drink or . . .?"

"Nothing for me," Corrine shook her head. "I'm goin' to leave now, actually, so you two can get acquainted."

"You sure?"

Corrine nodded. "Mm-hmm. But before I go, let me holla at you fo' a minute."

"Awrite."

Gia watched her grandmother lead the man whose blood she also shared over to the DJ booth.

"What's up?" René asked, leaning against the booth.

Corrine crossed her arms. "It was brought to my attention just before Dominique's . . . *accident* . . . that Duke and ya son had been speakin' fo' some time. Did you know that?"

René lightly scratched his brow. "Duke did mention it to me."

"I see."

"Cori, I assumed you knew. Duke never made it appear as if you didn't."

"Of course, he didn't. Why would he?" She shifted her weight to the other foot.

René sighed heavily. "Well, I'm sorry. I know how you feel about my son. And I am partially to blame for his misdoings. But we can't change anything that's happened. So my hope is that we all can just move forward now. For Gia's sake."

Corrine's brows furrowed. "How do you expect us to do that when he won't leave my chile alone?"

"Is that what she told you?" René asked, alarmed.

"She didn't have to."

"I'm sure he means well. He's made tremendous strides these last fourteen years."

Corrine uncrossed her arms and looked at him in disbelief. "How can you say that when you know he's to blame fo' Simone's mental breakdown? Fo' Dominique and Gia gettin' shot and almost killed?"

"Corrine—" René began as he repositioned himself.

"He followed Dominique back to New Jersey last month. Did you know that?"

"No."

She searched his face for the lie. "And the river?"

René ran his hand over his mustache. "I called 'im."

Corrine chortled.

"I did," René shrugged his shoulders innocently. "But it was just to see if he knew where she was. And thank God I did because he was the one who found her."

"Thank God?" Corrine crossed her arms again. "Ya son is a livin', breathin' *haint*. And he has been ridin' my chile since she stepped back on Louisiana soil."

René scratched the back of his head. Offended. "Antoine's many things, Cori. Troubled, yes. But he's not a monster. And surely not a haint."

"Oh no?"

"No," René spat.

"Did he tell you what happened at the river?"

René averted his eyes, setting them on Gia. She was studying the photographs on the wall.

"No."

Corrine waited patiently for his eyes to find hers again. "Ya know, as a midwife, I've dealt with many miscarriages. Many, many miscarriages . . . but very few stillbirths. However, those stillbirths never left me. They haunt me at night. Still. But I'll tell you somethin'. None of them, and I mean *none* of them, compare to the one that I bore witness to down at that river five nights ago." She looked past him to Gia, then back at him again. "The mighty Mississippi, in all her splendor and glory, pushed my child out wit' *not a single breath in her body*. Drained her *completely*. Her daughter lookin' on, hysterical beyond consolation. And li'l ole me . . . wit' only my prayers and tears." She forced a smile through her evident pain. "It took everything in me . . . *everything* to bring her back." René extended his hand to her, but she politely rejected it. "Now, ya son was in that water when we got there, René. You tellin' me, he didn't say anything to you about what happened?"

243

"He didn't, Cori. Believe it or not, Antoine doesn't tell me much of anything. Never has. He confided in Duke more than he did me."

"Well, Duke is dead," she snapped. "So I expect you to step up now and take yo' place as his father. I want you to tell him to stay away from my girls. *All of them.*"

René let out a quick, sharp snort. "He's a grown man, Cori. I can't tell 'im what to do. And to be quite honest with ya, I don't want to."

Corrine repositioned her pocketbook on her shoulder.

"Look, I know you're upset," René continued. "It's been one helluva summer for you and those girls. But I don't think Antoine had anything to do with Dominique's accident. He already blames himself for the shooting. And if you ask me, I'd say he truly loves her."

"But I *didn't* ask you."

"Well, I'm tellin' you anyway. And whether or not you want to admit it, she loves him too." René leaned back on the booth.

Corrine snickered and shook her head in disagreement.

"They're not kids anymore. They're gonna do what they wanna do. Doesn't matter what you or I say. So whatever's meant to be . . . let it."

"Over my dead body," Corrine scoffed.

René sighed in defeat.

"You know what the saddest part about this whole thing is?" Corrine smiled devilishly.

"What?"

"You don't know yo' son at all," she smirked.

"He deserves to be forgiven . . . just like you."

Corrine looked past René to see if Gia heard his last remark. But, to her relief, she was still admiring the pictures on the wall. "You told me you didn't blame me fo' what happened to her."

"I didn't, and I still don't," René replied honestly. "After all, I'm the one who came to you for help. But Duke did, Cori."

Corrine, taken aback by the admission, gently placed one hand on her hip and moved in closer. "She would still be here had she just followed my directions."

"Maybe," René shrugged.

"Or you'd stopped whorin' around," she spat.

"Maybe not," he shrugged again.

Corrine backed away and composed herself. "I want Gia back home in an hour."

"Yes, ma'am," René replied hesitantly.

Gia turned around just in time to see her grandparents' side conversation end. Her grandmother walked up to her and caressed her cheek.

"I'm goin' now. If you need me, just call me."

"Okay."

Corrine smiled reassuringly before leaving her in René's hands.

"Now, about that cold drink," René's voice rang in.

"I'll have a bottle of water, if you have one."

"I surely do. One bottle of water comin' up."

René walked behind the bar and retrieved a chilled bottle of water. He opened it for Gia, then handed it to her.

"Thank you."

"You're quite welcome. Would you like to sit in here or outside in the courtyard?"

"Inside, if you don't mind. It's a little too hot out there for me."

"Of course." René led them to a two-seater table at the front of the house and pulled out a chair for her. "Thank you again for comin', Gia. I've been waitin' for this day for quite some time."

"You're welcome," she smiled nervously.

"How is your mother?"

Gia took a swig out of her bottle. "Much better. She's up and about."

"Good," René nodded. "That's real good. I was worried about her. About you and your grandmama. You ladies have been through hell."

"Yeah," Gia replied quietly.

An awkward silence began to creep in. Gia fiddled with her bottle cap as René took all of her in, his eyes nonthreatening.

"I apologize for staring. You just look so much like ya grandmama, my first wife. It's uncanny."

"Funny, people always say I look like Mamaw . . . just lighter," Gia grinned.

"You do," René nodded. "But your resemblance to my late wife . . . It's almost identical. Would you like to see a picture of her?"

"Okay."

René pulled his wallet from his pocket and opened it. A photograph of a woman with Gia's face, hair, and complexion came into view. Gia's jaw dropped. For years, she felt like an anomaly. Her mother's child, yes, but only through the soul. Not in body.

"She's . . . beautiful."

"Yes, she is. Was. She was the love of my life." René basked in the photo, then pulled himself out of the myriad of memories. "I think I should apologize to you, Gia."

"For what?"

"For my son's shortcomings. I want you to know that his decision to abandon you and your mother was not your fault. It was not your mother's fault. My wife's passing did a number on 'im. On us both, actually. But I was able to bounce back from it. Antoine, not so much." He paused. "He messed up a good thing with your mother. There's no doubt about that. But I hope you will allow him to make it right between the three of you."

Gia placed the cap back on her water, then secured it

tightly. "The man who raised me is a good man. He's by no means perfect either, but he loved and raised me as his own. Do you know how much a man has to love a woman to accept her child as his?"

René remained listening attentively.

"A lot," Gia continued. "That says so much about his character. And the last thing I want to do, as his daughter, is hurt him. He can't be replaced. Not by Antoine or any of the other men who want my mother. And no disrespect, Mr. Brevard—"

"Please, call me René."

"—René. No disrespect, but I hope you don't think Antoine is the only one vying for her affection, 'cause he's not. And he never will be. My father's always taken the extra attention with a grain of salt. Could Antoine ever say the same?"

René smiled in defeat. Gia was no dummy, and he was proud of her for sitting in her and her mother's truths. "That's an excellent question, Gia. And honestly, I don't know."

"Well, I don't think so."

The front door opened slightly, pulling Gia and René from their conversation. Antoine stood in the threshold talking to a neighboring business owner with a rolled-up banner and brown paper bag in hand. "A'ight, Diggy. I'll holla at you later." He backstepped into the bistro, locking the screen door behind him. "Hey, hey, Daddy! I got the banner from the printer and picked up your prescription from the pharmacy," he threw over his shoulder. Antoine turned around and tried to conceal the shock that blanketed his face.

"Thank you, son. You can put everything over there on the bar."

Antoine did as he was instructed, then slowly made his way over to the table.

"Hey . . . Gia."

"Hi," her voice soft.

Antoine wiped his sweaty hands with a napkin, then tucked it inside his pocket.

"I, umm, I didn't expect to see you here."

"Same." Gia looked up at him and took in his features. She corrected her initial thought. He looked more like his mother than his father. And Gia wasn't sure if favoring either one of them sat right with her just yet.

"Why don't I leave you two for a while? Go pick up some lunch for us," René said, breaking the awkward silence.

Antoine cleared his throat. "Sounds good, Daddy."

"Gia?" René went on.

"That's fine."

"All right. I'll be back." René grabbed his bag of medication, a bottle of water, then left father and daughter alone.

Antoine pointed at the chair his father had just vacated and asked, "May I?"

"If you want," Gia shrugged.

Antoine made himself comfortable. "I've been worried about you and ya mother. I went to see about her at the hospital, but she'd already been discharged."

"Yeah," Gia nodded slowly.

"How . . . is she?"

"She's fine." Gia reopened her bottle of water and took another drink.

"Really?" Antoine asked, his eyes big.

"Really. As if nothing happened to her at all."

Antoine rubbed his forehead, trying to wrap his mind around the miracle.

"Wow. Umm . . . That's great. That's really great. I thought she was—"

"She's not," Gia sniffed.

"A'ight." Antoine watched Gia take in their surroundings before redirecting the conversation. "It's nice to have a moment to speak to you finally. One-on-one, ya know?"

"Yeah."

"How you like it down here?" He watched her closely, trying to detect any hint of nervousness. There was none.

"It's okay," she replied indifferently. She peered back into his curious, intense eyes. She was beginning to understand how her mother became undone in his presence. He was attentive. Undoubtedly present in the moment.

"Yeah. There's no other place like it in the world."

"That's for sure," Gia replied, rolling her eyes.

Antoine cracked another smile. She saw her dimples in his cheeks. "Where you been stayin'? At Toni's?"

Gia shook her head. "No, at my Mamaw's."

Antoine nodded slowly. He should have known. "Oh, okay. How you like it over there?"

"Fine."

"The house is huge, right?" he grinned.

"Yeah, it is," Gia said, smiling small. "She's taken good care of me."

"I wouldn't expect anything less." He watched her fiddle with her water bottle top. "Ya mother told me a lot of wonderful things about you."

Gia smirked. "I'm sorry I can't say the same."

Antoine ran his hand over his mustache. "I deserve that. But I hope that you'll want to get to know me like I do you since we have the opportunity now. That you'll give me a chance to make up for the lost time. Show you and ya mother that I truly am sorry."

Gia said nothing.

"The last time I saw you, you were a little bitty thing. Ya mother brought you to see me at the Audubon Zoo. You remember that? I gave you a li'l stuffed ballerina bunny rabbit."

"That was you?"

"Yeah," Antoine nodded proudly.

"I knew you looked familiar when you came by my aunt's

TASH HAWTHORNE

house back in June, but I couldn't remember where I'd seen you before." Gia took herself back to that day at the zoo. "I loved that stuffed bunny. She was my favorite."

"I wanted to make amends wit' her that day, Gia, but . . . She told me she'd moved on and was happy. What could I do at that point but accept it?"

"That or you could have told her you still wanted a relationship with me. My father would have understood. That's the type of man he is," Gia countered.

"I know that now. But ya grandmother—"

"What about my grandmother?" Gia's antennas shot up. He had her full attention.

"She would have made it so that I would have never had a relationship wit' you."

"If that had been the case, I'm sure she would have had good reason."

Antoine studied her for a moment. "I'm not a bad guy, Gia. Despite what she may have told you . . . I have thought about you and ya mother every day for the last fourteen years. I kept in touch wit' ya Papaw just so that I knew what was going on in you and ya mother's lives. It was important to me."

"Really?"

"Really. Ya Papaw understood forgiveness, ya know? He always extended grace. But ya grandmama . . . she's a hard woman. Always been that way."

Gia tilted her head in disbelief. "My grandmother saved my mother's life. She saved *my* life. There's nothing hard about that."

"That may so, but ask her how many more lives she's taken."

"What?"

"Ya grandmama ain't no saint, love," Antoine sneered.

"Neither are you," Gia spat.

"You right about that. But I ain't never claimed to be."

"We give life; we don't take it. That's what she's taught me,

250

what she's taught my mother. All the women in my family live by those words. My grandmother isn't a killer." Gia sat back in her chair, attempting to control the rage that was growing inside. This man was spewing lies about her grandmother, and she wasn't sure how much longer she could listen to him.

"Oh, but she is. And you know how I know?"

Gia remained silent.

"She killed my mama."

Gia leaned forward. "You're a liar."

"I'm many things, but a liar ain't one of 'em, baby." Antoine ran his tongue along his top row of teeth. "Ask her. Ask her what she did to my mama."

"This is some bullshit." Gia rose from the table and made her way toward the door and outside.

"Gia!" Antoine cursed himself as he followed behind her. He found Gia pulling her phone out and scrolling through names. "Gia, just listen to me for a minute."

"No! Get the fuck away from me!"

"Gia, if you just . . ." He snatched the phone away from her. ". . . listen!"

"Give me my phone!"

"No! Look look look! Ya mama doesn't know. I never told her," Antoine carried on.

"I don't give a fuck! Give me my phone!" Gia screamed at the top of her lungs.

Antoine surrendered, handing it back to her. "Ya grandmama's gotta hold on ya mama like nothin' I've ever seen before. It ain't natural." He watched her text away as he struggled to make her understand his dilemma. "Ya mama and I loved each other once, Gia. Very, very much. That's the truth. I'd do anything for her. But ya grandmama's hate for me overshadowed her love for ya mother. She destroyed us. She destroyed *her*. Why do you think she took you away from here? Moved all the way up North? It had nothing to do with me or Esai or her wantin' a better life. She had everything she needed down here —and more. She left to get away from *her*."

Gia looked up from her phone, wiping tears that were threatening to fall from her eyes. "I don't believe you."

"She's evil, Gia. That voodoo shit . . . That's evil too. You saw what it did to ya mother at the river. It had her levitatin' and shit. It almost killed her like it did my mama!"

Gia shook her head. "How do I know *you* weren't the one who tried to kill her?"

"Because I would never do that. I was trying to save her."

"You say that, but I don't really know for sure. Only you, my mother, and God know what happened that night. And granted, I don't know a lot about voodoo either, but I know it runs through my veins. I know it's sustained my mother all of these years, especially after you and my father left. It's kept me and my brothers for just as long without us even knowing." Gia placed her phone in her back pocket. "My mother taught me as a child that people speak ill about things they fear or know very little about."

Antoine sucked his teeth. "I'm goin' by what I saw, Gia. There's no good in that shit."

"Well, my mother believes there is. And she doesn't believe in a lot of things. She didn't believe you and my father would ever do her wrong, but *you* did." Gia watched him shift from one foot to the other. He was coming undone. "She didn't deserve the heartache you two caused. I didn't deserve it. And I'm ashamed to say, but I used to judge her. Judge the way she dealt with it. I didn't understand at the time that all she was trying to do was forget. All she was trying to do was *survive*. It took us to come back here and have hella shit happen to us for me to realize it."

"Gia—"

"I don't want her living like that anymore. So I'm gonna ask you to leave her alone. If you love her like you claim you do . . .

leave her alone. Leave *me* alone. We don't want you—and we don't need you. We have my brothers . . . my grandmother and aunts . . . cousins . . . and my *father*. We're good."

DOMINIQUE SAT on the top step of the front porch braiding the end of her hair and watching her mother treat a couple of fingers that had been pricked by the thorns in her rosebush. Dominique had been in bed for most of the day at her mother's insistence. But she was finally permitted to venture out of her room to see Gia off and spend time with her sisters. They were now gone. The atmosphere in the LeSaint-Favier household was light, very much alive. Dominique's miraculous recovery brought a newfound appreciation for life and the good that is often born of the bad, yet never spoken of. Her mother, visibly exhausted, had not taken her eyes off her all day, doting on her hand and foot upon returning from her early-morning errands.

"Want me to get you some more Band-Aids?" Dominique teased.

Corrine sucked her teeth. "No, I have enough. Thank you very much."

Dominique chuckled as she watched her mother struggle to wrap one of her fingers on the opposite hand. "I don't know why you just didn't let me go to the Garden Center to get you a new pair of gloves."

"Because I don't want you drivin'," Corrine admitted as she removed her gardening hat.

"I feel fine, Mama."

"Good. But I ain't ready for you to do too much, too soon." Corrine crumpled the Band-Aid's wrapping paper and placed it in the top pocket of her overalls. Then she closed her first aid kit and pushed it to the side before sitting down beside Dominique.

"I ain't the one doin' too much," Dominique smirked.

Corrine cut her eyes. "Don't be fresh."

"You're exhausted, Mama. You need to go inside and take a nap."

"I will as soon as Gia gets back," she said as she patted herself down with a damp cloth. "In fact, I'll be sleepin' fo' a couple of days after this is all over."

"I'm sure she's fine. Mr. Brevard's always been kind."

"Fo' true. But I can't help but worry. That child's been through hell and back. She don't need no more upset."

Dominique looked over at her mother. Her skin was glowing. It looked like melted dark chocolate, its richness soaking up the sun's rays. "She told me she saw me down at the river. When they pulled me out."

Corrine nodded slowly, remembering. "Yes, she did. After that, nobody could do anything wit' her. And they couldn't do anything fo' her." She looked over at Dominique and studied the sadness that found its place on her. "Did you tell her what happened?"

"Yeah." Dominique met her mother's wary eyes. "I didn't try to kill myself. And Antoine . . . he was just . . . there. He didn't have anything to do with me jumpin' in."

"Okay," Corrine replied quietly. "Okay."

Dominique turned her attention back to the road. "I wasn't prepared."

Corrine smiled, letting out a short chortle. "Neither was I. The ancestors gave me very little insight into what they had planned fo' you. And, I, uh . . . I don't know if I overstepped my boundaries by disruptin' that plan. But what I *do* know . . . is that I'm a mama first . . . " Corrine began to choke back tears. ". . . and when I got that call, nothin' else in this world mattered. Gettin' you outta that water and bringin' you back was all I wanted. Losin' you was *not* an option. You hear me?"

"Yes, ma'am," Dominique sniffled.

"Not then, not now, not never." Corrine kept her eyes forward. "You got my heart, baby girl."

Dominique choked back tears. She lay her head on her mother's shoulder as she slid her chocolate arm around her waist and basked in the kisses her red lips left on her crown. She'd waited fourteen long years to hear her mother say those words. And even though it wasn't the usual *"I Love You,"* its meaning was just the same.

A 1966 Mustang GT pulled up in front of the house and parked. Dominique wiped her eyes as her mother anxiously stood to her feet and made her way down the steps. Gia and René got out of the car, meeting Corrine midway. Dominique watched Gia bid René goodbye, then make short conversation with her grandmother. The woman looked concerned. Gia politely moved past her and made her way toward the house. As she closely approached, Dominique noticed the despondent look on her face. She rose to her feet and waited patiently for her child to meet her.

"You awrite?" Dominique took her face into her hands and checked her over.

Gia averted her eyes. "Yeah. My stomach's just bothering me."

Dominique studied her for a moment. The girl was lying, and she knew it. Something happened, but Gia was being tight-lipped about it. So Dominique decided to play along to see where the conversation would lead. "Well, what did you eat?"

"Nothing. I didn't have much of an appetite." Gia rubbed her forehead nervously.

"It's unlike you to turn down good food." Dominique cocked her head to the side.

Gia looked up at her mother. "Nothing Antoine has to offer is good."

"He was there?"

"Yeah. I'm gonna go lie down." Gia walked past her mother

and into the house.

Dominique was pissed. She placed her hands on her hips, briefly turning her attention to her mother and René. Their conversation had come to an end. He was retreating to his car as her mother was making her way up the footpath.

"René said they had a nice time, but Gia's came down wit' a little stomachache."

"Yeah, she just told me. It's probably her nerves," Dominique replied, hoping her mother couldn't read the lie.

"Yeah," Corrine sighed. "Well, I better fix her somethin'."

"I got it, Mama. Go lie down."

Corrine hesitated.

"Please?" Dominique asked sweetly.

Corrine pinched her chin and smiled. "Awrite."

Dominique watched her scale the steps and disappear into the house. She took in a deep breath, then released it. Antoine had, once again, overstepped his boundaries. And Dominique was officially tired of him. He'd said or did something to her child and she promised herself it would not go unpunished.

GIA RESTED ON PRAYING HANDS, watching her mother place a tray of food down on the dresser. She still wasn't hungry. The day's events replayed in her mind. Antoine had been very adamant about her knowing of her grandmother's past. But Gia found his confessions hard to believe, all of them except her grandmother's feat in ending his relationship with her mother. Her aunt disclosed that months ago.

Gia blinked back tears. Her grandmother was the center of her world. She owed her her life. Literally. His lies could never reach her ears. She promised herself that much. It would stay between her and her mother.

Dominique sat on the edge of the bed and began to rub

Gia's back. "I warmed up some red beans and rice for you."

"Thank you," Gia whispered.

Dominique caressed Gia's arm with the back of her hand. "Ya grandmama's nappin' right now. So, I think you should take this opportunity to tell me what happened at the club."

Gia bit the inside of her cheek. "He just . . . showed up. And Mr. Brevard decided he was going to leave us to get lunch." She shook her head. "He just left me with him."

"Jesus Christ," Dominique sighed.

"He talked about you the entire time. How much he loved you and how different things would be had Mamaw not interfered." Gia buried her feet beneath the covers. "Was he right?"

"Yeah," Dominique nodded. "But Mamaw saw somethin' in him that I couldn't because I was too close."

Gia marinated in her mother's response. "He blamed her a lot. He blamed her for everything." She shook her head. "Do you know how his mother died?"

"Umm, if I recall . . . He told me that she died from complications during pregnancy."

"Oh."

"Why?" Dominique's brows furrowed.

"He told me Mamaw killed her."

Dominique stopped rubbing Gia's back. "What?"

"He told me to ask her," Gia shrugged. "He said Mamaw performed voodoo on her or somethin' . . . and it killed her."

"Let me tell you somethin', Gia. Antoine's mama was a ragin' alcoholic, awrite? A big one. He told me so. And her complications came about because she couldn't put that bottle down," Dominique seethed. "Ya grandmama had nothin' to do with that. She barely knew the woman." Dominique shook her head. "She ain't no killer. And that ma'fucka needs to be ashamed of himself for lyin' on her like that."

"He hates her, Mommy."

"Yeah, well, the feeling's mutual," Dominique murmured.

"I told him I didn't wanna have anything to do with him. Neither one of us do."

"Good. You did good." Dominique kissed the back of her hand.

Dominique's phone began to vibrate in her shorts pocket. She pulled it out and answered. "Hey, Toni. Mama's asleep. Yeah. You comin' down with somethin'? Yeah, it sounds like it. You did? Awrite. No, I can drive over and feed 'im. Yeah. Is there any food in the fridge or . . .? Okay. Awrite. Bye." She slid the phone back into her pocket. "Ya aunt forgot to feed Damballah."

"Did she really?" Gia grinned.

The two shared a laugh.

"I'm gonna drive over and take care of 'im."

"Okay. What should I tell Mamaw if she wakes up before you get back?"

"Tell her the truth. I won't be gone long." Dominique retrieved the platter of food and handed it to Gia. "Enjoy." She kissed her on the top of her head, then headed out.

DUSK CREPT up on the Crescent City with no fair warning. Dominique pulled up to *Au-Delà Du Voile* and parked in her mother's designated spot. She hopped out of her father's old pickup, enveloped in one of her mother's white kaftans and matching tignons. She wanted to be dressed properly in case she ran into a customer or one of her mother's many followers, so she changed her clothes before leaving the house.

Dominique opened the iron gate, locked it behind her, then glided up the stone stairwell. She sifted through the myriad of keys on her mother's keychain before finding the one she needed. After jiggling the lock momentarily, the door opened, welcoming her back once again.

～

GIA AWAKENED to the clanging of pots and pans downstairs in the kitchen. She didn't remember falling asleep but was grateful to have been able to do so after the day she had. She threw her legs over the side of the bed and made her way down to the first floor. Her grandmother was cleaning chicken at one of the counters.

"Hey, Mamaw."

"Hey, baby. How's yo' stomach?"

Gia propped herself on one of the bar stools at the island. "Much better."

"Good," Corrine smiled.

"How was your nap?" Gia asked as she grabbed a praline out of the glass trifle bowl.

"It was pretty good." Corrine shucked a clean thigh in a bowl. "As soon as I get through wit' dinner, I'm gonna turn in fo' the night."

"That's a good idea," Gia giggled.

"Why, thank you," Corrine joined her. "Where's ya mama?"

"She went by the shop to feed Damballah. TeeTee forgot again."

"I told her I didn't want her drivin'." Corrine continued to prepare her meat but stopped momentarily. She put her knife down to process Gia's response fully. "You say she went to feed Damballah?"

"Yes, ma'am."

"That can't be. I fed him yesterday."

"You did?" Gia asked, wiping her mouth with a paper towel.

"Yeah." Corrine removed the house phone from its cradle and dialed Toni's number. "Hey, honey. I don't know just yet. Did you call Dominique and tell her you forgot to feed Damballah? That's what I thought. No, I'll call you back. Toni, I'll call you back!"

"What's the matter?" Gia said, her mouth full with another praline.

Corrine dialed Dominique's number and cursed herself when her voicemail picked up. "We gotta go."

~

DOMINIQUE FORGOT to lock the door behind her. She hadn't noticed Antoine watching her from his car parked down the street. She went to retrieve a mouse from the miniature refrigerator in the back office but was surprised to see it was empty. Confounded, she walked back out to the front of the shop and suddenly found herself face-to-face with a jilted Antoine.

"Simone sounded just like Toni, didn't she? That li'l call she made to you . . . she made it while Toni was in the bathroom," he smiled wickedly. "It's visitation day at River Oaks. I went up there to see her after me and Gia's li'l talk. Simone looks good. Healthy, ya know? It's a shame, though . . . All that beauty's gonna go to waste. Like her mind. I don't think she knows she's never gettin' outta that place." He looked around the quaint space, admiring it before settling his eyes on the oil painting of Corrine.

"Ya mama did a number on y'all. I mean, she really fucked y'all up. Shit, she fucked me up." He waited to see Dominique react to his statement, but she didn't. "Gia tell you what I told her? About my mama?" Dominique nodded. "Fucked up, right? I should'a told you the truth from the jump, I know, but I loved you too much. I couldn't tell you that the day ya pops brought me home to introduce me to the family, I recognized her but couldn't remember where I knew her from. I couldn't tell you that I finally placed her the day I came by to apologize for breakin' ya curfew. Right in my mama and daddy's bedroom." Antoine paused for a moment and wiped his wet eyes.

Dominique remained silent. She wasn't surprised by his

admission. He'd been rejected by both her and their daughter, his mother was gone, and so was the only man he'd confided in. He was desperate now and had taken desperate measures to get her to the shop.

"Gia looks just like my mama. She even sounds like her. It's like she came back to do this thing called life all over again. I don't blame her . . . to wanna get it right this time. She deserves a second chance. But this time . . . ya mama ain't gonna have a say." He reached for Dominique's cheek and stroked it. "You and Gia are all I got. And I ain't interested in sharin'.'"

His eyes were wild. Sensing impending doom, Dominique slowly sauntered up to him and placed her hands on his chest. She was going to use everything in her power to find the root of his obsession with her and dispose of it. Her fate was unknown. Whatever it was, she was not going to go down without a fight.

"Accept the things you cannot change, my love," she uttered, stroking his face.

His eyes closed, and his top lip curled. "Never."

Dominique brushed her fingers against his lips and sighed. "Then prepare yaself."

"For what?" Antoine asked, emerging from the trance he'd quickly fallen into.

"For me," Dominique replied seriously. "I am because she was. *Crains moi.*"

Antoine laughed incredulously. He didn't know they weren't alone. A spirit. *The* spirit. Marie Laveau. Dominique's great-great-grandmother was there—standing behind him.

Waiting.

THE STREET WAS BARRICADED on both ends by police cars. Corrine parked haphazardly on the sidewalk and jumped out with Gia on her heels. The neighboring businesses were all painted in red by the rotating fire engine lights. *Au-Delà Du Voile* was ablaze. The smoke that billowed from her business caused Corrine to stutter-step before pushing past a police officer and paramedics- in- waiting. As she ran past one of the ambulances, she noticed it was empty. She skimmed through the crowd in search of her child, but she wasn't out there. No one was being treated for smoke inhalation or burns. No one was speaking. No one was moving.

"My daughter! My daughter's in there!" Corrine heard herself cry out. It fell upon the ears of the fire captain, and he promised they would do everything in their power to save her.

Gia felt her legs giving way beneath her. There was no sign of her mother anywhere. She'd almost lost her to the water. And now, there was a possibility that fire found claim to her in an effort to both purify and counteract the sea's failed attempt on her life. Gia grabbed her grandmother's arm and held onto it tightly. She, in turn, wrapped her arm around her grand-daughter's waist, pulling her in close. They watched the fire-fighters battle the untamed inferno with precision and force. It wasn't long before they managed to stabilize the front entrance and enter. Gia and Corrine held their breath as they waited for the capeless heroes to reemerge with their beloved. When they finally did, the body in their clutches was not that of Dominique . . . but of Antoine. And in one of their gloved hands was an object neither Gia nor Corrine could identify. But just as their living nightmare was being placed on a gurney, the item slipped out of the firefighter's grasp onto the ground. It was then that Gia and Corrine both realized it was a partially charred gas can.

With tears in her eyes, Gia looked over at her grandmother. Watched her lose her breath. Her knees buckle. Then completely fade to black.

To Be Continued

DISCUSSION QUESTIONS

1. Vüdü Dahl opens with Dominique at work/her funeral home. Why do you think the author chose to open with this specific scene? How did this scene set the tone for the rest of the novel? Why is Dominique's profession such an integral part of the storyline?

2. The encounter between Dominique and Simone is a short, yet volatile one. Do you think Simone was right to verbally attack Dominique? Do you think Simone feels threatened by Dominique? How so?

3. When Corrine sees Dominique, she makes it a point to mention that her daughter "has lost her softness". What draws Corrine to Dominique's hardened disposition and/or physical appearance? Do you think she was being a concerned mother or an instigator?

4. Dominique and Gia's relationship is just as unstable as the one between Dominique and her mother. What does each one gain from the relationship? What does each one lose? Is it an intergenerational cycle of trauma or individual-independent behaviors?

5. At one point in the story the author writes, "Grudges are

sometimes held onto tighter than lovers' hands". Why do you think Corrine, Dominique, Simone and Gia are bound by said grudges?

6. In the beginning of the book, the author has included this quote by Toni Morrison: "Love is divine only and difficult always. If you think it is easy you are a fool. If you think it is natural you are blind. It is a learned application without reason or motive except that it is God. You do not deserve love regardless of the suffering you have endured. You do not deserve love because somebody did you wrong. You do not deserve love just because you want it. You can only earn—by practice and careful contemplations—the right to express it and you have to learn how to accept it." – Toni Morrison, *Paradise*. What do you think of this statement? How does it pertain to the story?

7. Vüdü Dahl is set mainly in New Orleans, Louisiana. What "role" does the city play in the story?

8. Describe Dominique and Antoine's relationship. What first drew them to one another? How would you describe their relationship when the story first begins? How does it change as the novel progresses? At the end of the story, the reader finds out that Antoine is the one who was been recovered from the fire. How do you think Dominique's mother and daughter would have reacted to him not being present at all?

9. "He's gonna be the death of you. You hear me? He's gonna be the death of you. And I'm not gonna be able to save you." Why does Corrine feel so bereft by Dominique's departure?

10. What aspects of the novel do you think touch upon your life or the life of someone you know? Is healing possible?

ACKNOWLEDGMENTS

To the Great Spirit/God be the glory for all of His amazing grace and mercy.

To my/the ancestors, I send you light and love from this moment back along my ancestral lines. I carry forth the spark of life which you have bequeathed in me. I am a product of endless generations of your converging paths, of a grand tree which roots and connects to all other trees here on earth. I thank you for my existence. I thank you for my life. I am because you were/are.

To my mother and grandmother, Leslie and Lorraine Hawthorne, I AM BECAUSE YOU ARE.

Thank you for my life.

To my sons, Xavier and Evan, thank you for speaking life into me during this long, emotional process. Where there was self-doubt, you provided reassurance. You kept me on course and for that I am forever grateful. Thank you for your patience and understanding, beloveds. It is truly an honor and privilege being your mother.

To my muses, Dr. Karen Turner-Ward and Adriana Inoa, thank you for being two tremendous sources of inspiration. You made yourselves available and were instrumental in setting a solid foundation for the LeSaint-Favier women's story to be told. Your insight into character development and language is unmatched. You made this struggle a beautiful one.

To Voodoo Queen Kalindah Laveaux, my spiritual counselor, thank you for giving me permission to share a story that has been on my spirit for some time. To give our people an insight into the good that is Voodoo/Louisiana Voodoo. You are always honest and patient with me. It is never a dull moment when we speak (lol). I couldn't have been blessed with a greater conduit to help me navigate through this world. I am forever indebted to you.

To my partner in crime, Tatiana M. Johnson, you are my second pair of eyes. You ask all of the difficult questions to which I don't always have the answers. You push me to dig deeper, think clearer and give myself some grace when necessary. Grace. I didn't know if or how I was going to finish this piece with the unexpected ascensions of Mark and my grandmother, but you told me to give myself a bit of that. Something I've never done before. THANK YOU. We have broken day behind many a time behind the inspiration of simple dreams, sounds or smells that have evolved into (necessary) stories. You are a blessing. I am honored to call you my sista.

To my superheroes, Mark Hagans, Jr. and Steve Donato, you two have been steadfast in your support of me. Selflessly spreading the word about my endeavors, may they be in literature, stage or film. Your encouraging words and blind faith in me have caused my cup to runneth over more times than I can count. Thank you for understanding me, not only as a (Black) woman, but as a creative, (magical) being. You two are the archetype for true friendship.

To Wahida Clark and the WCP Family, thank you for the companionship that has been 12 years in this ever-changing world of storytelling. You have given me a platform to be myself and stay true to my characters and their stories.

And lastly, to my readers, THANK YOU. Thank you for your patience during these last 3 years. You have been with me since KARMA's inception (12 years ago) and I am truly humbled by your loyalty, genuine belief in my gift, and demand for more! I do hope you enjoy this new journey that is the LeSaint-Favier women. A journey that is a reflection of our own (black women) and our mothers and our mothers' mothers and daughters.

ALSO BY TASH HAWTHORNE

The Karma Series

Karma: With a Vengeance

Karma 2: For the Love of Money

Karma 3: Beast of Burden

WAHIDA CLARK
PRESENTS
INNOVATIVE PUBLISHING

CLASSIC STREET LIT
—S-E-R-I-E-S—

FROM WAHIDA CLARK PRESENTS INNOVATIVE PUBLISHING